ALSO BY DELILAH S. DAWSON

Servants of the Storm

DELILAH S. DAWSON

SIMON PULSE

NEW YORK   LONDON   TORONTO   SYDNEY   NEW DELHI

〰️

SIMON PULSE

An imprint of Simon & Schuster Children's Publishing Division

1230 Avenue of the Americas, New York, New York 10020

First Simon Pulse hardcover edition April 2015

Text copyright © 2015 by D. S. Dawson

Jacket photograph copyright © 2015 by Thinkstock

For information about special discounts for bulk purchases, please contact Simon & Schuster Special Sales at 1-866-506-1949 or business@simonandschuster.com.

The Simon & Schuster Speakers Bureau can bring authors to your live event. For more information or to book an event contact the Simon & Schuster Speakers Bureau at 1-866-248-3049 or visit our website at www.simonspeakers.com.

Book designed by Regina Flath

The text of this book was set in Dante MT Std.

Manufactured in the United States of America

2 4 6 8 10 9 7 5 3 1

Library of Congress Cataloging-in-Publication Data

Dawson, Delilah S.

Hit / Delilah Dawson.

p. cm.

Summary: Near future thriller about a teen forced to become an indentured assassin who has only three days to complete her hit list—with the added complication of her sole ally's brother being the final assignment.

[1. Assassins—Fiction. 2. Science fiction.] I. Title.

PZ7.D323Hit 2015

[Fic]—dc23

2014022216

ISBN 978-1-4814-2339-7 (hc)

ISBN 978-1-4814-2341-0 (eBook)

Finally, a book I can safely dedicate to my parents!
Thanks, Nina and Big Ben, for teaching me frugality and
excellent money management. We work hard, but we
party hard too. And we carry very low balances.

1.

ROBERT BEARD

The carefully folded strip of paper in my lucky locket reads *I want to survive the next five days.* I kiss it and tuck it under the tight neck of my long-sleeved black tee with the solemn reverence my mom would give her rosary. Or, in the last six months, her Vicodin.

I sit on the cramped cot in the back of a refurbished mail truck, surrounded by band posters and crocheted afghans and half-finished knitting projects, trying to pull myself together. I can't stop shaking. At first, the truck smelled like welded metal and fresh paint. I stuck prints from my bedroom at home on the walls, draped my favorite quilt on the cot, and arranged my vintage pillows with a few stuffed turtles from my collection. I even tried hanging up some embroidery hoops, but they kept falling down. For a couple hours,

I pretended that it was a dorm room or my first apartment, the freedom and comfort I've always craved. But the illusion didn't last. Now, with fast-food bags crumpled up under the cot and a digital clock ticking down the minutes to failure, it reeks of hot garbage and desperation. It's one step away from being in prison. Or worse.

I'm already running out of time on my first assignment, with only thirty minutes left before the twelve-hour limit. I've been sitting here in my truck, waiting for . . . I don't know what. For my feelings to coalesce, for some sort of determination to set in. But it never has. I just feel empty and thin and shaky, as flimsy as the fast-food salad I could barely choke down for lunch. I knew I should have gone for fries. Fries would have given me strength.

I swallow again, fighting to force down the lump of fear in my throat. I've got a job to do, and not the one at the pizza place where I've worked since my fourteenth birthday, slinging pies with my friends Jeremy and Roy to help pay the bills. No, this job is far more disgusting. And dangerous. And I can't just quit.

"Shit," I mutter, the word echoing off the metal. A few minutes ago, the digital clock set into the dashboard started blinking, which is a noxious reminder to hurry. They've given me twelve hours each to complete ten deliveries, so five days to finish out my "shift," as they called it. But I supposedly get a bonus if I finish early, and I really need that money. And I need to finish. So I need to get started.

I squeeze back into the driver's seat, which is on the wrong side, and pull the US Postal Service hat down over my hair. Dark, wavy chunks straggle out underneath, and I wish it were long enough for a decent ponytail. This hat is required, and it's possibly the ugliest thing I've ever worn—and that's saying a lot, because I have a closet at home full of sweaters straight out of the eighties. At the last possible moment, I button the scratchy new Postal Service shirt over my long-sleeved tee. It's stiff and itchy, and I can't wait to take it off again. Just wearing the thing makes my skin crawl. Looking down, I make sure the top button is buttoned correctly, not blocked in any way, and I slide the small signature machine snugly into the front pocket.

The package I'm supposed to deliver is riding shotgun, and I can't stop staring at the printed card that goes with it. I've been reading and rereading it all day, but it barely makes sense and my brain is full of snow like a broken TV and I know I won't be able to remember it. And it has to be done perfectly, word for word.

I'll be lucky if I can remember how to read.

I shove the key in the mail truck's ignition and turn it, and the engine sputters to life. I drive around the corner to the house I've been watching all day and put the truck in park, leaving it running as I step onto the uneven sidewalk. With shaking hands, I lean in and pick up the fruit basket, the plastic crinkling against my fingers and short but wild nails. I painted them alternately bloodred and bright green with dollar signs just last night. It's not like I could sleep, anyway, what with the unusually large mail truck parked in an abandoned lot and me having a complete breakdown. The nails look a little Christmassy, but it's really my own personal protest against what I have to do. I'm still me—even if they're making me do something very, very bad.

I walk up between dried-out, overgrown bushes, holding the basket like a shield. This neighborhood used to be really impressive. We pass it all the time on the way to the store. The Preserve, it's called, like rich people are just milling around in a beautiful, protected oasis, dumb and magnificent as wild animals. I remember wondering how someone could ever earn enough money to have one of these gigantic, brick castles with a filled four-car garage. Now I understand that they couldn't. Which is why I'm here in the first place.

The yard is yellow and dry, half overtaken with clover killed by the first frost just a few nights ago. A small tree has fallen over, surrounded by earth gone cracked and hard without constant watering from the sprinkler system, but no one has done anything about it. I trip on an old garden hose and drop the fruit basket to catch myself painfully on my hands. If it were a real gift basket, I would be scrambling to pick up bruised pears and broken apple jelly jars. As it is, the entire thing is still in one piece, the plastic fruit glued firmly together and the foam now dented. The signature machine is still in my front pocket, and I wonder how much abuse it was designed to take. A lot, probably.

For just a moment, I stay on the ground, feeling the burn of cold concrete under my stinging palms, trying to breathe. I want nothing more than to run back to the truck, to run home, to cry, to scream, but I can't, so I stand and brush myself off. When I pick up the basket, carefully, as if it mattered, I turn it around so the dented part doesn't show.

There are two steps up to the house, steps that aren't even really necessary. The paint on the door is peeling, the doorbell dangling by wires. I seriously hope this guy is home. Robert Beard, the list says. With a deep breath, I step up to the door and knock. A cold trickle of fear drips down my spine, and I shift from foot to foot in mismatched sneakers, wishing this was just a bad dream and hoping I don't lose my salad.

For a while, nothing happens. I start to worry. What if he's not here? What if he's already moved on? What if he's at work? And for just a second, relief floods me as I imagine skipping back to the truck and driving away to get a milk shake and some fries. But the relief is a silly dream, not real, because that would just make my job harder, if he wasn't here. It wouldn't get me off the hook. It would keep me here longer, like a writhing worm stuck right through the heart. If worms even have hearts, which I can't remember. And I don't want to find out what happens the moment that blinking clock in the car stops counting down.

The curtain to the side of the door twitches to reveal the flash of reading glasses and squinting eyeballs. I smile and hold up the gift basket. *Guess what? It's a package for you, Mr. Beard!* He smiles back like a dog slurping over a steak and nods, and the door unlocks and swings open. The hot air inside hits me like a wall. He's still got enough cash to cover electricity, then. At my much smaller house, we just put on more clothes and live without heat until the pipes are about to freeze, but this dude is living in his own tropical paradise to escape the sharp chill of November, which isn't sharp at all in Candlewood, Georgia.

The man inside is big and disheveled. What once must have been a nice body has migrated to an old dude pregnancy. He looks like he hasn't left the house in weeks, with patchy stubble and dark blond hair that's too long for a rich guy. But his robe is the fluffy white kind you get at fancy hotels, and one of his teeth winks gold when he smiles. And something about him is eerily familiar, but I don't know why.

"Robert Beard?" I ask, voice squeaking.

"That's me," he says.

He holds out his hands, and I give him the signing machine. Without reading the message, without pausing for even a single heartbeat, he signs it, sealing his fate for the second time. I don't realize until he hands it back that I was holding my breath. Exhaling a tiny cloud of fog, I look down to make sure the digital stylus worked.

His signature is big and bold with a line underneath it. *Bob Beard.* And that's when it clicks.

This was the Vice President Bob Beard who fired my mom from her nicer office job downtown. She cried for days and never got over the fact that if she'd been prettier, younger, more put together, he might have let her stay. Behind his closed office door, he told her that being a personal assistant was a job for an optimistic young woman with up-to-date skills, a winning attitude, and a fresh-faced appeal. A go-getter.

And my mom knew exactly what that meant, so she boxed up her mementos with what was left of her pride and walked out before she was forced to train her big-boobed twenty-year-old replacement. We started looking for new jobs that afternoon and ate nothing but peanut butter sandwiches to make her two weeks of severance pay last as long as possible. Her next job was a step down in every way, with insurance so bad that my mom's had a broken tooth for two years but won't get it fixed. She winces when she drinks ice water now. Since her car accident, we've switched to even cheaper peanut butter.

All thanks to Bob Beard.

I press the accept button harder than necessary and nestle the signature machine in my pocket. My pulse speeds up as I angle my body toward him. I've hated this guy for years. He holds out his hands for the basket, a little closer, a little more insistent. Bob's not used to waiting for anything.

"Well?" he says when I don't shove the goodies at him and run. I shift the basket to my hip, holding it one-handed so I can read from the card. And so he's directly in front of me.

"Robert Beard," I start, my voice low and angry, all squeak long gone. "You owe Valor Savings Bank the exact sum of $643,762.80. Can you pay this sum in full?"

His eyebrows go up, and he snorts like a bull.

"Of course not," he says, confused and angry, like I'm not supposed to know the true depth of his failure as a responsible human being. Like it's my fault. He licks his lips and pulls the sleeve of his robe down over the shiny gold watch on his wrist. "Are you with a collections agency?"

I clear my throat and take a step back as I read from the card, just a little too fast.

"By Valor Congressional Order number 7B, your account is past due and hereby declared in default. Due to your failure to remit all owed monies and per your signature just witnessed and accepted, you are given two choices. You may either sign your loyalty over to Valor Savings as an indentured collections agent for a period of five days or forfeit your life. Please choose."

"What?"

I look down at the card, wishing there were more for me to say, more than all the tiny-print legal crap on back, the language so thick and official I can't begin to understand it. It's so confusing, really. They probably did it that way on purpose. I push the basket up against my chest, right over the top button of my shirt and, underneath that, my lucky locket.

"It's pretty simple, Bob," I whisper. "You either agree to work for them as a bounty hunter or I have to kill you."

"What? Who the hell do you think you are, kid? You can't just walk up to my door and read shit at me and threaten me in my own home! What about charge-offs? What about declaring bankruptcy? That's how it's done. There's a system. Valor isn't God. This is America, for Chrissakes."

I sigh. There's no helping this guy. He sure didn't help himself. When you look back at the chain of events that brought me here, he's one of the biggest dominoes that fell. If he'd let my mom keep her job, if he hadn't been so goddamn greedy, if he'd paid back his debts, I wouldn't be standing on his doorstep at all. I move the basket back to my side, let that top button get a good look at his snarl, at his gold tooth, at his I'm-a-wealthy-white-guy-so-I'm-protected-from-everything rage.

"Robert Beard, you have two choices."

"Screw you."

"I'm going to take that as a no," I say.

"Great. It's a no. Can I have my goddamn basket now?"

I take a deep breath and reach behind me, to the waistband of my jeans. I pull out the Valor-issued 9mm Glock and point it at his chest. We're so close that I can't even extend my arm all the way. My hand is shaking like crazy, and the gun feels like it weighs a million pounds, and my fingers are numb and slippery. Bob Beard's hands shoot up, his body going tense.

"Wait, kid. Let's talk about this. I might have some cash. . . ." He wiggles his arm, and his sleeve falls down, showing his watch.

My vision goes weird, like I'm looking down a long tunnel, and at the end is this guy I've never met but have hated for years, and for just a second, I can see the tiny red veins in his nose lined up in the pistol's dead-black sights. I lower the gun, close my eyes, say a prayer to whoever is listening, and completely fail to pull the trigger.

A soft beep starts up from the truck, the siren getting louder and louder, like an alarm clock that hasn't reached full volume yet. How much time do I have? A minute? Less?

I swallow hard and whisper, "I'm sorry."

Eyes still closed, I pull the trigger and shoot Bob Beard right in the chest.

The gun barely recoils, and I take a few steps back. God, it happened so fast. And it's so unreal. And he still doesn't understand. He gurgles and clutches the door frame before sliding to the ground, one hand to his heart like he's about to say the Pledge of Allegiance. I lean over him, angling the top button of my shirt, the glossy black one, so that it's right over the bloodstain blooming on the front of his fluffy white robe. I wait until he stops breathing. I want to make sure they know.

With trembling fingers, I place the printed card from Valor on his chest for his next of kin. Not that the explanation is going to help much unless one of them is a lawyer. Maxwell Beard has the same address and is tenth on my list, and I'm guessing it must be his son. For just a second, I consider stepping over Robert Beard's body and going inside to find Maxwell and get that bonus. But I'm pretty sure I'm going to throw up, and I don't want to do it in a dead man's house. Seconds have passed, but it feels like forever.

I leave Bob lying there, his door wide open, and jog back to my truck with the basket under my arm and the warm gun in my hand, finger firmly off the trigger. My feet are numb, my heart trying to pound out of my chest. I feel cold all over, cold and empty, except that there's something warm all over my face, and I know I'm crying, but I don't have a free hand to wipe away the tears. The lump in my throat is about to come up, a writhing ball of lettuce and fat-free ranch. Killing a person—it was both a million times easier and a million times harder than I'd thought it would be. And because it was him, because it was Bob Beard, God help me, it almost felt good. And that scares me.

Today is the first day of government-sanctioned assassination, and the faster I can get through my list of ten debtors, the better my chances of catching them like this, unaware. I can only hope that they'll all be this uncomplicated—one person, alone, at home, confused, with no warning or rumors. It will be so much easier if they haven't heard mysterious gunshots all day or found some accidental slipup on the Internet. The guy from Valor Savings said they would prevent that, but we all know that the Internet was made for conspiracy theories, even ones that are eerily true.

I slow to a walk to stick the gun in the back of my jeans and unbutton the Postal Service shirt with one hand. God, it's just the itchiest, scratchiest, we-don't-give-a-shit-about-your-comfort-est piece of clothing imaginable, even with a tee underneath. Plus, since I know that the camera in the top button never turns off, I'll just feel better when it's wadded up in a ball on the floor under the seat. I've still got my pride, and I don't want them to see me puke, whoever they are.

"Dad? Dad!" someone shouts behind me.

I don't turn around. I walk faster.

"You! What did you do?"

I break into a run and sling the basket and shirt into the passenger seat as strong hands yank me down, flailing, from the open sliding door of my still-running truck. The guy spins me around and holds the front of my T-shirt bunched in one fist, shoving me against the truck hard enough to make it rock, hard enough to hurt. Rage sings through me, and I don't need to throw up anymore. I need to fight.

"What did you just do?" he yells, slamming me against the truck again.

I gulp down my anger and grab his wrist with my left hand, struggling to put some room between my body and the cold metal of the truck. Reaching behind my back for the gun, I whip it around and put it to the side of his chest, tight, so he can't jerk away. So he can't see my hand shaking.

"Let me go," I say, quiet and cold.

I look at his face for the first time, and my heart wrenches in my chest. It's like looking at a ghost. He looks like his father, like what his father used to be when he was my age. Dark blond hair falling over buttery brown eyes, tall and broad-shouldered like an athlete. And yet he's wearing the shirt of a band I like, a shirt I have too. Or used to have. It's at my old house with my mom and most of my stuff, just another part of the life I was forced to leave behind.

His fingers fall open as the gun kisses his ribs. I yank my shirt away and step back. But the gun doesn't budge. The kid's hand is open between us, frozen in place, and I'm transfixed by a prominent Adam's apple that bobs all the way down and back up.

"What just happened?" he says, staring into space.

"Your dad had a debt, and Valor Savings called it in. This is totally legal."

"Valor Savings? The . . . the bank? But why? You can't just go around shooting people." Rage and sorrow war on his face, and he's panting like a dying animal.

"Go read the card, Max," I say.

"What card?"

· 13 ·

I exhale, a soundless sigh.

"The one I left on his chest. Just read it, okay?"

I climb into the truck backward, my eyes locked with his and the gun still pointing at his chest. He doesn't move. He doesn't turn to his father's body. He definitely doesn't go read the card, which would explain how Valor Savings Bank, now just Valor Savings, paid off every debt the US government owed to every other country on earth and now owns everything from sea to shining sea, plus Alaska, Hawaii, and Puerto Rico.

If he would just read it, the dumb asshole, he would know that Valor Savings is now calling in debts and that, thanks to a tricky and vague little clause in a credit card application that no one bothered to read before signing, they can legally kill their debtors. Even if Max did read the card, he still wouldn't know that he'll be making his own choice in exactly four days, if not earlier.

Kill or be killed, and God bless Valor.

I could shoot him right now. Could just pull the trigger while he stands there, stunned. Easy pickings. I could have done it a moment ago, while he was holding me by my shirt and the adrenaline and defiance were shooting through my veins, making my trigger finger as itchy as my Valor-issued shirt. I should have done it then, before I looked into his eyes. It would have made my life a hell of a lot easier.

But I couldn't do it. And I still can't. Not while he's wearing that T-shirt. It would be like shooting my favorite band, like killing my

· 14 ·

old self. And Valor may force me to do things I don't want to do, but they can't take away the things I am. Or the things I love.

That's what I tell myself as I get in the purring mail truck and drive away, my Postal Service shirt crumpled up on the passenger seat by the dented foam gift basket. Max stands there, watching me, until I turn off his street, the big game hunter leaving the Preserve behind until I come to claim the next dumb but magnificent animal in four more days. I swerve to the side, quick, and barf up my salad into the bushes by the neighborhood's elegant, brick-framed sign.

As I climb back into the truck, the clock on the dashboard stops blinking and calmly begins counting down from 12:00:00.

When the GPS tells me to turn right, I do.

Goddammit, I do.

2.

ELOISE FRAMINGHAM

The next name on my list is an old woman's name—Eloise. And I kind of hope she *is* an old woman, so old that she won't even be able to see my face through milky-white eyes. Maybe I can just smile and hand her the glued-together basket of plastic fruit for a few minutes, make her feel like she won something, like maybe somebody cares. And then I'll whisper the words on her card, right into the top button so she won't actually hear them with her cheap-ass hearing aid. And then I'll shoot her in the back when she goes to get me a glass of milk.

That would make it so easy.

But it's just another dream.

I pull into her neighborhood, just a few streets over from Bob

Beard's. The Preserve is practically abandoned these days, but this cookie-cutter subdivision of much smaller homes is thriving and tidy. Bob's house probably has ten rooms in it, not counting bathrooms. These houses might have three, if they're lucky. I already know what they're like inside: just like the house where I grew up, where I lived until yesterday morning, where my mom is waiting for me, exhaustively praying to Mother Mary while high on prescription narcotics.

Point is, this could be my house. Probably has scuffed parquet by the front door, a coat closet full of junk, torn linoleum in the kitchen, sparkling-clean toilet bowls next to faded wallpaper. The people who live here are what my mom used to call "the proud poor" before the economy went sour and then downright bitter. Before she took a lesser-paying job and finally realized that she was one of them.

Eloise's house is sloped and unbalanced, basically a big lean-to striped with weathered gray wood boards. It reminds me of when Pa built log cabins in *Little House on the Prairie*, like one day soon they'll build the other side of the house and make it symmetrical. Which, of course, they never will. The yard is trim, and there's a birdbath and a reflecting ball relaxing amid strategically partying garden gnomes. There's a For Sale sign, too, pretty faded. And wind chimes made of sea shells.

Please, please, let Eloise be an old woman.

I stop the mail truck in front of her house and unwad my Postal Service shirt. It's been riding shotgun beside me as I follow the directions on my Valor-issued GPS unit. They want to make sure I know exactly where each of my marks lives, and they want me to get to them all within the time frame, before word gets out and people start hiding from anything that looks governmental. Or anything with a Valor logo. My instructions say that if a debtor runs or I can't find them within their twelve-hour period, I set fire to the house. Which makes me think of my mom and that stupid, fraying heating pad she sleeps with for her back and how easy it would be for my own house to go up in flames that no one would ever question or investigate. Now that I'm carrying a gun and I know what Valor can do, nothing familiar feels safe.

She's why I'm doing this, of course. My mom did a great job of raising me after my piece-of-crap dad left us when I was four, but when the recession hit, it hit us hard. First Bob Beard sent her packing and we were on unemployment. We were even on food stamps for a while. She took a job that was far away and paid less, but the stress really ate at her. Her last job wasn't awesome, and the insurance was even worse. When she totaled the car on the highway six months ago and spent two weeks in the hospital, it was pretty much the last straw. Now she can barely walk, she's depressed and addicted to pills, and I'm maxing out my hours at the pizza place just to keep the electricity on.

Or I was. I told Roy and Jeremy that I had to cancel all my shifts and go out of town for a funeral, but I didn't mention it might be my own.

My mom always told me that if you worked hard and paid your dues, you would be happy. A good person. And then, a couple of months ago, she asked me if she could borrow something from my savings and use some of my work money. And to bring home an extra pizza when Jeremy dropped me off after work. She'd always said my work money was my college money, and when she asked for some of it, the wrinkles around her lips quivering, I knew things were worse than she was letting on. But I had no idea how bad they really were.

Up until two nights ago, I never could have guessed that she was more than $100,000 in debt. That she had taken out a second mortgage. That she had pawned the title to our new piece-of-shit car. That she'd been fired for missing too much work after the car accident—and kept it from me. That under the influence of generic Vicodin, she had done everything they tell you not to do to stay afloat in an economy this bad and had hidden it from me out of shame. My mom had raised me to be humble, determined, hardworking, and tenacious, just like her.

Turns out that was just a bunch of bullshit.

And here I am today, seventeen and driving around a repainted mail truck, killing strangers for the megacorporation that now runs my government. I can't even begin to grasp what sort of threats, voodoo, and cold, hard cash are behind the fact that everyone in America—excuse me, Valor Nation—doesn't seem to know to whom they are now pledging allegiance. But somehow, Valor has managed to give themselves at least five days of complete radio silence in which to set the new regime in motion by getting rid of the irresponsible scum dragging down the economy with unpaid bills.

It's finally open season in America the Beautiful.

And lucky me. I get to be part of it.

The representative who came to our door in a black suit like the CIA guys wear in movies was as composed and careful and neutral as a plastic figurine. I was sitting cross-legged on the couch when the doorbell rang, working on a knitted cozy for the flagpole at school, knee-deep in bright yellow acrylic yarn. My mom opened the door, and he scanned the room before walking right past her without being invited inside. He had wires sticking out from his ears and a precision to his haircut and sideburns that made me think they had programmed his hair to grow along a dotted line.

"Patricia Klein?" he said, standing right in front of me, more a statement than a question.

I was so surprised and freaked out I could only mutter, "Patsy," under my breath, like he cared about my nickname.

"I'm here to offer you a wonderful opportunity," he said.

He perched on the edge of the sagging recliner, and my mom looked out the door. Whatever she saw in the front yard made her close the door, lock it, and sit by my side on the couch, pulling my hand away from my knitting needles and clutching it tightly like she already knew terrible news was coming. Good news arrives with TV cameras and big, brightly painted vans. Bad news arrives quietly, in dark sedans with black windows. Worry and guilt rolled off my mom like fumes, her shoulders slumping like she'd been caught doing something bad. When I was little, my ex–best friend, Amber, had a puppy who used to look like that when he peed on the rug while wagging his tail. But he ran away, and later on, I had to admit that he was smarter than he looked.

"An opportunity?" my mom said slowly, like it was a word she'd never heard before.

"I represent a very high level of the government, and we'd like to recruit your daughter," the man said. He never gave a name or offered a business card. But he did hand me the same card I leave with my victims—with my mom's name and six figures on it. And then he handed me another one with lots of legalese and double-talk. And he watched me read it, his face as impassive as a turned-off TV. I dropped it into the puddle of yarn in my lap, my yarn bombing forgotten.

"I'm sorry," I said. "Congress? Amendments? Banks? I don't get it."

His smile had the greased movement of a machine. There was no kindness there, no empathy.

"Patricia, has your mother not spoken to you about her debts?"

"Don't drag her into this. Whatever needs doing, I'll do it," my mother said before I could even turn to her in utter disbelief. And yet, was it utter? Underneath it all, there was some tiny *click* as everything came together. As it made sense.

The man slowly reached into his matte black blazer and pulled out a matching matte black gun. Of course I knew what it was. Jeremy and Roy from work had taken me shooting a few times. Not at a range, since I'm underage. But out in the fields behind their trailer park, where they had some old bales of hay and one sad, three-legged plastic deer set up. It felt good and rebellious, blasting a few rounds of cheap bullets into a row of off-brand soda cans while my pizza-tossing geek friends from math class drank stolen beer and cheered me on. It was my one concession to my white-trash roots, shooting that gun in my hipster getup and sale-rack gladiator sandals. Learning how to handle a gun made me feel powerful, offered a different sort of high than the one I get from yarn bombing and selling rude embroidery patterns on Etsy, channeling my frustration into doing something beautiful and defiant with my hands. Most of the time, I prefer creation to destruction. Valor Savings feels differently on that topic.

As I sat there, cradling a half-made yellow flagpole cozy and a doomsday card in my lap, the man pointed his gun at my mom's chest. And just like Bob Beard, that's when I knew it was real.

"What's your choice, Patricia?" he said casually.

My heart jumped into my sinuses, and I picked the card back up, fingers shaking. The words all blurred together. It still didn't make any sense. It was printed in green ink with a weird seal at the top and the Valor Savings Bank logo at the bottom. Except the word "bank" ,was gone.

Just Valor Savings now.

"I can't even . . ." I trailed off.

I guess the robot guy understood what I wasn't able to say. As I watched my mom clutch her chest and stare down the barrel of a gun, he explained it with the clear implication that he would indulge me only once.

"Due to overwhelming national debt, Valor Savings Bank combined with several private shareholders to relieve the government of their obligations to other countries."

"You mean they bought us?"

A cold, reptilian smile.

"'Bought' is such an ugly word, Patricia. They saved us. From ourselves."

My mother crossed herself and started praying under her breath.

"One of the first acts of the Valor Savings Congress was to draft Amendment 7B, which calls in a tricky bit of fine print from the

Valor Savings Bank Platinum Credit Card Agreement issued in 2007 through 2013. Debtors owing significant amounts and in arrears for more than three months can, in effect, be considered indentured servants and can, therefore, be legally killed in recompense. And Valor Savings is now calling in several of those debts to relieve the country of deadweight. Our algorithms have pinpointed you, Patricia Klein, as an optimal debt collector."

"She's just a child!" My mom's voice was painfully high, her swollen fingers tight around mine. "I'll do it. Don't . . . This is my business. It's not her fault. It's mine."

The man swiveled to face her, his gun never wavering. "You're old, slow, overly religious, damaged, and drugged. You have neither the emotional fortitude nor the stamina to accomplish this simple task. But Patricia is an ideal recruit. And, if she fails, she's no great loss to the future economy. Consider this . . . an internship."

"Like in a call center?" I said, voice shaking.

"More like a bounty hunter," he said. "Did you ever watch that show on Bravo? *Dog the Bounty Hunter?*"

I gave him a blank stare. "The wrestler? Like with a mullet? Who never kills anyone?" I said. "Like Boba Fett?"

Something in his jaw twitched then, and I decided to speak as little as possible from there on out.

"Allow me to be frank, Miss Klein. Your mother owes $167,892.33

to Valor Savings. We already own the car and the house. And, per her signature, we own her."

The gun pointed at her chest never so much as trembled the whole time. But I did.

"Mom, is that true?"

"I think it's gone up a little since I quit paying it," she said, her voice childish and wavering, like a recording of herself. Her fingers left mine to clutch her rosary against her wrist brace.

The man smiled again, showing even, white teeth.

"Now, I'm sure you don't want me to shoot your mother," he said. "Not only because no young girl should be orphaned, especially not one who hasn't seen her father since she was four. But also because there will be no witnesses. Who knows what might happen? You could get shot too. The house could burn down."

"You're going to shoot us both?" I asked. My hands started to lift up of their own accord, like we were in an old Western movie and he had told me to reach for the sky. But he lowered the gun, shook his head as if it were a joke, and smiled like a car salesman.

"Valor Savings doesn't want it to come to that. We don't want to lose our bright young stars before they even get a chance to shine."

I gave him as much of a deadpan look as possible, considering his gun was still mostly pointed at my mom, held loosely in his hand. If he'd done his homework, he'd learned about *my* homework. I'm not a genius, but I try hard. I mostly get A's and B's because I really want to get into community college, maybe get a grant or a scholarship to a state school. No awards for me, no after-school activities. I stay out of trouble, although I was once caught selling parsley to some freshman idiot in the last stall of the girls' room, having convinced her it was weed as a joke. While the other girls in my class went for jobs at the mall or the Cracker Barrel, I'm content to sling cheap-ass pizza because that means I can walk home if I have to. If I was a star, then the sky was getting pretty freaking bleak.

"We don't care about your grades," he said as if reading my mind. "We have your test scores. You have the exact qualities we're looking for."

I turned to my mom and gave her my usual, careful smirk.

"And you were worried about my career prospects," I said. "I'm being recruited!"

I guess that was what broke her and, in effect, me. My mom sobbed and doubled over, dropping the rosary, her arms wrapped around her belly. She'd gained a lot of weight since the accident, and she couldn't really hug herself anymore. As she rocked back and forth, crying, I realized that it was the saddest, most hopeless, most desperate I'd ever seen her. When Dad left, when she'd lost her good job and had to take a worse one, when I saw her in the hospital, covered in dried blood and bruises—all these experiences had been torture for me to watch, helpless.

But this was worse.

"Karen, this is no reason to cry," the man said, and I sensed a cruel glee under his carefully manicured facade. "It's not like she had any real future. It's not like she was going to college. And you'll be able to afford the treatments you need now. If she succeeds."

My head shot up. "Treatments?"

Mom just sobbed harder and turned her face away like she was trying to bury it in her shoulder.

"She didn't tell you about the lump they found in her breast?"

I scooted closer to her, laid my head against her shoulder.

"Is it true, Mama?" I said as quietly as possible. It should have been a private moment, not one acted out in front of the government's new robotic grim reaper.

She laid her head against mine and whispered, "Oh, Patsy. I should have told you."

I wanted to be angry at her. I wanted to pitch a giant fit, slamming doors so hard that things fell off the thin walls. But I couldn't. All that hugging herself, hiding in her robe. I thought it was just the pain left over from her broken clavicle and busted ribs. But she'd been keeping it from me. The money, the gun, the terrifying wax robot man in our beat-down living room—none of that mattered compared to what was going on under her worn terry-cloth collar.

The gun twitched in the man's hand. "Look at it this way. If I shoot her, she won't be in any more pain, right? That's better than a long, slow death by cancer."

"You know I won't let you do that," I said, low and deadly.

"The algorithms indicated you would feel that way. And you will be compensated for your time. Your mother's debts will be released. You'll receive all the supplies you need. As long as you satisfy the terms of our contract within the time frame specified while meeting certain prearranged criteria, this could possibly be the best thing that's ever happened to you. You might even get a bonus."

"So I should thank you for ruining my life?" I asked.

He put the gun in my lap and smiled. I didn't touch it. But I already hated it, cold and heavy on the pile of bright yellow yarn.

"You can thank democracy and greed for that," he said.

After he left, my mom showed me her scans, pointed out the lump cradled by broken bones that even a blind person wouldn't have missed. She showed me the printouts from the oncologist, how much it was going to cost to have surgery and undergo chemo without insurance. Even with the best insurance around, it still would've been impossible on our budget.

I sat there on the threadbare couch, shaking my head. On the coffee table in front of us, the gun rested on a thick envelope of crap I was supposed to read but couldn't. The robot man made me sign something before he left, and after everything I'd learned, I should have read the fine print. Maybe it was suicidal, but leaving my signature without bothering to read the document first felt like my last act of freedom.

They pretty much owned me anyway.

"I'm so sorry," my mom started, but I just grabbed her hand like a kid being torn away in a crowd, like holding on to her puffy fingers was the only thing I had left.

"I don't want to talk about it," I said. "It just sucks, and it's happening, and talking won't change it. You'll get what you need. Don't worry."

"But they want you to kill people." She tried to pull her hand out of mine, but I wouldn't let her.

"Better them than you," I said. "Better them than us."

She nodded. I don't think she agreed. But my mom has always tried to be a good person and play by the rules. She goes to church and leaves something in the offering plate. She pays her taxes—or she used to. Mama taught me from a very young age that if I worked hard and pulled my weight, I would eventually succeed. We scoffed at people who got evicted and at our neighbor, who sometimes chose a new phone over paying her water bill and had to borrow our shower.

Turns out we were screwed either way.

Now I'm more practical, more ruthless. I've always liked little rebellions and sticking it to the Man, whoever he is. And if I can solve all our problems in five days, then I will do whatever it takes to live through it and keep my mom safe.

Or so I told myself two nights ago.

X X X

The next morning, I pulled the yellowed scrap of notebook paper out of my locket, uncurling it and running a finger along uneven, childish script.

I want to find my dad.

More than anything, that was what I'd wanted every day since he left. Just to see my dad again. For every birthday, I didn't want a party—I just wanted him. I asked Santa and the Easter bunny and even left a note for the tooth fairy. He'd become this mythical, larger-than-life figure of my imagination, and I was too faithful to give up the dream, even after thirteen years without a single card or phone call.

But the suddenly grown-up version of me had bigger problems than wanting love and answers for childhood abandonment, than wishing for a picture of my dad to put in the locket he left behind for me. I scratched out my old dream and turned the paper over to write something new.

I want to survive the next five days.

Now here I stand, on the doorstep of Eloise Framingham's house. I kiss my lucky locket and tuck it back down my collar. The welcome mat I'm standing on is worn, but the small porch is swept clean. There are two cars in the driveway, a minivan and a compact, both with ghosts on the hood. I shift the fake fruit basket to my hip, check the gun in my waistband, and ring the doorbell. It feels like three years pass by the time a shadow darkens the window glass. I pray for the hundredth time that she's ancient and nearly gone.

A guy in his twenties answers in a ratty sweatshirt. "Can I help you?" he says. He looks like he's forgotten what sleep is.

"I have a delivery for Eloise Framingham." My smile is so big he has to know I'm screaming inside.

"Jesus, who would send that?" he says, voice raw. "She can't even eat anymore."

"Oh, I'm sorry. I'm just . . . I just deliver them."

"So leave it on the porch or whatever. I don't care."

He turns to go inside and is about to shut the door in my face. I can't let that happen.

"There's a message, too," I say, desperate. "A singing telegram."

I don't even know if they have those anymore, or what you would sing to someone who's dying, but I've got to get to Eloise. Now.

"A message? You can give it to me."

I shrug in apology. "Sorry, if it's not in person, I don't get paid."

"Fuck your getting paid!" he shouts, his face screwed up. "Just let her die in peace. She deserves that much."

"Who is it?" a reedy voice calls from inside the dark house. "Is it Stephanie?"

I shove the guy aside and shoulder my way through the door,

using my big plastic basket. He shouts and follows me, but I'm too fast. Grief makes people slow, like moving through water. My mom was like that when my dad left. I was just a little kid, but I remember.

I barrel down the hall, toward a room where machines hiss with quiet rhythm. An old woman huddles in the center of a swaybacked bed, surrounded by pillows. The smell of urine and worse lurks under the cheap air fresheners lined up on a windowsill. I slam the door shut and twist the lock, and the guy curses and yanks it from the other side.

"Stephanie?" she says, squinting.

"Are you Eloise Framingham?" I ask, breathless, before I lose my nerve.

"Yes," she rasps. She's got tubes cascading down her face, and a pink silk scarf struggles to stay tied around her bald head. She's nothing but bone, just paper skin collapsed around a flat, hollow frame. Her smooth, well-manicured hands are the only sign that she's much younger than she looks, that she's being eaten inside by disease. One hand flutters to her concave chest, the nails fake and thick and a beautiful, rosy pink. "Is that for me?" she asks.

I smile and nod, my lips wobbling. "Could you sign this, please?"

Her signature is just a jerky line, and she falls back against her pillows with a gasp of pain at the effort. I have never pitied someone so much in my life. And I hate myself for being grateful that what

I'm about to do will be as much of a mercy as it is a murder.

I hold the first button of my shirt up to my mouth and whisper, "By Valor Congressional Order number 7B, your account is past due and hereby declared in default. Due to your failure to remit all owed monies and per your signature just witnessed and accepted, you are given two choices. You may either sign your loyalty over to Valor Savings as an indentured collections agent for a period of five days or forfeit your life. Please choose."

"I'm sorry?"

I've read it so fast and low that there's no way she could have heard anything over her machines. I walk across the worn carpet and hold out the card, and she takes it, her beautiful fingers trembling. And there's no way she could do what I'm doing because there's no way she can even stand up.

"What the hell did you just say to her?" the guy shouts through the door, his body slamming against the wood. I just need it to hold a little longer.

Eloise looks over the card, and my heart wrenches in my chest at how spastic and yet elegant her movements are. She must have been a dancer once. She's like a dying queen, like a deer struck by a car trying to stand on severed legs. Her carved ivory eyes scan the card from purple hollows, and she meets my gaze and nods.

"I don't mind." She holds her chin up. "And I forgive you."

She closes her eyes. I sit the basket gently on the ground. The flimsy door is banging and slamming behind me, the lock about to break. Just as it flies open, I whip out the Glock and shoot Eloise Framingham in her bird-bone chest. She falls back onto the pillows with every bit of grace I imagined. Her lips curl up in a smile. I'm trembling, but she's not. Not anymore.

"What did you do?" the guy shouts. "What the hell did you just do?"

He runs past me to the bed, holding the woman's broken body to his chest and sobbing.

"What was that?" a worried voice calls from the hall, and a college-age girl in a tracksuit appears in the doorway.

"Call the police!" the guy yells. "She shot my mom!"

The girl gasps behind her hand and disappears, running down the hall.

"The police won't come." I stick the Glock back in my jeans and pick up the basket, a thousand years older than I was when I walked in the door. "Read the card. It explains everything."

"Read a card? The police won't come? What the hell is happening?"

He takes the card from Eloise's limp hand as the girl shouts from far away, "The police aren't answering. It was just a message, like for a bank. For Valor Savings. But I called 911, like, three times. What do I do, Matt? Tell me what to do!"

He doesn't answer. He's reading the card. Tears are slipping down his cheeks, he has one arm around his dead mother, and still he's reading the card.

"What does this mean?" He looks up into my eyes like I'm a priest, like I'm God, like I know anything. Like I have power.

"It means you need to start paying off your debts."

I can't stay here a second more, watching a son mourn his dead mother. I can't watch her head flop against his shoulder as he tries to keep her upright.

"I'm sorry," I mutter, and I hurry down the hall, the basket in my hands.

The girl in the tracksuit is nowhere to be seen. The front door is still open. I jog back to the mail truck and pull the Postal Service shirt off over my head and throw it onto the floorboards so it doesn't record my sobbing. My hands are shaking as I put the truck into drive, and I swerve around a cat and nearly hit a mailbox. I can barely drive through the tears, and my mind won't let go of her beautiful hands holding the card as everything else fell away to nothing.

I know she said she didn't mind. That she forgave me. Hell, it was probably a mercy for her. If she was in hospice care, trapped in a bed, strapped to those machines, it's not like she was living a great life. He said she couldn't eat. Eloise Framingham wasn't just going to miraculously recover. That woman was already dead. It was just a matter of time before her brain realized it. Maybe I did her a kindness, doing it quick like that.

But what about her son? Now he's got a dead mom, and he'll probably go into debt just to hold her funeral, and that little paper card isn't going to be much comfort to him. He's probably already ripped it to shreds. If you'd asked me yesterday, I would have said better him than me. But now, seeing the reality of another kid watching his mom die of cancer and then the senseless, cold-blooded government murder in the back bedroom, I'm not so sure. Maybe they weren't ready to let go yet, either of them.

Less than five minutes ago, I stood on her doorstep, wishing she would be ancient. But seeing Eloise Framingham die there, in her bed, with as much dignity as she could muster—now I wish she had been mean or a drug dealer or something, anything that I could hate. I wish she had been like that nasty creeper in the big coat who comes into my work on Kids Eat Free night and rubs himself under the table and tries to corner little boys in the bathroom. I wish it had been someone who deserved to die, instead of someone who simply couldn't afford proper medical care or who never had a chance to beat her disease. When she racked up her debt, Eloise Framingham didn't want a bigger TV or a fancier purse. She just wanted a few more years of life. I'll never even know if she got what she wanted. If it was worth it.

I back away from the mailbox I almost hit and turn around, and my mail truck is stuck right in front of Eloise Framingham's garden gnomes while I frantically try to escape. The guy in the sweatshirt steps onto the porch with a rifle in his hands. He opens his mouth to shout something, but I slam my foot on the gas before I find out what it is. He must fumble the gun, or maybe it's not loaded, or maybe he's too sad to pull the trigger, because the shots I expect never come. I'm down the street and around the corner on two wheels as fast as a mail truck can go, my heart pounding in my chest.

I want out of this tidy, happy-looking neighborhood, fast. Back on the main road, I pass the fallen grandeur and yellowed, empty yards of the Preserve and aim for the place where I parked the mail truck last night as I counted down the hours until the clock started blinking and I had to knock on Bob Beard's door. It's in one of those subdivisions they started before the economy got bad, where they half built three gigantic houses and abandoned the property to grow wild between fancy streetlights. Like the Preserve's equally self-important sister, they call it the Enclave. But it's empty now and has become the sort of place where kids park to make out or smoke weed and drink beer where no one can see them. No one ever lived in those three houses, and they're covered in graffiti tags now.

There's this paved lot behind the most finished house, all screened in by those thick privacy bushes that rich people put up so they don't have to see their neighbors. I guess they were going to have an RV back there or something. But now it's just a convenient, private place for me to park.

The clock resets itself, the red lines blurred through my tears.

Before I give in and punch the shit out of it, I slip between the seats and into the back of the truck. Some of my stuff flew all over the place when I was turning around and speeding away from Eloise Framingham and her son and his gun, and I try to put things back in order. I tuck the pillows into place, shove yarn balls back into my tote, and push the fast-food bags farther under the bed—after trolling for leftover croutons. They're clammy with old dressing, but I'm starving and still overcome with emptiness, so I swallow the few chunks I can find and then cough them right back up into the bag when they won't stay down.

Hating myself completely, I shove the gun under the pillow on my bed, a narrow cot with a thin mattress that came welded into the back of the truck. When I first saw the setup, I thought it was kind of cute. Homey. Now I see it for what it is: a prison.

I sit down on the carefully made bed and realize that my hands are still shaking.

I just killed someone. I killed two people in one day. Eloise was dying in the same way my mom might die. I'm living in the back of a truck. All I've eaten today was fast food, and I puked most of it back up. My blood sugar's probably low, or maybe I'm in shock. I've got eight more people to kill, and one of them is a guy around my age.

I don't know why killing Maxwell Beard should be any worse than killing anyone else. A life is a life, right? It's not like Jesus thought there was a big difference, if I remember what little I learned when

my mom still made me go to Sunday school. For what I'm doing now, age and attractiveness and goodness and great taste in bands don't matter.

Still, I'm dreading seeing him again, putting the gun to his chest and actually pulling the trigger this time. Deep down, I know it's worse because he's my age and we like the same music. Maybe he's just another keep-up-with-the-Joneses douchebag, like his dad. But I saw the fear in his eyes, the devastation. He's just a kid, like me, and kids should be allowed to make their own mistakes. Whatever he did, we're both victims of our parents' weaknesses and bad decisions. And that strikes a little too close to home. I hope I can convince him to do what I'm doing, work off the debt in a horrible but surprisingly quick way, and be done with it. He might believe me if I tell him it's not so bad.

I snort. That's one big lie to swallow.

I yank up the back door of the truck so I can stare at the high grass sloping down to a forest. Maybe some fresh air will help me relax, make my stomach stop churning. I just need a nap. I haven't slept since the man in the black suit showed up. When I found the list in the envelope yesterday morning, I tried to Google these people, to find out more about them, but our Internet was mysteriously down. Was it just ours, or everyone's? Is Valor Savings taking over the media, too? Do they now own the television stations, the news, the radio? Are the phones even working? Have they shut down the cell signals? I know the police aren't answering the phones, but what about the hospitals? Has a bank really taken over the entire country overnight, just like that? Out here, in the backyard of an unfinished house in an abandoned neighborhood, I have no way of knowing what's happening in the real world, whatever that is now.

I set the alarm on my phone for four hours from now and toss it back into my yarn bag. Other than making sure I'm awake in time to visit the next victim during Postal Service hours, my smartphone is now completely useless. No bars anywhere, all day. I'm more alone than I've ever been in my life, and if I don't eat something, I'm going to barf acid, so I open the mini-fridge that's bolted to the back of my truck. It and the tiny microwave are both run by thick cords that snake through the truck, and I'm not even going to try to understand how all that works.

The mozzarella sticks I bought at the drive-through earlier are almost frozen, so I microwave them until they melt. They're mealy and mushy and burn my tongue, but I snarf the entire box and drink a can of soda, which makes me shift uncomfortably. That's the one thing this mini-RV doesn't have: a bathroom. But I do have a four-pack of toilet paper. I think about breaking into the house and using their facility, if anyone bothered to put in a toilet. But I can see missing windows, and I know other, less responsible people have already broken in. The toilets are probably ruined and already full. So I just pee out back in the weeds, glaring around, feeling both like the only person in the world and like a rabbit waiting to get eaten by something bigger.

Back in the truck, I lie down on the bed, holding an embroidered pillow to my chest and staring at the posters I've taped to the ceiling. I wonder what will happen to bands, to music and musicians, now that Valor Savings owns the country and democracy is dead as a doornail. Will life mostly go on as it always has, or will we suddenly have new rules, new standards for living? Will we be like Socialists, or something new, some freaky breed of responsible capitalists in matching Valor uniforms? Or will it be full-on dystopia?

So far, I've focused on getting through the next five days and then taking my mom to the oncologist the moment my bonus arrives from Valor. I don't know how I would live without crafting and music. Without the giddy joy of yarn bombing a cart at the grocery store or slipping embroidered bookmarks into the soulless bestsellers at the bookstore. Without the glory of going to shows, of charging into the pit, of swaying or slam dancing or just singing along with a crowd. But living without art and music would be easier than living without my mom. And a lot better than dying.

I have a brief mental image of my favorite local band chained up in jail for singing anti-Valor songs and shiver. My history teacher once said that wherever there's oppression, there are going to be people who won't put up with it. Even my yarn bombing is its own form of protest, although I probably wouldn't get in too much trouble if I got caught.

Thunder cracks outside, the world gone gray with almost-rain. When I turn over to sleep, all I can see is the list of names I found in the envelope. I've already got it memorized. The last two names are the ones that worry me the most; now that I've met Max, I know both of them.

But Ashley Cannon is next, and I don't know if that's a guy or a girl. I'm going to assume it's a girl. She lives about five miles from here. With less than twelve hours to go, I should just get it over with. I assume Valor is tamping down the rumors, keeping people from using technology to spread the word that it's open season on debt and the police aren't going to be there for protection. The faster I get my list done, the easier it should be. But I'm on the verge of collapse, and I'd rather go unconscious by seeming choice.

The first raindrops rattle on the flat roof of the truck, reminding me all too much of gunshots. I get up to yank the back door down before it can rain inside. The truck is borrowed, but the mementos inside are mine, and they're more important now than ever. The posters carefully taped to the walls might represent the last shows I ever go to, the last few times that music was completely free to say whatever it wanted to say and that I was innocent and unrestricted enough to enjoy it on my own terms.

The storm smells so good that I leave the door cracked open, maybe a foot up from the floor. Just enough to let in the gray light and the sweet scent of rain on fall leaves. I shuck off my jeans and long-sleeved T-shirt so that all I've got on are panties and the white tank I wear instead of a bra. There's a painful zit coming up on my chin, the kind that hurts like hell, so I dab some white zit cream on it and scrub my teeth with one of those fingertip disposable toothbrushes. If I were on a road trip or a vacation, this might be fun. But I've never done that, never even slept in a hotel bed. This is as close as I'm going to get.

With a shiver that's only half from the cold, I crawl under my favorite blanket, the flowered quilt my mom bought for me off the sale rack at T.J. Maxx when I was nine. I gave an identical one to my best friend for her birthday that year. We embroidered them one afternoon, our initials and BFFS 4EVER in purple thread, and I wonder if she still has hers. I haven't really had a close female friend since I started high school, and I run fingers over the clumsily stitched letters, remembering what it was like when everything was easy. When I didn't even know what debt was.

Pulling the gun out from under my pillow, I curl around it, running a finger along the barrel. PROPERTY OF VALOR SAVINGS is stamped on it in gold. Although I know exactly how many bullets there are, I eject the clip and count them. Thirteen bullets left. Eight more lives on the line. That's all they gave me, but it's not the only weapon I brought.

With a deep breath, I mutter the prayer my mom used to make me say every night before bed.

Now I lay me down to sleep

I pray the Lord my soul to keep

Watch and guard me through the night

Awake me with the morning light

When I was little, I would follow it up with "God bless" and then list the names of everyone I cared about. Mommy, Daddy, Gramma and Gramps, Aunt Patty, Amber, my other friends, my teachers, my neighbors, the stray cat I sometimes fed but that my mom wouldn't let me bring inside. Over the years, as I lost the people I cared about most, it ended up with me just asking God to take care of my mom.

But instead of "God bless" and a bunch of names, tonight I say, "Please forgive me for Robert Beard and Eloise Framingham. Amen."

God doesn't answer. He never does.

And his silence doesn't last long this time.

3.

ASHLEY CANNON

Something heavy lands on my chest, and I jerk awake with the hard bite of metal against my throat. My heart pounds in my ears, nearly drowning out the heavy rain drumming the roof of the truck, and I almost piss myself in terror.

"Why'd you kill my dad?" he says, voice low and fierce.

I knew it was him even before he spoke. Who else could have found me out here? Who else would have cared? Eloise Framingham's son couldn't even pull the trigger from thirty feet away; there's no way he could put a knife to my skin. But Robert Beard's son can. He's big, straddling my waist with all his weight, and I can barely breathe.

"I told you to read the card," I say through clenched teeth. I struggle beneath him, and the knife, or whatever it is, stings my neck and makes me hiss.

"Don't move," he says, followed in the same breath by, "Where's your gun?"

I swallow and roll my eyes. Did he bring friends? I don't think so—the truck isn't moving, and I see only one bedheaded hulk with a knife. The red digital clock is reflected in the wetness of his eyes, the seconds draining away.

"It's under the front seat," I say. "Can I pull up my blanket now?"

He looks down and realizes that the blanket is puddled on my side and I'm not wearing much. It's cold out, and the tank's mostly see-through. I don't have much, but even in the low light, it's showing. The knife jerks away like I'm going to cut him instead of the other way around.

But I lied. The gun is in my right hand, still under the blanket, just like it was when I fell asleep. I tighten my grip and find the trigger. Thankfully, much like his old man, Max Beard is a sucker. No one expects a girl as skinny and ridiculous as me to be any kind of a threat. I take a deep breath, letting my boobs stick out inches from his arm.

"Oh God. Sorry." He fumbles the knife, and it clatters against the metal floor of the mail truck. It's lost now, in the dark under my bed, and he knows it. I smile.

"No problem," I say, much cooler than I feel. My heart is beating so loud I'm surprised the sound isn't filling the truck like something out of a Poe story, and I've gone all cold again. My finger is cramped where it holds the trigger, and I make sure to point the gun away from myself, in case I lose all feeling and do something stupid. He scoots down farther, still straddling me, but not so heavily and around my knees instead of my waist. At least I can breathe.

I pull the blanket up over my chest with an embarrassed smile that's both real and fake at the same time. But when I go to shove the gun in his face, I find it pinned under his leg. That's when I look down and notice that the straddling and wiggling had other consequences that he probably didn't think about when he was trying to intimidate the psycho chick who shot his dad. He's in flannel pajama pants, and it's my turn to look away, embarrassed from catching him in a deeply private moment for the second time today.

In that pause, everything changes.

He should have been an easy kill. I should have marked Maxwell Beard off my list and collected my bonus, easy as that. But seeing the confusion and anger and grief and naked, unwelcome desire on his tearstained face crumbles me from the inside out. No one has ever looked at me like that before, like I'm something, and even if the circumstances are impossibly horrible and horribly impossible, I can't help it. I can't lift the gun. I'm stunned and weirdly flattered and mortified, and at the base of it all, I don't want to be the kind of girl who kills a guy with a pajama boner.

The silence spreads out in the dead air of my mail truck, broken only by the steady drip of rain falling from sky to pine tree to government-issued vehicle and our hearts banging like monkeys in a drum. The longer we don't speak, the more awkward it gets, like the never-ending slow song in the middle school cafeteria at a dance you didn't want to go to where no one asked you to dance. He's cuter than the boys who usually ask me out and who I usually turn down, and I can tell by the way he tosses his bangs that he knows he's cute, but he doesn't know what to do, either, because I killed his dad this morning and his hormones are overriding his brain. I guess this isn't a situation you can plan for.

I realize for the first time that what my biology teacher said is actually true: no matter what we think or what we say or what we hope to become, at the root of everything, we're only animals.

He finally clears his throat and scoots back, shifting his shirt over the telltale bump in his britches. I sit up and scoot back, too, pulling my knees up and clutching the old quilt to my chest for real now, knowing that the cool air, thin shirt, and bizarre rush of closeness are giving me headlights that he can't help staring at.

"So," I say.

"So," he says, and to his credit, his voice doesn't break.

"Well? You attacked me. You go first."

"Why'd you do it?" He looks away. "You owe me that much."

"If you read the card, you know why. That's why there's a card."

I sweep sleep-sweaty bangs away from my forehead. It suddenly occurs to me that I've gone to bed with white zit paste speckled across my chin, and I mentally curse myself for being the world's vainest, most idiotic bounty hunter. That doesn't stop me from rubbing my chin against the quilt, hoping it will flake off.

But why do I care if I look like a freak? Why am I letting him get to me at all? He's just an assignment, and an easy one at that. My pity should have fled with his embarrassment. I could still end it, right now. My finger twitches on the gun under the quilt, the one he's apparently forgotten about. He edges off my legs and sits on the end of the bed, feet firmly on the floor.

"My dad was a dick, and he did a lot of bad things," he says, his eyes cutting to the ceiling and walls of the truck, where tape and putty hold my favorite band posters to the dinged-up white metal. He smiles, but only for a second, barely a flash of teeth in the cloudy darkness.

"Yeah, and your dad should have read the fine print when he took out credit cards from Valor Savings," I shoot back, surreptitiously wiping my chin with the back of my hand and frowning at the grit of the zit cream that's stubbornly left behind.

"Banks don't kill people," he says confidently, like he's not used to being wrong. Something about his pompous surety makes me lash out before I can stop myself.

"You're right. Banks don't kill people," I say. "They make other people do it for them in exchange for not setting their houses on fire, shooting them, and letting their mothers die a long, slow death by cancer."

He sucks in a breath, and I know immediately that I've said too much. It's more than I'm allowed to say, more than I meant to say.

"Shit," I mutter under my breath, hoping the camera/mic in my shirt is wadded up tightly enough under the front seat to keep me from getting in serious trouble. The Valor guy didn't mention that button at all, and the references in the paperwork are random and worded with purposeful confusion. "Constant surveillance" and "limited monitoring" and "unrecorded kills will not satisfy contract requirements." I have no idea what that button is capable of. Just as they have no idea what I'm capable of.

But Maxwell Beard doesn't know about the button. He just knows more about me than he should.

"I'm so sorry," he says, and I'm mad at him, and I'm mad at myself, and it's all because I can't fathom how to be angry at my broken mother and the new corporate government that's shaking me like a rag doll. I'm not used to pity from supposedly rich guys, and I don't like it.

"Piss off, Max," I say.

Confusion passes over his face.

"You called me that before. But Max is my brother," he says. "I'm Wyatt."

I exhale and let my head fall against the back of the passenger seat, my mouth twitching into a smile that lasts mere seconds. It shouldn't matter. It's not going to make things any easier. Today I killed his dad. One day soon, I have to kill his brother. If I live through it, he's going to hate me even more than he already does. But all I feel is relief that I don't have to kill this guy, now or later. And I can't tell him that. And still I'm fighting the smile, and he's looking at me like he wants to smile too, but can tell that, deep down, he shouldn't.

We are possibly the two most messed-up people on earth.

"What?" he asks.

"I'm sorry."

"What are you sorry for?" He swallows hard. "My dad?"

He stands, paces, and slides down to sit on the floor against the far side of the truck. The air is charged, crisp and tinged with pink. I wait until he's got his pants arranged, and then I turn to face him. Things were happening too fast for me to catalog details after I shot his dad and ran away to keep from puking all over him. He's about my age and more of a Wyatt than a Max. He's definitely cute, although he looks and smells like he hasn't bathed today. Jesus, who would? With your dad lying dead on your doorstep and the police nowhere in sight as you call 911 again and again, praying someone will answer? Knowing that no one is investigating, dusting for finger-prints, promising to find the murderer? Still, he doesn't look or smell awful. Just raw. Broken. He fills the truck in a way I don't.

His hair is wheat-gold and straight, falling over puddly brown eyes that are serious and sharp. He's big, like an athlete, and tall, and I know firsthand that he weighs more than I expected. But what kind of guy is he, really? The clues I would normally get from his style are absent. Plaid pajama pants, bare feet. He's wearing a faded black T-shirt, probably replacing the band shirt he was wearing before, because I bet he held his dad, hugged him, dragged him inside, got covered in blood. But he has something tattooed on the inside of his arm, near his elbow. There's not enough light for me to make it out, but it's black, probably words. He's giving me the same once-over, and it's intense.

And somehow, without my noticing it, he got his knife back. It's clenched in his right hand, against the cold metal of the truck floor. My own hand hasn't left the gun hidden under the quilt. The moment would be agonizing enough without weapons added to the mix. As it is, I can barely breathe, and I don't know whether to talk or run or cry. I want to connect with him, touch him, beg him for absolution, shoot him a dozen times for looking at me that way. Instead I just stare at him, waiting for something to happen.

I wonder what I look like to a stranger. A normal girl. Thin, but I usually wear big sweaters or coats, the sort of clothes that hide my body for the sake of showing off my style. My dark hair is scraggly and asymmetrical on purpose, and I wear red lipstick like a dare. I can tell that I'm not the type of girl his type of guy would go for, not a Snow White fit for his Prince Charming. But I bet the see-through white tank top helps. Right now, startled from sleep, I'm as absent of social signals and pretense as he is. Stripped bare.

In the back of this truck, ripped from my normal life, I could be anyone. I ache for the armor of my belongings, to be more than just a scrubbed-clean, nearly naked murderer in a mail truck. Valor wanted an invisible soldier, of sorts, and I guess they got one. But I'm doing this on my own terms. And whatever Wyatt sees, his eyes don't seem to accuse me. He looks more wounded and curious, just as tense as I am.

His fingers drum against the truck's floor. He's waiting for me to say something.

"Why a knife?" I finally ask.

He holds it up; it's your basic serrated steak knife, flashing with the red of the clock. "My dad sold all the guns, back when he was still trying to pay the mortgage. This was all I could find." He puts it down again, like he's embarrassed. "I didn't really think it through. I keep it in my glove box in case my car ever goes off a bridge, so I can cut the seat belts. Stupid, right?"

Now it's my turn. But I don't show him the gun. And I don't think he's stupid.

"I'm just sorry," I say, kind of flustered, kind of defensive. But completely sincere.

"Sounds like they didn't give you a lot of choices," he offers gently, and it's more than I deserve.

"No, they didn't," I whisper. "Just look away for a minute, okay?"

He shrugs and lets his chin drop to his chest, eyes closed. I grab my jeans off the floor and scramble into them under my blanket without knocking my gun to the ground or letting it make noise, which sounds a lot easier than it is. I leave the gun under the blanket before lurching into the front seat. Ass in the air, I check that my mail shirt is wadded up tightly and stuffed under the driver's seat, making sure that the top button is wrapped inside the bundle. I have to keep it dry and near. If the camera button gets too wet or stepped on, it will break, and I'll be in trouble. But I don't want them to know about Wyatt. While I'm up there, I check the rearview mirror and lick my finger and scrub away the last of the zit cream before turning back around.

"Did you just do a mirror check?" The corner of Wyatt's mouth barely turns up, and I realize I have no idea what he looks like when he's smiling for real, or if he's the kind of person who laughs a lot. I only know what he looks like when he's crying and murderous. And that he was watching me when I asked him not to. And that he didn't say anything about me going for the gun supposedly under the front seat.

"Yeah. No. I was checking my shirt. It's bugged. Or whatever." I look around the van, wishing I knew if anything else was likewise

bugged. Too late. "Look, I'm not supposed to tell you anything, but I'm going to anyway."

"I'm listening."

I sit on my bed, leaning back against the opposite side of the truck from him and pulling my blanket up over me to trap the heat. The frosty metal bites through my thin tank top. His legs are stretched out, his bare feet crossed under the bed. I crook my knees so our feet don't touch. My socks don't match, but they never do.

"So you read your dad's card. I got a card too. Turns out my mom's in serious debt after a car accident and has cancer but was trying to hide it all from me. The guy from Valor who came to my door put a gun to her chest and said we would both die if I didn't do this. He threatened to shoot us and burn our house down."

Now's the part of the conversation where he should say something, but he doesn't. The silence feels wrong. I keep talking to fill the space.

"It's not like I want to do it. It's not like I want to kill people. But my dad left when I was really young, and my mom is all I've got, and I can't let her die. For the next five days, I am the bank's bitch." I stare at my painted fingernails; I've already chewed off most of the paint. "Probably after that, too."

"Why don't you just kill yourself?" he asks quietly. Did I imagine him rubbing his wrist?

I snort. "They already thought of that. Much like the church, suicide doesn't count. You die in duty, you're excused. You off your-self, they treat it the same as running away." I mime a big explosion, fingers shaking imaginary hellfire down on my mom's house.

Wyatt's eyes glaze over at the thin red line his knife made on my neck before wandering up to my posters, and he almost smiles again. He runs a hand through his hair, making it stand up in ragged spikes in the red glow of the clock. I probably look like a corpse, but it's not like I'm trying to win a beauty pageant. I just want us both to get out of this mail truck alive, without hurting each other any more than we have to. And maybe, just a little, I want him to understand.

"You didn't know your mom was in debt?" he finally says.

"I knew we were poor. And I knew her insurance sucked and the hospital time and meds were a serious problem after her accident. I didn't know she'd been fired, lost her insurance, and pawned the car title. We were doing pretty good a year ago. You've probably passed our neighborhood. River Run? It's just around the corner from you, but my entire house would fit in your living room."

"Yeah, we pass it all the time." He tosses his hair. I wonder if he straight irons his bangs. "That's why I don't know you. We go to different schools."

I snort. "Yeah. You go to Haven with all the rich kids, and I go to Big Creek with all the losers."

"There's nothing wrong with that," he says. "I didn't ask for . . . It's not like . . ."

"Like what?"

"I'm not going to say I don't want to be rich, because we both know that's stupid. Everyone wants to be rich. But I knew what my dad was doing. I knew he got fired for embezzling, and I knew he was blackballed, and I knew the bills were racking up. I saw them in the trash, the ones that they start sending in pink instead of white. Like you just forgot to pay them because they weren't a bright enough color or something. But my dad . . . It's not like I could have said anything. I mentioned it once, that we might need to make a budget or cut out . . . some stuff. And my dad went ballistic and smashed my laptop."

Now it's my turn to stare at him. I feel curious about this strange fake-rich boy who somehow tracked me down in the rain, possibly to kill me, and who is now waxing philosophic about his father's debt. Did he actually think he could kill me? Does he really have what it takes to do that? Pulling the trigger on his dad was one of the hardest things I've ever done, and that was four feet away with a gun. What does it take to put a knife through someone's throat? He's playing with it now, cleaning out his fingernails like it's just the most normal thing to do with a steak knife. But maybe he knows how to use it on more than steak. I probably look pretty harmless from the outside too.

"Why am I telling you this?" he finally says.

He looks up, and our eyes meet somewhere in the center of a repurposed delivery truck.

"Stages of grief?" I venture, fiddling with my locket.

"Let's see. What am I feeling? Well, I watched my dad die, and I felt confusion, fear, anger, and sadness. I got in my car in my pajamas to drive to the hospital because they wouldn't answer the frigging phone and saw a familiar girl driving a big-ass mail truck past my neighborhood. That was anger again. I followed her into the middle of nowhere to kill her in some weird action-movie-revenge scene with the knife from my glove box. So that was more anger, and I'm pretty sure I felt insanity in there. I sat in my car for two horrible hours, crying and thinking and raging and waiting for this stupid truck to do something, anything but sit there in the rain."

I open my mouth, and he stops me with a finger in my face.

"And I finally charged over here to kill you before the rain quit and I had to see your face in the sunlight. That was desperation. When I failed, there was more anger. And now that we've talked and I know we like the same music and that your mom's dying and you don't have a choice, there's nothing but confusion."

"Those aren't the stages of grief they taught us in health class," I say like an idiot.

"Oh, well, you go to poor school." He gives a comic eye roll. "At rich school, we take notes on hundred-dollar bills using unicorn tears, and our grief is vastly different and more complex. I was talking to Chauncey just the other day, and—"

One lone chuckle escapes despite my best efforts to keep it tamped down.

"Shut up," I say. "This is serious."

"Maybe I'm off base here." He recrosses his feet. "But things are majorly effed up. I don't see how being serious is going to make our situation any better."

"So."

"So."

He looks around the mail truck again, taking it all in.

"Did you see their show at the Masquerade last year?" he says, inclining his head toward a poster.

"Of course. It was amazing."

"Were you part of the conga line?"

"Of course." I mimic his earlier eye roll. "We poor people live to conga. Because it's free. We conga to the food stamp line. I already sold my hair to buy tickets for this year's show, but I need to live long enough to go and conga. So what are we going to do?"

This moment with him has lasted way too long. I used to dream of being trapped in a small, dark space with a guy who wasn't completely wretched. Not that I'm saying I like Wyatt, or that I even know him, or that there's any point in pretending that anyone meets their soul mate on the first day of the apocalypse, but at least he's not a mouth-breathing troglodyte or a dropout or a druggie. Probably. He can form coherent sentences. And he's cute.

But I don't forget for a single second that there's a gun under my hand and a knife in his.

Apparently, he can't forget it either.

"We could pull a Romeo and Juliet," he says brightly, holding up the knife. "But not suicide. Like . . . a homicide pact."

"That's the dumbest thing I've ever heard."

"Whatever. It's romantic as hell."

I sigh dramatically. "That's a story. This is real. We can't just sit in the truck forever, making polite conversation and bad jokes and reliving awesome concerts. I'm on a pretty tight schedule." I incline my head toward the bright red clock in the dash, the numbers ticking down. Ten more hours until it starts blinking again.

"Places to go, people to kill?"

"Seriously, shut up, Wyatt."

He lets out a long, controlled sigh that ends in a groan, signaling that the flirty banter is over.

"You've got a lot of nerve," he says. "You think you can just tell people to shut up and they're actually going to do it? Just because you have a gun and work for the bank that, according to you and a printed card, now owns America? You can't tell me how to feel. Which is back to anger, by the way, so thanks for that."

"At least I didn't try to slit your throat while you were sleeping," I shoot back.

"But I'm on that list," he says. "Aren't I?"

I swallow hard and look away, my gaze landing on the stuffed turtle my ex–best friend gave me for my eighth birthday. She was as close as I've ever come to having a sister, to having anyone to love outside of my mom. How does Wyatt feel about Max? And if I tell him the truth, will he let me just drive away and get on with my business?

"Nope," I say. "You're not on it. If you were, I would have shot you already. I get a bonus for that sort of thing."

"Jesus freaking Christ." He bangs his head back against the truck. "They've turned life into a video game. And you just keep playing, or your guy dies."

"It sucks. But that doesn't change anything," I mutter.

"I felt the same way about calculus."

"Do you think this is a big joke?" I shout. "Seriously?"

The look on his face alerts me to the fact that I'm now waving around a loaded gun that's supposed to be under the front seat. He clears his throat, and I lay the pistol gently on my flowered quilt.

"I know it's not a joke," he says quietly. "I just don't see how laughing hurts anything."

"It's just so stupid," I say. "Like—"

But he doesn't get to hear my next great simile, because I'm interrupted by the sound of a car skidding to a stop, brakes squealing. Bass thumps the air, and my eyes meet Wyatt's.

"I thought this neighborhood was abandoned," he says.

"It is."

Gun in hand, I scramble up and peek between the front seats of the mail truck. I can't see anything yet, but car doors slam on the other side of the house, probably in the driveway.

"What is it?" Wyatt asks.

"Can you shoot a gun?"

"What?"

"Can. You. Shoot. A gun?" I say.

"Of course. This is Georgia."

When the first guy appears around the side of the house, I glance back at Wyatt. He's standing in the middle of my truck, stooped over and out of place in his plaid pajama pants and faded shirt and sleep-wild hair. He looks so big and helpless and clueless, and my heart clenches.

"Can I trust you?" I whisper.

Two more guys follow the first one, their arms straining to hold bulging black trash bags. The guys are in all black, with hoodies pulled down over their weird white masks. Gold chains glint around their necks, women's jewelry in disarray. When they see my mail truck, they drop their bags and shout at each other and pull guns as they approach. My throat goes dry.

"Can I trust you?" I ask again, more urgently. Wyatt hasn't answered, hasn't moved.

"No," he says quietly.

Six guys with six guns are creeping up on the truck, maybe fifty feet away. I still trust him more than I trust them.

"Wyatt, listen. There's a gun in the microwave. It's loaded. Don't worry if you kill anyone. The police aren't going to be involved."

I don't take my eyes off the men whispering as they surround the truck, but I'm satisfied to hear the microwave door open and the magazine sliding out of the gun as Wyatt checks that it's loaded. I go cold all over, knowing that now is the decisive moment. Just as I had my chance to shoot him and didn't, now he's got a clean shot at me. I tense, refusing to turn my head to see if he's aiming for the mess of loose hairs tangled around my exposed neck.

"You going to confront them or just start shooting when they get too close?" he whispers from right behind me. I wait to feel the kiss of metal against my back, but it doesn't come, and I let myself exhale. But the cold tension doesn't leave me, and it won't until I'm dead or these guys are gone. Maybe not even then. Maybe not for four more days.

With a deep breath, I slip into the front seat and squash the US Postal Service hat down over my hair. The windows in the sliding doors have no glass, of course, so most of my body is exposed, and the transparent tank top doesn't help against the chill. Almost without thinking, I reach under my seat, slip on the Postal Service shirt, and paste on a shaky smile as the men skid to a stop in front of the truck.

"Can I help you?" I ask.

"What the fuck, kid?" one of the guys asks, his eyes black pools behind his mask. He's thick all over, with beefy shoulders and a belly running to fat. The women's necklaces look ridiculous piled around his bull neck, and I wonder briefly if they're loot or kill trophies.

"Just taking a quick lunch break before I finish my rounds," I say. "Lots of mail to deliver."

"Bullshit," the guy says. "It ain't lunchtime." His eyes wander down to my chest and stay there. The other guys stare from him to me, but most of them can't stop looking at me like I'm a Thanksgiving turkey with its legs tied together.

"I was sleepy," I say defensively. "And I think it's more my manager's business than yours, anyway. What are you going to do, call the Postal Service and complain? 'Cause here's a hint: you're going to be on hold a long time."

The guys edge in closer, snickering like hyenas behind their masks.

"I got a package for you," the first guy says with a leer.

"So where's your mail, honey?" another guy asks.

"Um, in the back of the truck?"

"Let's go back there and check," one of the guys says, moving closer and giving me a sort of smoldering look through his mask. "I'll give her some mail. Hot, American male." He reaches toward my leg, and I scoot away like I'm edging around a puddle of barf.

"What are y'all doing out here, anyway?" I ask. "This house is abandoned."

"Hey, we don't bust you for sleeping on the job, you don't bust us for hanging out in an empty house," the first guy says. "Bank owns it. Bank won't mind."

"No phone over here," a guy says, and I realize he sneaked around my truck to the passenger seat while I wasn't watching. I'm surrounded.

"Jeans are too tight to hide a phone, anyway," says the smoldery guy, leaning closer into my open door.

"Let's go in back and I'll show you that package," the leader says. "Now."

I feel a new kind of panic, one I've never personally felt before but as old as the word "no." I'm not sheltered or stupid, and I know girls who have been raped. But I've always been careful, not going to dangerous places alone after dark or hanging with roofie hogs. I've been really lucky. Up until this week, I guess. But I have several advantages that I didn't have before. Guns. Diplomatic immunity. Wyatt.

Seeing my hesitation, the lead guy pulls his own gun out of the back of his pants. It looks shockingly like mine.

"I said now, sweetheart."

With a shaky breath, I edge between the seats and into the back of the truck, keeping my gun hidden in my waistband under my postal shirt while we're still in full view of his friends. I've heard of guys like them. I can tell by their clothes and accents that they're not trailer trash, not a gang. More like middle management and IT gone wrong, computer guys with desk-job paunches. Since the economy mostly collapsed, too many people are out of work, and the police can't keep up with looting and theft. Gold is worth more than money, and judging by the metal each man wears like a badge, they do pretty well. I'm just another spoil of war, as far as they're concerned. So I won't feel too bad about killing them.

Or so I tell myself.

Something rustles in the truck behind me, and I realize that it's darker than it should be. Wyatt must have shut the door. I only hope the rest of the gang isn't going to come around back, reopen it, and watch the fun. I want surprise on my side. Our side, I guess, since Wyatt is in it now too.

The truck lurches as the leader climbs into the front seat. I duck farther into the blackness of the truck, shuffling into the back corner and pulling out my gun, holding it behind my butt.

"You gonna act shy, huh?" The guy rubs himself through his jeans. "Baby, they're gonna hear you moaning all the way to downtown Atlanta."

He squeezes between the front seats, barely fitting through. As my eyes adjust to the near darkness, I note Wyatt waiting behind the passenger seat, his face twisted up with rage. For just a second,

I'm surprised—it seems like a pretty aggressive place to be for a guy who recently tried to kill me himself.

"You can't hide, honey," the guy says. "Don't even try. It doesn't have to hurt."

Before I raise my own gun, Wyatt shoots him in the chest. It's muffled a little by the guy's shirt, but the light blinds me for a moment, and the sound is amplified by the metal walls of the truck. The hard scent of gunpowder and metal fills the trapped air, and I rub my nose with the knuckles of my gun hand, stunned.

Shouts erupt outside, but I can barely hear them over the ringing in my ears.

"Dave, what happened, man? Did you shoot her or what?"

I cram myself against the wall of the truck, wishing to hell I was farther away from the slumped figure of Dave. Wyatt crouches in place, still as death, as we wait to see if another guy is going to try the front doors. Behind me, one of the guys jerks on the back door, and I spin as it ratchets open. He reaches for my arm, and I shoot him in the belly before I really know what's happened.

"Shit, man. Shit. Forget it. Come on!"

The remaining thugs take off, leaving Wyatt and me alone in the back of the truck with a corpse. I'm mostly deaf, white spots dancing in my vision, and the gun quakes in my hand like it wants to jump to the ground and beg forgiveness. I slide down the cold wall and collapse into a ball on the floor.

"Did that just happen?" Wyatt asks, and he sounds as empty as I feel.

"You saved me," I say, voice quivering.

The reality of what almost happened falls on me like a concrete block. Nearly raped out in the middle of nowhere by a gang of unemployed suburbanites. The guy I shot in the stomach writhes on the wet grass outside, cussing and moaning; his friends didn't even try to save him or drag him away. On the other side of the house, a car squeals off, without the thumping bass this time.

"We've got to get out of here," I say. "They might come back."

"What about the one outside? Do we call 911 for him?"

"For the rapist thug? Really?" I wipe away tears.

Wyatt walks across the truck, his steps shaking the metal floor. My hearing must be back with a vengeance, because his bare feet seem to boom. He holds out a hand and pulls me to standing, and I wobble against him on unsteady legs. He wobbles right back against me, and I laugh weakly at how we've gone from strong to weak in a matter of seconds. My left hand is on his right arm, and his left hand is on my right arm, and neither one of us has let go of our gun. His skin is warm under my hand—hot, really—and I can feel the veins in his forearm.

"It just seems like the right thing to do," he says, looking at the body in the shadows. "Calling someone."

"You are still not getting this." I have to tilt my head back to look up at him from under the brim of my hat. "He's dead either way—911 doesn't work anymore. You call it, and you get a message from Valor Savings. We're on our own. The police aren't even going to show up. For at least a few days, you're pretty much free to have as much anarchy as you want. If there's anyone you want to kill, just go for it." He lets go of my arm, and I sink right back down to the floor. "Open season on assholes."

"I just killed a guy," Wyatt says, towering above me.

His plaid pants are too big, and I can't even see where his legs are inside of them. For a moment, I think that he might be utterly insubstantial and unreal, but then I notice that there are dark hairs on his toes, and it strikes me as too weird to be my imagination, that he's a real person, and that he might be as devastated inside as I am, unable to comprehend a world with no consequences and no safety.

"How do you feel?" I ask.

"Empty? Blank?" Wyatt turns away and pokes his pinkie in a bullet hole in the truck's metal wall, right behind where Dave was standing. "I have no idea." He collapses beside me and runs a hand through already-wild hair.

"That's how I've been feeling too. Just totally lost."

"It's like, I know they deserved it. They were bad guys, and they were going to . . . Well, you know what they were going to do. But I've never killed anything bigger than a mouse for my snake, and I always feel a little bad about that, anyway."

Wyatt's eyes sweep over to the dead guy by the truck seats, and I can't help looking too. The body is hard to ignore with our feet almost touching it. Him.

He's facedown, with a bald spot on the top of his head and these weird spiky things that look like a fence coming out of his scalp, which I guess must be hair plugs. Behind his mask, he probably looks like your average derp. But I'm glad I can't see his eyes.

I realize my finger is still on the trigger and have to pry it off. I've shot this gun three times. I've killed three times. Each time, I've died a little inside. How much of me is left?

"Why'd you put on your shirt and hat?" Wyatt asks, and my eyes dart up to him.

"I don't know. I wanted to cover myself. Maybe look official to scare them away."

And that's when I realize that the shirt isn't choosy. It sees everything that I see, maybe more. Maybe someone's watching. And maybe they're seeing Wyatt.

Oh, shit.

"Do you trust me?" I whisper.

"No," he says.

"Good. You shouldn't."

I stand up, aim the gun, and pull the trigger for the fourth time.

Light and sound explode again, and the truck rocks when Wyatt slams into the wall. Even before the gun can recoil, I've turned, a hand

around that bugged button. I pull the shirt over my head and wad it up into a ball with the button in the very center of the shirt and my fist.

"Jesus freaking Christ," Wyatt says, voice shaky as he huddles on the floor, arms covering his head. "What the hell was that?"

I shove the shirt into the fridge before looking at him—really looking at him—by the light of dawn. His eyes are huge, the pupils tiny pinpricks in the center of speckled brown. Less than a foot away from him, there's a bullet hole in the truck, with a weird little metal rip around it. I notice that it looks nothing like those fake sticker bullet holes tough kids at my school paste all over their moms' old sedans. Now Wyatt's got his hands over his stomach like I actually shot him, just like I shot the guy outside.

"My shirt," I say, surprised that I can breathe, much less talk. I was cold before, cold and tense, but now I feel hot and quick and hyper, like my wires got crossed and I'm overheating. "I told you it was bugged. The top button is a camera, maybe a microphone. It saw you. And if they knew that you were alive, that you were here in my truck, that you knew what I was doing, what I was sent to do . . ." I pause, my chin quivering. "They'd kill you. Or make me kill you. Maybe they'd send someone else. I don't know. I was just told not to tell anyone else what I was doing. Hand over the card and leave. Or else."

He uncovers his head, rubs his ears. "What's the *or else*?"

"How would I know? Do you think they answer questions? Do

you think there's a freaking FAQ online where you can go click on 'Indentured Assassins' and see frequently asked questions? It just seemed like pretending to kill you would be a lot better than waiting around to see the consequences of letting you live."

"But you could have shot me!"

"I'm not an idiot, Wyatt. If I wanted to shoot you, you'd be dead."

"So I'm really not on your list? Like, inheriting my dad's debt or whatever like you did with your mom?"

He stands slowly, his back dragging against the metal. We stare at each other across the truck. At each of our sides, a gun hangs limp. Mine is still warm.

"No," I say, and I feel like I owe him more, so I tell him the truth. "But your brother is."

The gun waggles on the end of his arm, like it's trying to shake loose of him. His face scrunches up, and he rubs his eyes with the back of his gun hand.

"Max."

"Yeah."

"So when you saw me yesterday morning and you called me Max, you thought that . . ."

"Yeah."

"And still you didn't . . ."

"No."

He lets his head hang forward. "Shit."

"Yeah."

Wyatt sets the gun down gently on my pillow and shuffles halfway across the truck. But then he stops, right in the middle. Right between me and Dave's corpse.

"Why are you—" he starts.

"Because I have to. Quit asking me that."

"I was asking something else."

He looks so open and wounded, standing there in his pajamas. If I wanted him dead right now, I wouldn't have to shoot him. He's as dumb as one of those cows people are always talking about tipping over. I could just walk over and nudge him, and he'd topple to the floor like a dead tree. I'm pretty sure I did that, too, when I went outside to catch the bus to school and saw the mail truck parked on the curb, no postman in sight. The keys were in an envelope on the worn welcome mat in front of our front door. Funny how my last mail delivery was an actual mail truck.

But I was home alone then, when I stood woodenly, dumb as a cow. There was no one there to push me over. No one to watch me fall.

I didn't even get to tell my mom good-bye. Now that I think about it, there was no reason she should have been gone. She didn't have to pretend to be at work anymore. So did she leave on her own, or did Valor make her? Did they take her? A tiny part of me wants to believe they set her up with a doctor's appointment. The rest of me knows that her being gone wasn't a coincidence or a mercy.

I was alone. And in my heart, I know they planned it that way.

And I'm pretty sure we've been standing here for a year, Wyatt and me, taking up all the sulfur-tinged air in the back of the truck. I want him to move first, to speak first. I don't want to ask the next question. I really don't want to answer it.

"What now?" he finally says.

"You keep saying that."

"You keep not answering."

I can't help a small smile. Bantering with him is fun, if painful. It would almost be flirting, if it wasn't about death and guns. If I didn't feel so empty inside.

"I have to get to the next house, Wyatt. You can do whatever you want."

There's a little lilt at the end that escapes before I can stop it.

"I'm going with you. I can't let you out of my sight."

It takes a few breaths before I realize what he means, why he suddenly looks sharp and hard again.

"So you're going to stop me from going after your brother. Is that it? That's what you're going to do?"

"If you want to look at it that way."

I stare at him, taking stock, wondering if he could actually do it. Right now, he's got one of my guns— my dad's old gun, the one that my mom kept in her underwear drawer, which I hope Valor doesn't know about. And he did shoot a guy. Is he still in shock, like I was after I shot his dad? Could I get the gun back from him if I needed to? Is he as strong as he looks?

And that's when it occurs to me.

"You can't leave, anyway. You have to come with me."

"And why's that?" he asks with the same amused, flirtatious lilt I had a minute ago, back before I realized how thoroughly his presence had screwed up my situation.

"Because if I let you out of my sight and you tell your brother what's up and he runs, then I can't make my entire list, and then my mom and I are . . ."

Even after everything, I can't say it.

He just nods, lips pursed, considering. Not agreement. Almost understanding.

"So it looks like we're stuck together." I try not to sound too pleased. It's been hard, doing this alone, not being able to tell anyone or talk to my mom without her breaking down into tears and useless apologies. Just having someone to talk to changes everything—I hope for the better.

"But what about Max? What do we do when it comes down to that?"

I snort. "I've got to get through seven more before then. Maybe one of them will be gone, or maybe someone will shoot me first, or maybe Valor will get whatever they want and cancel the whole stupid job. Maybe they're just trying to make a point, incite anarchy so that they can squash us. Maybe someone will storm Wall Street, take it all back. Stage a rebellion. Maybe something will change."

"I wouldn't have pegged you for an optimist," he says.

"You don't even know me." I aim for flirty, but it comes out a little sadder and more woe-is-me-ish than I had hoped.

"Who's next on the list?" he asks, mercifully ignoring the very thing I would have ignored if he had said it.

"Ashley Cannon," I say.

We drag Dave out the back and dump him beside his friend. They're as anonymous as china dolls behind their matching masks, and I'm grateful that I never saw their faces. The high grass is jeweled with dew around them as they disappear in my side mirror.

Wyatt leaves his car right where my mail truck used to be, hidden behind the abandoned mansion. It's exactly what you would expect a guy like his dad to give his son—an older gold Lexus with leather seats and a nav system that doesn't work anymore. My nose wrinkles up just a little bit when I see it, but then I remember how angry he was about his dad. He probably didn't ask for a fancy-ass gold car. I guess he's just as much of a victim of his parents' choices as I am of mine. He'd hidden it a few houses away before he came for me, which tells me how very serious he was when he put that knife to my throat.

It's . . . chilling.

And it's weird, having him in the mail truck's passenger seat, barefoot in his pajamas. I kind of want to ask him if needs to stop by his house for some jeans, because those thin plaid pants are just too flimsy for propriety. At least while he was moving his car, I managed to brush my teeth, put on a sweater, and clean up with some shower wipes. I don't feel quite so exposed now that I'm put to rights and feeling more like myself. But he looks like I imagine a boyfriend would look after you slept with him—rumpled and open and vulnerable. Just being this close to him feels more intimate than I've ever been with a guy. And I can't deal with that right now.

The mail truck's special GPS leads us a few miles away, onto the highway. The fall leaves glitter with raindrops, reflecting a pale, shy sun trying to break through dark clouds. We don't talk, and as I drive, I scan the road for any sign of anarchy or government breakdown. The only hint I see is an abandoned plastic fruit basket just like mine, sodden and crushed by the side of the road. A shudder threatens to yank me apart, but I snap my teeth together and ride it out. It's like when they say a goose walked over your grave, but this was one big effing goose.

How many people know that the government is no longer the government? Where are the policemen and the ambulance drivers? Will they ever answer the phones at 911 again? Are the oncologists and pediatricians still handing out chemo and lollipops? And what part do the armed forces play in this weird, dystopian takeover? Will tanks soon barrel up the road? What's happened is like something right out of a sci-fi book or movie, except that it's happening right now, and nobody knows the rules and aftereffects yet. Will I ever pledge allegiance to the flag again?

But everything just seems normal. We pass by a Starbucks, a Walmart, neighborhoods and fire stations. There aren't drones or guns or scorch marks. Just regular people in regular cars, going about their regular business, most of them talking on cell phones, which makes me think that mine was purposefully tampered with. The drive-through at McDonald's is packed. My stomach grumbles, but I remember how watery and nasty it was losing my salad yesterday and figure I'll hold off on eating for just a little longer.

In a nagging British voice, the GPS tells me to turn down a scrubby, unkempt road. We pass another abandoned neighborhood where they cleared the land, paved the street, put up the streetlights, and ran out of money after building one lone town house. It looks like a single tooth in an empty mouth, poking up uselessly from the dry red dirt. Beyond that, there's a rundown redneck compound: a combination mechanic, deer-processing business, taxidermist, and, oddly enough, notary public. And that's when it gets really country. Wyatt shifts uncomfortably in his seat, one hand holding on to the handle welded to the wall. I can almost see him thinking about jumping out. Poor people must make him nervous.

We turn into a subdivision that has definitely seen better days—probably back in the fifties. The houses are small and crooked, melting back into yards grown high with weeds. Cars on cement blocks flock around them like lost sheep, and the colors are sun-bleached and sad, still dripping with rain. When the GPS snottily tells me that I've reached my destination, I park the mail truck in front of a faded gray ranch and sigh, staring at the threadbare Christmas wreath still on the door. One more month, and it will actually be apropos again.

"So what do I do?" Wyatt's hands shuffle around his hips like he's looking for jeans pockets, and I wonder where he's stashed my other gun.

"Stay here, I guess," I say. "Just stay out of my way. I know what I'm doing now."

He sucks air through his teeth and leans back against the passenger seat, which is where the driver's seat usually is. It was weird, driving the mail truck the first time and trying to figure out where the yellow line in the middle of the road was from the other side of the vehicle.

"You think these people deserve it?" he asks.

"Not my business."

"But if you had to guess?"

"No one deserves to be shot down from behind a fruit basket," I say, holding in my temper behind clenched teeth so I don't rile up the neighbors. "But my mom didn't deserve to get cancer, either. It

· 79 ·

doesn't matter if it's fair or not. It just . . . is what it is. If I don't do it, someone else will."

"I guess cows don't think it's fair that people eat them."

"Just let me get this over with so I can eat a burger," I say, and by the way his nose wrinkles up, I figure he's a vegetarian, or maybe he only eats organic.

I slip into the back of the truck and yank my Postal Service shirt out of the fridge, shrugging into it like it's made out of slime and yellow jackets. It's cold and smells like gunpowder. I keep my chest pointed away from Wyatt as I tuck the gun into the back of my jeans, slide on my shoes, roll up the door, pick up the basket, and get the card ready. The entire process is smooth compared to the bumbling joke I was this morning in Wyatt's front yard.

I jump down, my feet unsteady on the overgrown sidewalk. The Preserve has been running wild for only a few years, but this nameless neighborhood has languished for decades. It's weird to think of people going to the trouble of buying a house and then just letting it go to shit, but that tells me a little bit more about how the economy came to suck. Everybody just took so much for granted.

Wyatt watches me from the passenger window like I'm a wild animal that might be rabid. It occurs to me that I left the mail truck running with my only key in the ignition, and he could easily slam on the gas and get the hell out of Dodge, leaving me without my stuff, my GPS, my other gun, and a way to escape from Ashley Cannon's crappy house before the neighbors show up to take me down, country-boy style. But he's just sitting on the passenger side, one bare foot up on the dash, and he smiles, just a tiny smile, like he's glad to see me watching him back. Somehow, deep in the pit of my belly, I know he's not going to leave me here, dead in the water, even if it would make his life easier.

The walkway up to Ashley Cannon's house is both completely different and utterly the same as the one up to Robert Beard's house. Yellowed grass pokes up through the cracked and puddle-riddled sidewalk, and the screens over the windows are all ripped up. The house is a faded gray that could have been any color, twenty years ago. I think I'm going to feel worse about Ashley Cannon than I did about Robert Beard. Whatever Ashley used credit to buy, it didn't improve anyone's life very much.

I ring the doorbell, and a dog starts barking and scratches at the door. A guy yells, "I'm coming. Shut up, dog. Goddamn!"

The distinctive *shick-shick* of a twelve-gauge shotgun behind the door silences the barking. It's a pretty common greeting for strangers in my county, but sweat breaks out all over me. Balancing the fruit basket in one hand, I whip out my gun and hold it sideways under the basket, my jittery finger on the trigger. Does this guy know what's going on with Valor? Are his neighbors dropping like fiscally irresponsible flies? Will he even open the damn door, or is he going to just shoot me right through it?

While I wait to feel a hole blown in my chest, I struggle to straighten my posture and smile, which feels so wrong and awkward under the circumstances that it's more like a chimp pulling back its lips to show scared teeth. The door snaps open just a few inches, and two black chasms poke out slowly over the chain. Behind the shotgun barrels, the man's eyes are wary and bloodshot.

"That for me?" he asks.

"That depends," I say with cheerfulness I don't feel. "Are you Ashley Cannon?"

The gun pokes out a little more, and I take a step back.

"Who's asking?"

"Just your friendly postal carrier." I waggle my eyebrows and lean the basket forward enticingly, covering the gun as I get a better handle on it. My hands are so sweaty that it keeps slipping. My face is starting to hurt from smiling so much. I just want this to be over. And I can feel Wyatt's eyes boring into my back like two red-hot pokers.

Ashley undoes the chain and opens the door enough to stick his head out over the gun. He's your average country guy, in his late forties, wearing a camo hat and sporting a dark beard. There's something familiar about him, but honestly, I've seen a thousand guys like him at the pizza parlor and at Walmart and at church on Sunday mornings, when my mom forces me to go. I look down and am unsurprised that he's wearing a NASCAR shirt.

"Do I know you, missy?" he says, leaning closer and squinting.

But he doesn't drop the gun. A river of sweat runs down my back, but my shoulders are burning and my hands are freezing and I'm about to drop the gun again.

"I don't think so," I say. "Because I don't know your name, and you still haven't told me if you're Ashley Cannon or not."

His eyes light up with recognition, and his face breaks out in a snaggletoothed grin as he puts the shotgun down. "You're Jack's girl, aren't you?"

I was cold all over before, but now it's like an egg full of lava cracked over my head, and I can feel my face filling up with red and all my nerves firing at once. I bounce on my toes and swallow hard.

"Ashley Cannon. Yes or no?"

His arms reach for me, and I stumble back. "Of course I am. Don't you remember when you were just a little thing, and—"

It happens so fast that I'm not sure which of us pulled the trigger until I see a hole bloom in his chest, inches from Rusty Wallace's teeth. Ashley fumbles for the shotgun and falls to the ground, his mouth opening and closing like a fish trying to breathe and his eyes all but popped out of his head.

It was me. Oh God. It was me. My finger slipped. I couldn't hold on to the gun, and I squeezed too hard, and I feel like my fingerprints have melted into hot metal. I drop the basket and stare at my traitor hand, clamped around the gun for dear life, the finger shaking like a worm on a hook.

"Patsy," he says, barely a whisper.

I drop the gun and fall to my knees on his doorstep. He reaches for me, his hand trembling as hard as mine as it makes a clumsy grab for my shirt, for that top button, like he wants to pull me closer.

Oh, shit. Are they watching? Does this count? I can't find his card. Everything is a mess of blood and tears and snot and sweaty, murdering fingers. I yank my face away, point the button down. He's still breathing, but it's no comfort.

Because he knows my name. And even though his lips are moving, nothing is coming out of his mouth except more blood.

"Ashley Cannon, you . . . you owe an assload of money to Valor Savings, and Amendment 7B, and we all know you sure as shit can't pay it," I say, stumbling over the words and ending in a jerking sob.

His reaching hand falls, and his eyes go dry and empty.

And I am empty.

But the gun isn't. I snatch it up and stuff it down my waistband under my shirt, half wishing it would accidentally shoot me, too. They said suicide didn't count, but they didn't say anything about being so stupid and scared that you slip up and blow yourself a new asshole.

Trembling from head to toe, I find his card in my back pocket, toss it down, and hurry back to the truck. I pull off my shirt and wad it up and sling myself into the driver's seat. Remembering the signature machine in the shirt's pocket, I pull it out and write *Ashley Cannon* in wobbling script and click accept. The machine logs it normally, and I roll it up in the shirt and remember to breathe. But before I can put the truck into drive and break some more laws, if there are any laws left, Wyatt's hand lands on my arm and stops me.

"What happened back there?"

"Nothing." I shake my head, look away, swallow, tremble. "The gun went off by accident. It's done. Let me drive."

"No," he says. "Something went wrong. You totally freaked out. I could see your neck go red. Are you okay?"

"I just killed somebody. My fourth murder today. Of course I'm not okay!" I shout.

He wants to say something, but he doesn't. He just stares at me like he's interrogating me with his eyes, but also like he's hugging me with his eyes. It reminds me of when I was six and I tried to steal a flying monkey figurine from the drugstore and my mom made me take it back in. She wasn't mad at me, but the disappointment and tragic love in her eyes was heavier than the house that landed on the Wicked Witch. Now Wyatt's eyes are squeezing me like that too.

I lick my lips and reach back to tug my hair out from its ratty half ponytail. I don't want him watching my neck so closely.

"He knew my name," I say quietly. "He said he knew me."

"Did you ask him how?"

"He knew my dad's name too. I haven't seen my dad since I was four." I can't help sniffling. "He . . . Ashley Cannon has my eyes. Or I have his. And the same dimple."

"And you just shot him and ran off? Without asking him about your dad or why he knew you?" Wyatt looks down, shakes his head. "You don't seem like a coward."

Under my hair, my neck goes from red to maroon. I can feel the rage creeping up, itching. I hold up the gun, ignoring the way it quivers in my hand.

"I'm not a coward. I'm a shitty assassin with slippery hands. And you don't want to be calling me names right now," I say, reedy and desperate.

Wyatt looks at me, looks at the gun, and then turns back to look at Ashley Cannon, who's strewn out in his own doorway. A big, bear-shaped black Lab is nuzzling his side, and the dog's upset whining carries across the still space of the yard. This is the longest I've stayed behind after an assignment, and I'm a little surprised that none of the neighbors have come outside to see what all the fuss is about.

It's the dog that finally changes my mind. The way that big, thick tail slowly waves back and forth and the way those floppy black ears are laid back against its square head. When the dog falls to its belly and crawls forward to lick the dead man's face, I mutter, "Shit," and get out of the truck. That damn dog's devotion cuts me to the heart more sharply than Eloise Framingham's son with his stupid gun and stupider girlfriend.

Wyatt hops out without a word and follows me back up the sidewalk, bare feet dodging around a broken beer bottle. It seems like a longer walk than it did when I was on my way to kill a stranger, like I'm crossing continents or tectonic plates as they heave and sway. My tummy feels a bit like that too, like it's falling apart into bits and pieces. Wyatt suddenly spins around and jogs back to the truck, and I have one moment of heart-wrenching terror as I think he's going to abandon me here. Instead, he just pulls the keys out and hurries back to my side, and I feel small and fragile in his shadow. And I realize I'm glad that he's there.

The dog looks up at us, whining. It's a girl—*she's* a girl. Her tail thumps against the door frame, her eyes trusting and the color of Hershey's syrup. She belly-crawls to me and licks my hand like she's asking for help, and my heart wrenches in my chest.

"Good girl," I say. I pull her frayed camo collar around and see that her name is Matilda.

"He's gone." Wyatt stands up from where he was squatting by Ashley Cannon.

"I know," I say. "He was gone pretty quick."

I leave out the part about how I watched the second Ashley Cannon's eyes went dull, drawn in by the fact that they're the same cloudy blue as my own.

"Hello?" Wyatt calls, careful not to stick his head too far in the door. He might be rich, but I guess he knows that trespassers around here don't get prosecuted. They get shot.

No one answers. Matilda whines. I realize that I've been stroking her head as my unfocused eyes linger on the red splotch on Ashley's NASCAR shirt. I clear my throat and pull my hand away, but when she whines again, I put my hand right back where it was. Her head is like a cross between a seal and a shoe box, and I don't want to stop stroking her between her silky ears until the world goes right again.

"I don't think anyone's home," Wyatt says. "Do you want to go in? Look around? Maybe y'all are related or something."

I put a numb foot through the door and smell barbecue potato chips. Somewhere farther back, Garth Brooks is playing.

"I guess we have to," I say.

I am terrified to set foot in the dead man's house, but I don't want Wyatt to think I'm a coward, either. I don't want him to think any less of me than he already does. Underneath that false bravado, the sullen, bruised child in me wants to know why the hell this guy knew my name and my dad's name. I need to know if he still knows my dad. Most of all, I need to know if we're related, because he's as familiar as a dream I've forgotten, as a face smudged in a mirror.

I remember my daddy like some kids remember meeting Mickey Mouse on vacation—larger than life, magical, perfect. My mom never talked about him, but I imagined him in Vegas, or out in Arizona. Someplace wild, like he'd just gone into the jungle and become a vagrant or a wizard or a crazy shaman.

I never let myself think about the fact that even crazy shamans can send letters or e-mails, every now and then.

Shaking, I step over Ashley Cannon onto carpet the color of nicotine-stained fingers. Matilda doesn't budge from my heels, her tail wagging side to side lazily and her head held low. Wyatt dodges the fruit basket and bends down to pull the body inside, grunting as he settles it against the wall. I close the door and turn the dead bolt. Already I am aware that Wyatt is doing the hard work for me, but I can't think of a way to thank him that doesn't sound monstrous.

Scanning the room, I take in the faded paintings of landscapes, the plaid couch with a distinctly butt-shaped dent in the middle, the huge flat-screen TV that doesn't fit with the other, older, broken-down furnishings. A football game is on but muted, a bag of bar-becue chips open on the dinged-up Goodwill coffee table. Garth continues his sad bastard wailing from a back room. A row of dusty pictures staggers across the mantel in cheap plastic frames, and they draw me over like a bass on the line.

The first two are old, two boys and a girl eating Popsicles in threadbare bathing suits and then posing by a lake with a wolfish older man a few years later, sometime in the seventies, maybe. The girl looks a little like me—rangy, with crooked bangs hacked into dark hair and a ponytail. At first I think the next picture actually is her, but then I notice that it's much more recent.

And it's me.

Ashley Cannon has my ninth-grade school photograph on his mantel, horrible sweater, braces, and all.

I lurch forward to pull that picture down. My fingertips leave streaks through the dust, and the frame feels heavier than it should. With Wyatt standing over my shoulder, I turn it over and pry the metal lever open. Photos burst out, five more school pictures hiding behind this one. They're not from every year, more like every three years since kindergarten. On the back of each one, unfamiliar handwriting in blue ballpoint pen spells out my nickname and the year.

Patsy. Patsy. Patsy.

My mom named me Patricia. My dad nicknamed me Patsy, and I wouldn't answer to anything else, even after he left.

"You were cute when you were little," Wyatt says quietly, and I am suddenly overcome with shyness about the differently flawed, younger versions of me laid out for him to see. I force them all back into the frame and twist the lever shut. When I put the frame back in the dust-marked place where it lives, I see the one on the other side of it, and my hands stop, fists clenched, inches away from it.

It shows three men in camo and neon-orange hats. They're smiling, arms around one another's shoulders, behind an impressive buck. One is Ashley Cannon, maybe five years younger than he is today. One is the older guy from the photo with the kids, gray and grizzled but broad as a bear. The third is a face I only remember from dreams. My heart lurches and the world goes sideways as I realize that I'm looking at my dad for the first time in thirteen years. My mom didn't save a single picture of him after he walked out on us. In the photo, my dad is smiling, older than I remember him and with a dark beard that matches the men who must be his brother and father. When I wrench the smooth photo paper out of the frame, the date tells me it was taken six months ago.

My mom used to call him Jack when they were together, but I've always wondered what my dad's last name was. Now I know. *Cannon*.

I didn't think about it at all for the longest time, that my mom and I shared the same last name as her parents and sister. Not until I filled out my driver's license forms last year did it become a problem, a puzzle. My mom turned her face to the rain-streaked window of the DMV and told me to put "deceased" for my dad's name. At the time, I was more interested in getting my license than driving my mom to tears before my exam. I guess that means they were never married, or maybe she kept her name. And it shouldn't matter, but it does.

I always wondered what my dad's side of the family was like. I knew my mom's parents, who lived thirty minutes away and gave me Juicy Fruit gum and haunted their small house like they were already ghosts before they died. I knew my aunt Patty, the one I was named after, before she moved across the country to California and had a heart attack. All Kleins. But I'd never had a passel of cousins like most kids, and I'd always wondered if maybe somewhere my dad's family was getting together for a reunion picnic by a lake, maybe having three-legged races and spitting watermelon seeds together and generally being impossibly idyllic without me. Waiting for me.

Looks like at least three of them were getting together, and they were doing the same thing I'm doing right now.

Hunting.

"Jack Cannon," I say to myself.

It's a manly, violent name. It sounds like he's the brother of G.I. Joe, like he walks around with a cigar clenched in shark teeth.

I fold the photo in half and stuff it in my back pocket before spinning around, hungrily eyeing the room as if there might be a trail of clues for me to find. Like at the end of the road, my dad's going to pop out of the closet with a bouquet of balloons and explain that he still loves me and wants to take me to a picnic to meet the cousins.

There's a pile of bills and letters and papers on the kitchen table. From ten feet away, I can tell that a lot of the bills are that familiar pink that means Uncle Ashley owed more money than he was worth. Just as I'm walking over to see if maybe there's a birthday card from my daddy with a return address on it, someone knocks on the door.

My eyes jerk wide and meet Wyatt's. He points to the sliding glass door, and I quietly remove the antitheft bar and slide it open.

"Ash, man, you hear that? You shooting squirrels again? Cuz you know my mama don't like that," a kid yells through the front door as we slip out the back. When I reach to slide the glass door closed, the dog squirms out behind us, her tail wagging hopefully.

Wyatt goes to jump the chain-link fence where it's a little short, but I shake my head and motion to the gate at the far end of the yard. As far as I figure, I'm the closest thing Matilda's got to family, and I'm not leaving her behind.

I jog to the gate with a tall boy and a fat dog loping beside me in the high, wet grass. Wyatt's bare feet squelch in the mud. We leave the gate open, and I run around the next two houses and try to compose myself to walk to the truck. I'm still wearing my Postal Service hat, if not my shirt, and I hope it looks like I'm just coming back from a delivery, or at the very worst, like I've been making out with my boyfriend in the woods between deliveries. I guess there's no explanation for the dog trotting at my heels like she's always been there.

As we come around in front of Ashley's house, the kid on his front porch turns to watch us. He looks like he's just out of high school, or maybe a dropout. Quite frankly, he doesn't look like the sharpest hammer in the drawer.

"What y'all doing with Matty?" he asks, scratching a thin and hairy neck.

"Is that her name?" I say, putting emphasis on the Southern accent I usually try to cover up. "That ol' dog's been following me all up and down the street. Get on, dog."

My heart's not in it, and Matty knows it, but hopefully the kid's dumber than the dog. Wyatt gets in the passenger seat, and I roll up the back door and motion Matilda—Matty—inside just as the kid starts walking down the sidewalk toward us, his head to the side like he's thinking so hard he might overheat and blow a gasket.

"Did y'all hear a gunshot a few minutes ago?" he asks.

"Wanna go for a ride, girl?" I whisper.

At the word "ride," Matty yips and jumps in the back of the truck, and I crawl in behind her and roll the door shut and lock it. Just as I hoped he would, Wyatt shifts into the seat behind the steering wheel and turns the key he's been holding all along.

"Naw, man. That was just the truck backfiring," he says, whipping out his own accent.

"My friend Ash ain't answering his door," the kid says. "Hey, where'd Matty go?"

"Dumbass dog," Wyatt says. "Probably diggin' up somebody's yard."

And I stroke Matty's head in the back of the truck and murmur, "He doesn't mean that, sugar." She thumps her tail and licks my wrist like she doesn't mind that I just killed her owner. My uncle. Like she was supposed to be with me all along.

Wyatt pulls away, the truck jerking as he gets used to the clunky steering.

"Hey, come back!" the kid yells, and I imagine him chasing a few feet before stopping in the middle of the cracked road, scratching his neck like he accidentally misplaced his trachea.

I can't help wondering how many days he'll stand in front of Ash's front door, ringing the doorbell and hollering about squirrels. How long before he breaks down that door or tries the unlocked sliding glass door in back? How long before he calls the police and can't get anybody on the phone?

Not until Wyatt pulls back onto the highway do I realize that we left my fake fruit basket on my uncle Ashley's nicotine-yellow carpet.

4.

KELSEY MACKEY

"That was close," Wyatt says, and it sounds so much like a TV sit-com that I laugh.

"We woulda got away with it, too, if not for that redneck yokel," I say, and Matty leans her bulk against me and thumps her tail on the floor like she thinks it's a good joke. It occurs to me that I now have my first dog. And my first inheritance from a family I've never met.

And then it occurs to me that since I was wearing my Postal Service shirt when I killed Ashley Cannon, whoever's on the other side of that button heard me freak out and now knows a lot more about me than I'd like them to. Of course, from what I've seen so far, they knew more than enough about me already. I pull down the list on the wall.

Out of three victims, one was the jerkass who fired my mom, one was dying of the same thing as my mom, and the other one was my uncle? I cross out the first three names and trace number four with my bitten-up fingertip before sticking it back on the wall.

Kelsey Mackey.

So a girl then, probably not too old. And I don't know her—that I know of. There's a name I do know on my list, much lower down, but I'm doing my best to forget about that one. Like with Wyatt's brother, I don't want to count my dead chickens before they hatch. No point in worrying about the next-to-last kill when I've got six more assignments to get through alive in a world already filled with thugs and people hard up for cash.

"So how am I going to get Kelsey Mackey to open the door without a sexy gift basket?" I say half to myself, and Wyatt glances back at me. He's got to notice that I'm avoiding talking about what just happened. But he can also see that I'm curled up on the cot, quietly shaking with an arm around my dead uncle's dog.

"Just hold an envelope," he says. "People will open the door for anyone in a mail truck."

"Good point."

I uncurl myself and shrug on a huge, colorful sweater before pulling my envelope out from under the thin mattress. It's unmarked—no name, no address, not so much as a wrinkle in the orangey-tan paper. I dump out the rest of the cards and pick up the one for Kelsey Mackey.

The card looks so boring, so normal. But it's just another death sentence, printed on fancy paper.

The truck shudders and chugs at a stop sign, and Wyatt says, "So where to? You want to hit your next kill or grab some food or what?"

Put that way, it sort of takes away my appetite. But if I don't eat something soon, I'm going to get even worse shakes.

"Pull into a gas station," I say.

I dig around for my cash while he drives up the highway. Matty hops up on the bed and falls instantly asleep, and even though she's getting rain splatter and mud all over my stuff, I let her. Being in the back of the truck makes me kind of queasy and carsick. My feet slide a little on the metal floor whenever he makes a turn, and every bump in the road jars my butt bones. I sit on the bed and try to relax among my throw pillows and stuffed turtles, but it's hard. I've been in control for so long that I'm not even sure how to let someone else take the steering wheel.

After my dad left, my mom didn't do that thing where women get makeovers and start dating and aiming higher at work. I don't remember her really having hobbies or friends or going out or leaving me with a babysitter she had to pay. She just had work and me. My mama never had any ambition; just put one foot in front of the other, hoping to stay in the same place. Naturally, she fell behind. By the time I was eight, I was pet sitting for cash and doing gardening for old ladies in return for cookies and crumpled dollar bills. When

I was eleven, I started babysitting, and that's when I really started being helpful. From the beginning of third grade, I got myself up in the morning, made my own breakfast and lunch, and walked my own self to the bus stop while my mom was already at work.

I started at the pizza place when I was fourteen, when Jeremy and Roy promised they'd take care of me, and we'd mostly just sit around, flipping dough in the back room and cracking jokes. I was like a mascot, almost, and it felt good to pay for my own clothes and craft supplies and fill the car with gas, once I started driving and before my mom wrapped the old Tercel around a median when a big rig ran her off the road.

My mom took care of me in the only way she knew how, with no help, no support, and no luck. When I think about the way she looked in the hospital after the accident, my throat closes up and my eyes burn. It was bad enough when she had insurance. She needs me now, more than ever. And I want to be done with this job as soon as possible so I can take care of her in the only way *I* know how.

"Gas station first, then next house," I say more firmly.

Wyatt just says, "Cool."

The tank of gas is practically full, so Wyatt pulls into a parking space and turns in his seat to stare at me, eyebrows up.

"Stay with Matty," I say. "I'll be right back."

I come uncomfortably close to him as I squeeze between the seats on my way to the passenger door, and it's almost alarming, how warm he is. I can smell the boy funk rising from his clothes and wonder for a moment who does the laundry at his house. Probably not his dad. Maybe him or his brother. And one of them let something sit too long, wet, in the washer. Does he even have a mom? I never asked. I hop down to the sidewalk and turn back to look up at him.

"Hey, do you want anything?"

"A Coke and something to eat would be good."

His eyes dart to the cash in my hand like he's wondering how much I have, how long it can keep both of us going when it was set aside for me alone. And I hadn't even thought about Matty, and I'm hoping gas station dog food isn't too crappy and doesn't cost too much. I'm also hoping Wyatt doesn't see me as just a poor girl to pity. I learned pretty early on that if you couldn't afford cool clothes, it was better to aim for a quirky style than to try to make do on the cheap copies of what the popular kids wore. But standing in the iridescent puddles of a gas station parking lot in my jeans and baggy sweater and mismatched socks, smelling like two days of stink and gun oil, and knowing that Wyatt is staring at me, I just wish, for once, that I felt like enough. I dash my bangs out of my face, wondering angrily what it would be like to have them professionally cut instead of just hacking them off myself over the bathroom sink.

I dart inside. Being in a public place is making me cagey. I've been shoving down my guilt over what I'm doing, pushing it down deep so I can finish what I have to do. But surrounded by people, by parents holding sticky little kid hands and old men comparing candy bars, it surfaces for just a moment that each person I've killed has a family who will miss them. For Ashley Cannon, I'm part of that family, and even though I didn't know him proper, I already regret that he's gone. Barely looking at what I'm picking up, I grab some king-sized candy bars and a couple of hot-all-day biscuits and some Cokes, not to mention a gallon of water and a bag of the cheapest, nastiest-looking dog food ever. I guess Uncle Ash didn't feed his fat old dog fresh organic chicken, but I don't want her to get sick.

I dump my bounty on the counter. As the clerk rings it up, I can't help watching the TV over his head. There's some dude talking about something, too low for me to hear. The video playing behind him shows a squirrel on a skateboard, and the guy laughs a big, fake laugh that makes his teeth look like horse teeth in a human mouth. Nothing about the government, Valor, or random killings, no insurgents lobbing Molotov cocktails at army dudes behind a barbed-wire barricade. Just a goddamn squirrel on a skateboard.

Something catches my eye, and when I look away from the TV, he's there. The Valor dude. Or maybe it's not exactly the same one, but it might as well be. Crisp black robot suit, perfect tie, cyborg earpiece, dark sunglasses. This one's hair is the color of nothing, white-blond and thin. He steps into line two people behind me, moving sideways like he's being controlled with a joystick.

I go all rigid with terror. Is he here to punish me? To warn me? To deliver a list of my penalties? He leans forward as if to grab a pack of gum, and I jump and drop my wallet. There's a flash of white, and he tries to hand me a card.

I have never been as scared of anything as I am of that card.

"That all for you, hon?"

It's my turn to pay, and I just grab my wallet, toss a twenty at the lady, and run back to the mail truck. Whether because that's what he wanted or because he's programmed to do so, the Black Suit doesn't move from line. His head swivels to follow me like a security camera as he places a pack of gum on the counter.

Back at the truck, I swing into the passenger seat and drop my bag on the floor, stunned and twitchy with ebbing fear. I scan the lot for a black vehicle, for any sign of the Valor suit, but he's totally disappeared.

What the hell was that? Why didn't I take the damn card? Could I be more spastic?

I hand Wyatt a sausage biscuit and a Coke and pull myself together enough to say, "I hope you're not a vegetarian."

"I'm pretty sure bacon is a vegetable," he says, biting off half the biscuit in one bite, and I smile. I guess I was wrong about that part.

In the back of the truck, I pour Matty's food into a plastic cereal bowl I brought from home. She starts snarfing it down, wagging her tail so hard against my leg that I'm afraid I'll get a bruise. Maybe cheap dog food is like fast food for dogs. She seems pretty happy, at least.

Wyatt joins me in the back of the truck, wadded biscuit wrapper in hand, and says, "What else did you get?" I throw him a foot-long Snickers bar. I was bolting my own biscuit, but now that he's watching me, I try to take daintier bites. But, of course, you can't eat a biscuit all in one piece if you take dainty bites—it just crumbles to bits and makes a mess. I drop a big chunk, and Matty slurps it up before I can grab it.

"I can pay you back," Wyatt says. "I mean . . . I don't have money with me right now, but I'm good for it. I eat a lot."

"No biggie," I say. "We can get by."

I lick my pinkie and dab up the last of my biscuit crumbs before Matty can get to them. They're dry as they coat my throat, and I swig my Coke too hard. The burn feels good, but the knowledge that I'm going to have to use a gas station bathroom soon doesn't. I guess it's better than going outside in the open again. The Black Suit hasn't reappeared. Damn, those dudes are like Teflon. I'd rather pee myself than get within touching distance of another Valor robot.

"Watch Matty, okay?" I say. "I'm gonna hit the bathroom."

"I'm next," Wyatt says with a smile, collapsing on the floor of the mail truck to tussle with the big dog. She likes him, but I get the feeling Matty likes everybody.

I take my backpack with me to the bathroom and clean up as best I can in the cramped, smelly room. Full-body wipe, deodorant, face wipe, hair brush, quick change of clothes, and some coconut-scented drugstore body spray. As I put on a long-sleeved tee under a band shirt, I wonder if Wyatt has the same one. I lean close to the mirror, noticing that my eyes have purple bags under them and are crisscrossed by little red veins. I'm not surprised, but it's weird. I look years older than I did the last time I stood in front of my own bathroom mirror. I slap on some red lipstick and purse my lips and make kissy faces, turning my head back and forth to see whether my jagged brown hair looks cleaner up or down.

Someone bangs on the door, and I rush out with my face down, cheeks hot. As soon as I hit the truck, Wyatt sprints to the guys' room. He finished off his Coke and mine as well. That means he's about to hit a men's gas station bathroom barefoot. I shudder and look away.

The keys are on my bed, and I realize that I could end it all right here. I could drive back to his house, kill his brother, and know that I was one step closer to finishing my term of service. Wyatt wouldn't get in my way, wouldn't try to stop me. He'd be stuck, barefoot and penniless, at a gas station. I'd never have to see him again.

But I know I can't do that. What I'm doing—it's not fair, and it's not good. But I am, or at least I want to be. I've done some harmlessly mischievous stuff in my time, but at my heart, I'm fair and good, and even if I have to do horrible things, I'm not going to be a horrible person.

Would anything be different if I wasn't, as I grudgingly admit to myself, suffering a crush on this boy? Maybe. If he was a bully, if he had hurt me, if he was mean—maybe then I could just peel out onto the highway and take care of the loose end that is his mysterious brother, Max. But he didn't leave me behind when he could have, so I won't leave him behind now. Instead, I just chew on my Milky Way and scan the road for shiny black SUVs and wait for Wyatt to return. At my side, Matty thumps her tail as if she can read my mind and approves of this course of action.

Whatever I have to do in the next few days, I want to make sure that the girl who comes out the other side is as similar as possible to the one who went in.

"So," Wyatt says, landing in the driver's seat and making the whole truck shake. "Where does this Kelsey chick live, anyway?"

"It's in the GPS. Just turn it on and click on her name."

"It's preprogrammed?"

"Apparently."

He inspects the GPS from all sides, taps on the red clock, and messes with the dashboard buttons for a few minutes before finally just backing out of the space and turning onto the road. Although I know I don't have much time, I pull out my knitting bag and select a new ball of yarn. Powder blue. That's how I feel today, like the color of tears in old cartoons. It looks even sadder next to the bright, hot yellow I was using the night Valor dropped a gun in my lap. I've been planning this piece for a while—it's supposed to go around the flagpole at my school. I even measured it and counted the stitches to make sure it would fit as snugly as a sock. The plan is to go in one morning at dawn and stitch it around the pole so that when everyone else comes in, it will be there, a kid-sized, rainbow-hued jacket around the cold, silver flagpole.

The idea sounds so simple, and yet yarn bombing makes me so happy. That's what appeals to me—the concept of taking something boring, something everyday and dull, and making it beautiful for no real reason. I am a deeply practical person in all respects except for this one. I don't have any great talents—I can't draw or write or sing or win science fairs. But I can make the world better with little touches of color here and there. It certainly can't cancel out the harm I'm doing this week, but if I can keep yarn bombing, it's one more way to keep being myself.

And now that I know that the flag is meaningless, this small act means even more.

Maybe one day I'll sell PDFs of cross-stitch patterns that say KEEP CALM AND DON'T RELY ON VALOR or DEBT SWEET DEBT. If Valor doesn't arrest or kill people for that sort of rebellion, of course.

As I knit, the GPS gives Wyatt directions in a stuffy British voice. He even talks back to it a few times, which makes me giggle. "Taking the motorway," he says, mimicking the clipped accent. "Turning right at my earliest possible convenience."

The truck rolls to a halt, and I finish my row of stitches before looking up. Wyatt squeezes into the back of the mail truck and squats across from me. He reaches into my knitting bag and pulls out several balls of bright acrylic yarn. They look tiny in his huge hands.

"Do you juggle?" he says.

I slide the row of stitches down on the needle and grin.

"Nope. I yarn bomb."

He drops the balls of yarn back in my bag and holds his hands up like I've got a gun pointed at him, which actually hasn't happened in a while—which is kind of nice.

"Are you saying these are bombs?" he says with mock horror. "Because I don't know whether to cut the red wire or the blue wire or the neon-green wire."

I snort.

"You're ridiculous. And you seriously don't know what yarn bombing is? I mean, have you heard of the Internet?"

"That's where the cats and porn are, right?" he shoots back.

"Boys," I say to myself, rolling my eyes. "Yarn bombing is this thing they do in bigger cities, where people crochet or knit stuff and then put it in public places. Like over subway seats or tree branches or those big metal rings by docks. Just to make things more interesting. More pretty."

"The yarn bombing assassin," he says, reaching out to touch the flagpole sheath I've been working on. "I like it."

Matty shoves into him, and he puts a hand on my shoulder to keep from totally falling over on me. His touch melts down into my skin through two T-shirts and my tank top, and I blush red and scoot away.

"Sorry," he says, almost as red as I feel myself.

"I think Matty's got a crush on you." I hide my face in her neck. "Don't you, honey? Are you a good girl? Are you?" Her tail beats the crap out of him, and he retreats to the other side of the truck, which still isn't very far away.

"So that was awkward," he says.

"Um, are we at Kelsey's house?" I ask, because I don't really want to make things more awkward by talking about how awkward they are.

"I stopped a few houses down." He points to the left. "She lives right in front of her neighborhood's playground."

"There are kids on it, aren't there?" I say with a sigh.

"Really cute ones," he agrees. "With sharp eyesight."

"Shit."

The sun has burned off enough of the rain to make the playground a total mess. The laughter of little kids carries, along with sharp screeches from their annoyed moms. The kids probably have soggy butts from the puddles on the slides. If only we could turn around and go somewhere, anywhere. But there's no good excuse other than cowardice. Those kids will be there the next time I come, too. I have to do it now. I want one more name crossed off my list, want to be one step closer to being back in my own bed, worrying about grades and my work schedule, or whatever normal, debt-free people will worry about in the new United States of Valor.

I peek out the windshield, and all the kids on the playground are tiny, smiling and shouting as their moms push them on swings or chase them around. A girl from my freshman health class is there with a baby on her hip and a phone in her hand, and I rack my brain, trying to remember if she got a new brother or missed the vital info on contraceptives and dropped out. And that's one more reason to hurry up: I don't want to miss anything important in class. The only way I'm ever going to get out of Candlewood is to get into college, if there's still college when all this crap is over and life settles back down. I'm not going to let anything else get in my way.

Wyatt is trying not to look at me, but I can tell he totally is. I wonder what he sees—a regular girl, a victim, a weirdo, or a cold-blooded killer. I get these little hints that he might have a crush on me, too, but he has to know it's impossible. If I don't kill his brother or turn him into a murderer, my mom dies. So why is it like we're trapped in a moment, paused together while the rest of the world goes on? All we have is the back of this mail truck and a fragile truce. And yet there's something in his eyes that tells me he sees something else entirely.

"Keep it in drive, okay?" I say. "Let's run on this one. No matter what."

He nods and settles back in the driver's seat. I give Matty some more food to distract her, then shrug into my mail shirt and grab Kelsey's card and the envelope, holding it firmly over my top button. I'm halfway up the sidewalk before I remember that I need my gun.

Wyatt grins at me as I hurry back and nudges me with his shoulder as I crawl between the seats with one hand over the shirt's top button. As I slip the gun into the waistband of my jeans, I'm extra aware of Wyatt watching me, and I can't forget that this gun spends a good deal of time next to my sweaty ass.

As I slither past Wyatt, he nudges me and whispers, "Break a leg, tiger."

I march up the street and slow when I hit her front walk, trying to force my feelings to behave. I'm a little giddy from being nudged by Wyatt, but the cold calm of killing is settling into my bones, step by step. It's so stupid, how my brain, heart, and body can all panic over different things at the same time.

This house, Kelsey's house, isn't rich or poor. It's right in the middle, respectable, the kind of house I would love to have one day. It's not ridiculously huge, but the kids probably wouldn't have to share rooms. The roses in front are a little wild, but the pansies are planted in beds that probably held marigolds just a few months ago, when it was still hot. Kelsey, it seems, still cares.

Holding the envelope like it's something important, I will my hand to stop shaking, kiss my locket, hop up the steps, and ring the doorbell. I have to admit it's a lot easier to carry an envelope than it was to tote that gigantic basket. But I do feel more exposed, with nothing to hide behind. Inside, a girl calls, "Coming!" and footsteps bound down the stairs.

The door opens to a breathless girl, about college age. She's so pretty and all-American and happy that she should be in movies or on billboards maybe. God, I hope she's not Kelsey. Shooting her would be like chopping down a fruit tree at full blossom in spring-time, when it's so pretty and pink that it hurts your heart. I would love to be this girl one day, to be this happy in such a pretty house.

"Oh my gosh, is that for me?" she says. "I've been waiting for my scholarship check all week. Yay!"

"Um, are you Kelsey Mackey?" I ask, my voice raspy. I have to clear my throat.

"Yeah," she says. "Do I need to sign or something?"

I realize I've forgotten the signature machine; I didn't put it back in my pocket after forging Ashley's name. Wyatt's got me all dis-combobulated. I'm totally losing it.

"Oh, one second. Sorry." I jog back to the truck with the enve-lope under my arm and my hand around the button, half wishing I could just jump in and gun it. My butt sweats against the gun, and it slides around in my waistband.

Wyatt gives me a quizzical, concerned look, but I can't talk about it right now, so I just shake my head and wrench up the back door and grab the signature machine, petting Matty on the head for luck and whispering, "Stay, good girl," as I close it.

Back at the door, Kelsey waits with rosy cheeks and bunny slippers. She thinks I've got a scholarship check, that I've brought the money she needs to continue getting her education. She probably wants to be a teacher or a nurse, something that would genuinely help make the world a better place. Something that I myself would like to be.

I hand her the machine, and she signs her name with a hurried flourish.

"Kelsey Mackey, you owe Valor Savings the sum of $49,876.02," I say, reading off the card. "Can you pay this sum in full, immediately?"

"Um, no." She pauses, waits for me to say something else. "Is this some kind of joke?"

I feel sick to my stomach, and the Coke burns its way back up my throat. The rest of it comes out so fast that by the end, I have to gulp for air. "By Valor Congressional Order number 7B, your account is past due and hereby declared in default. Due to your failure to remit all owed monies and per your signature just witnessed and accepted, you are given two choices. You may either sign your loyalty over to Valor Savings as an indentured collections agent for a period of five days or forfeit your life. Please choose."

"I don't understand," she says, hands on her hips. "It's a student loan. They said I would have thirty years to pay it back. I'm not even out of school yet. And I barely carry a balance on my credit card. My dad said it would help raise my credit score so I could buy a house after college. Is this for real?" She's babbling now, and I can tell she's not the sort of person who's usually yakkity.

"Can you pay this sum?" I say again, voice breaking.

"I could write a check for five hundred right now," she asks. "Is that enough? Do I make it out to Valor, or . . . ?"

They didn't tell me what to say if this happened. I wrap sweaty fingers around my top button.

"I don't think it works that way," I say, voice low. "It has to be paid in full, in cash. Which is impossible. But you can do what I'm doing. Work off your debt. And then you'll be free again in, like, five days. Maybe less."

"What do I have to do to work it off?" she asks. "I'm already working two jobs. And I plan on paying the loan off once I'm out of school. I'm not a mooch, seriously. I'm almost done with my master's."

"I know," I say. "I know. If you want to work it off, you have to kill the people who can't pay their debts. It's kind of like being a bounty hunter. Like that Dog guy. Or Boba Fett from Star Wars."

She giggles, a high and strangled sound. "Are you joking? Is there, like, a camera somewhere? You can't seriously expect me to believe that a bank is just going to have me killed."

"I'm serious." I glance around the street to make sure no one else is looking, then pull the gun out of my jeans and show it to her. She runs one finger along the stamped words VALOR SAVINGS. I hand her the card, and she reads it, turns it over, reads it again as I put the gun back in my jeans, under my shirt.

She looks over my shoulder, out to the mail truck. Then she looks at the playground, where little kids are climbing on the monkey bars and zooming down a bumpy slide. She leans heavily against the door frame, and I see a shiny diamond ring winking on her left ring finger.

"Fine," she says, almost a whisper. "I'll do it. Whatever I have to do, I'll do it."

"Really?" I ask. Because I never dreamed, when I accepted this job, that anyone else would ever take this path, that they would even believe it was a real option. I thought I was the only one.

"I didn't work this hard just to get shot for no reason." Kelsey's voice is steady, but she's shaking, her skin gone white as skim milk. "My dad told me student loans were a rip-off, but I thought I knew exactly what I was doing."

"Nobody reads the fine print." I shrug. "My mom didn't."

"So what now?" she asks. "Do I get in your mail truck and go with you? Or what?"

"I don't know," I say. "They never told me what would happen if someone agreed to it." Just for good measure, I aim the top button of my shirt at her face. "Say it again. I want to make sure they know."

Kelsey snorts and shakes her head. She leans forward, staring into the button.

"I'll do it," she says. One tear slips down her red cheek. "Just don't kill me."

I nod and smile at her, then turn to go.

"That isn't even my scholarship check, is it?" she asks, nodding at the envelope I never handed over.

"I'm sorry. It was supposed to be a basket of fake fruit, but I lost it. I didn't want to do this."

"I know," she says. "I don't either."

As I walk away, my hand around the bugged button, she calls, "Is it horrible?"

"Yeah," I yell back over my shoulder. "But it's better than the alternative."

I've got the mail shirt over my head and wadded up before I reach the truck. I stuff it under the passenger seat and climb in with a heavy sigh.

"What happened?" Wyatt asks.

"She took the deal." I sigh. "She's going to be . . . one of me. Or whatever."

"Then why do you look so sad?"

I watch Kelsey as we drive away. She sits on the front step, her eyes far away as she spins the ring around and around her finger. She and I have more in common than I would like. I pity her, and I also admire her. I hope she doesn't regret her decision later. I hope I don't have cause to regret mine, either.

"Because it hurts almost as bad as if I had shot her," I finally say to Wyatt. "I might not have killed her, but I definitely killed something inside of her. Now we both have to live with it."

His hand finds mine as he drives. We both watch the road, ignoring the fact that we're holding hands. His touch, his warmth, is the only thing that keeps me from crying.

"Sometimes good things come from horrible situations," he says. "Sometimes, when the worst thing happens, the only way to go is up. At least now she has a chance. Things could be a lot worse. Let's go get some McNuggets."

As we stop to turn out of her neighborhood, an all-black SUV glides down the curve of the road toward us.

"Duck!" I shove Wyatt down, but it doesn't feel like enough. Since the driver's side is really the passenger side, I stand up and hope my huge sweater blocks him. I wait for the SUV to stop, for a window to roll down, for blinking lights or a machine gun or, hell, I don't know—a giant grappling hook to sprout out of its sunroof and punish me for all the rules I've broken. But there's no sign of life beyond the tinted windshield, and it turns smoothly into Kelsey's neighborhood with no outward indication that the mail truck exists. With no sign that *I* exist.

I fall back into my seat and start breathing again. I don't even feel like a person. I'm just a cog in a machine, a tiny animal doing my part in a grand orchestra whose symphony is too complex for me to grasp.

"Goddamn McNuggets," is all I can mutter as the red clock resets.

5.

KEN BELCHER

Wyatt asks me something, but he sounds like he's underwater, and it's like I've forgotten how to feel things and what words mean, and I can't answer. It makes no sense that the first person I *didn't* kill is the one that really messes me up. I give his shoulder a squeeze and reluctantly let go, sucking my tummy in so I won't touch him as I move between the seats. Numb and shaking, I curl up in my bed in the back of the truck, huddling deep in my quilt. Matty pads to my side, her toenails clacking on the metal floor and her legs splayed wide to keep her balance. She puts her face up next to mine, cheek to cheek, and gives me one little sideways lick. I rub her head and sigh. I guess she knows what it's like to lose something too.

I can't help wondering what will happen to Kelsey Mackey,

what's happening to her right now. Is it the same robotic Black Suit in the SUV, or a slightly different model, like the one at the gas station? Will she have the same gun with the same gold-stamped Valor logo? Will her jobs be complete strangers, or will she, like me, start to wonder how so many coincidences can crowd one short list?

I don't think I know Kelsey, and I've never heard her name before. But maybe she's a cousin I never knew, or maybe she babysat for me once when I was too little to remember. Maybe some sicko at Valor just wanted me to see what happens to nice girls who work hard to make their dreams come true, who think a little loan is a reasonable sacrifice for a brighter future. Maybe they wanted me to think I was doomed. And maybe her surprising choice backfired on them, when I didn't have to shoot her after all. Despite the ball of dread in my stomach, Kelsey Mackey gave me a little hope.

Wyatt stops the mail truck, and I don't even look up. I don't want to know where we are. I just want some time to myself, curled up in bed. He leaves the truck running, and the whole thing wobbles when he jumps out. For just a second, I think he might be running away, gone forever. But deep down, I no longer think that's going to be a problem. A thousand years, or maybe two minutes pass, and then he's back in the truck. He swings a backpack onto the floor behind the front seat and drives away faster than seems necessary.

"McNuggets?" he asks.

"Please," I whisper.

In no time at all, he's parking the mail truck. I blink again, and he's shouldering between the seats with bags of hot, greasy food. I don't remember him asking me for money or ordering from a drive-through. I think I might have fallen asleep, just for a few seconds. And he's wearing jeans, boots, a lacrosse hat, and a fresh band shirt—another one I like too. And it's dark out.

"Holy shit," I say, sitting up on the bed. "Did you go home?"

"Yeah," he says with a grin. "You didn't even notice. Totally catatonic. It's like you were asleep but your eyes were open. I tried calling your name, but then I realized I don't even know what it is. I kinda let you sleep for a couple of hours. Seemed like you needed it. And your clock looks like it gave you until noon tomorrow. I guess mail trucks can't deliver anything between six at night and six in the morning."

He hands me a bag, and I eat with the robotic detachment of a stump grinder by the meager glow of the tap light I brought from home. I should be angry at the lost time, but I'm half asleep and numb. I guess it's a good thing, ending the day early and on a win. Beside me, Matty licks her chops hopefully, and I feed her some fries. Her tail goes berserk against the floor of the truck.

"What did you do while I was asleep?"

"Played my DS. Read a book. Got upset and threw rocks. Stared at you creepily and made dolls of your hair." My eyes snap to his, and he's trying not to laugh. "Just kidding. Look, I didn't know what you wanted to drink, so I got a Coke and a Sprite."

I take the Sprite and glare at him as he eats half a cheeseburger in one big bite. Jesus, does the boy even chew his food?

"Did you see your brother? Did you tell him?"

His eyebrows go down, and a look I can't puzzle out passes over his face. He swallows a huge lump of burger and clears his throat.

"I didn't see him," he says.

"But you were going to tell him, weren't you?"

"I don't know. Can we just eat, please? I'm starving. Aren't you starving?"

I shove a nugget in my mouth and chew mechanically. My stomach is growling, so I know I'm hungry, but it might as well be gravel. The sky beyond the dashboard is as black as the inside of a closet, and I don't see any streetlights outside.

"Where'd you take us?" I ask.

"There's this part of my neighborhood that they cleared out but didn't build on." He wads up the empty wrapper and pulls another burger out of the bag. "Kind of like the one where you were hiding out. Me and Max used to come here to hang out and cool off. Nobody really knows about it but us. Seemed like a good enough place to let you sleep and crash for the night. And then tomorrow morning we can go after . . ."

He stands and walks over to my list, where it hangs from the wall by putty.

"Ken Belcher," I supply. I memorized the list a long time ago, before I ever met Robert Beard. Or his son.

"What kind of guy do you think Ken Belcher is?" Wyatt tears his new cheeseburger in half. He gives one big chunk to Matty and stuffs the other chunk in his mouth like a snake swallowing a table lamp. I've never seen a boy eat like that. Watching Matty gulp down her half of the burger while her butt waggles in joy makes a smile creep up on me of its own volition. But when I consider his question, the smile turns back upside down.

"I don't care what kind of guy he is." I burrow back onto my bed and tuck myself into the covers, and put a pillow over my head. "It doesn't matter. Whether he's rich or poor or young or old, he's got two choices, and they both suck."

Wyatt walks across the truck and towers over me. I peek out from under the pillow. His shadow engulfs me, the red from the dashboard clock outlining him like a Lite-Brite. His band shirt is tucked in just a little in front, with a belt over low-slung jeans. His torso is impossibly long, and I think of him as a megalith, as some sort of powerful boy-god whose next words will drop wisdom on me like melting snow.

"You look like you need a hug," he says slowly.

And that's not wise at all.

I snort and burrow my head back under the pillow so he won't see me laughing. And before I even register that he's serious, he sits on the bed and just sort of falls over me, drowning me in the scent of Mountain Fresh laundry detergent.

"Oh my God, get off!" I shout from under the pillow.

"Did you say *hug harder?*"

He drops all his weight on me, and it must take a hundred cheeseburgers a day to fill him up, because he weighs a ton. I'm afraid the cot is going to come unbolted and crash to the floor. It's as if that big statue of Abraham Lincoln at the Capitol fell on me, and his pointy chin is killing me, pressing into the hollow between my neck and shoulders. Beside us on the floor, Matty's tail goes berserk. Wyatt's breath drifts over the back of my neck and I freeze, suddenly realizing how very, very close he is, closer than I've ever let anyone get since my best friend broke my heart.

Then his fingers dig into my ribs, and I can't stop laughing. I laugh until I'm breathless, until my belly aches where it's squashed against the metal bar under the bed.

"You have to stop," I say. "You're smothering me to death. I can't breathe."

He sits up, and I turn over and sit up too, because I can't lie down while he's this close to me, can't lie on my back with my heart and my boobs on parade.

"Are you better now?" he asks, a little breathless too.

"No. Hugs and tickles can't make this sort of thing better." I pick at the quilt to avoid some charged movie moment where we stare at each other and slowly move closer.

"Yes, they can. Do I have to hug you again?"

He moves closer, just the tiniest shift.

Is he *actively seeking* a movie moment?

"My name is Patsy," I blurt.

He cocks his head. "Seriously? I've never met a Patsy before." He holds out his hand. "Hi, Patsy. I'm Wyatt."

I reach out to shake his hand, but he won't let go. His wet-brownie-mix eyes go soft, and he moves even closer, and I have to tell him something, can't go another second without telling him.

"I'm really sorry I killed your dad," I say in an itsy-bitsy, super-tiny voice.

"I know." His voice breaks just a little. He leans back out of kissing range again and clears his throat. "Things are messed up right now. We're both victims. I feel like I should feel worse about my dad. I feel guilty for *not* feeling worse. But he left my mom to sleep with his secretary, and he's an asshole to Max, and I hate living with him, and he's a lying sack of shit. He's already had one heart attack. I just want . . ."

He traces the quilt, too. We start playing a game where we don't look at each other, don't touch, just move our hands around the ratty old blanket like it's a chessboard with no pieces. It's awkward, but almost a comfortable sort of awkward. His pause stretches out, and I feel his gaze on me. I can't stop staring at a sesame seed by the corner of his mouth.

"I just don't want how messed up the world is to mess me up too," he murmurs.

"Me neither. But how can it not?" I have to clear my throat to get past the lump. "We might be victims, but that doesn't mean we can just ignore it. This isn't a case where we can put on headphones and tune out how much grown-ups screw shit up. We're paying the price for what they did. Kids don't have debts, but we have to suffer for theirs. It's not fair."

His face goes red. "So what? I mean, people used to have kids just to do their farm labor. Or to work in factories. My friend Mikey's mom ended up having to pay the bank twenty thousand bucks because her mom got dementia and maxed out her credit cards buying crap from the Home Shopping Network because her cats told her to. Our parents are paying the price for what their parents did, too."

I put a pillow over my face and scream. It's only half fake. "Kids shouldn't have to worry about the economy. About debt. We should be allowed to party and be stupid." I sound like such a puss, but if I can't say it to Valor, I'll say it to the only person around. I didn't even party and act stupid when I had the chance.

He huffs. "'Should' is a useless word. There will always be poor people, and their kids will always have to worry about shit. And rich people's kids will have a different pile of shit to worry about. And then we'll grow up and get new shit."

"Shit."

"Pretty much."

"My brain hurts," I say softly. "I don't want to think about it anymore."

I drop my head and sneak a look at him through my scraggly bangs. He's studying me like I'm a puzzle, or maybe a confusing piece of art.

"What?" I say.

"I don't get you. You're willing to fight, to do whatever it takes to live, but then afterward, you regret it." He adjusts his hat, takes it off, and looks at it. "If you foul a guy in lacrosse, you don't sit around apologizing like a dick. You spend sixty seconds waiting for the chance to get back out on the field and score. You don't let it stay in your head when it's already done and can't be fixed."

"Yeah, so? This isn't lacrosse. I didn't smack some dude's arm with a stick. I feel fucking terrible for killing people. You think that's wrong?"

"No. I think it's a waste of time. You can't change the past, so you might as well live in the present. And if you don't like the present, make a different future."

"I'm pretty sure that my future is going to suck."

He puts a wide, hot hand on my leg, and I freeze. "So change it."

"How? How are you so goddamn sure? What makes you the world's foremost authority on how to live with yourself after you murder innocent people?"

Wyatt just stares at me like I'm an idiot, his lip curled up. I keep forgetting that he killed the guy who was going to rape me in the back of my truck and then throw me to his friends as leftovers. And I need to find a way to thank him for that. This close, I notice that his nails are bitten down, and I get a closer view of the marks on the inside of his muscular arm, some sort of homemade tattoo, unfinished and jagged. I can't tell what it is, but the skin is pebbled and scarred. Ugly.

"Who do you think I am?" he says finally.

"I don't know."

"If you had to guess."

"Wyatt Beard," I say. "Ex–rich boy, music geek, lacrosse god, and walking stomach."

His eyebrows draw down, and his entire body takes on this weird, cagey energy.

"What if you're wrong?"

I fidget with my hair, the knots on the quilt, anything. There's something sinister about him, like it's been lurking underneath the other Wyatt. I think of the way he straddled me, knife to my throat, of how quickly he shot that guy, and it sinks in that I might not be the most dangerous person in the truck.

"Fine. Who do *you* think you are, Wyatt?"

He snorts. "I'm not even sure. But the thing is . . . I got into some bad shit." He glares up at me, his eyes half daring me to stop him and half begging me for forgiveness. "I'm not proud of it. Hung out with wannabe thugs, got in fights, got sent to juvie for shoplifting and vandalism. Smashed my bass through a window. But I decided to turn my life around. I went from straight F's to straight A's and dropped all my former friends. Even switched schools. Now I'm one of the best lacrosse players in the state and VP of the student council." His fingers trace the jagged lines on his inner arm. "This was supposed to be the anarchy symbol. My friend Mikey was doing it with pen ink and a hot needle. I have to look at it every day now. It never goes away. So when I tell you that you can change the future, I fucking mean it. You just have to want it bad enough."

"Oh," I say dumbly.

"Let me guess. You've been a goody-goody your whole life. Probably never even took a sip of beer or smoked a cigarette. This is your first time doing anything really bad, isn't it?"

It's hard to wrench the word out of my gut, but I do it anyway.

"Yes."

"And no offense, but you're good at it. So why not turn it against them? Why not fight Valor?"

My eyes dart to the front seat, where the bugged shirt is wadded up on the floorboard. It can't see us, and I hope to God it can't hear us. If it can, we're already totally screwed.

"How could I fight . . . them? A huge, rich, faceless corporation?" I snort. "How could anyone?"

"I don't know. But between the two of us, we could figure out a way. You might have spent your entire life being good, but there's a rebel somewhere inside you. Your inner yarn bomber says so."

The food sits heavy as red clay mud in my stomach as we stare at each other. In the dark of the night, we're nothing but shadows. My feelings and thoughts are as tangled as unraveled yarn, loose ends and knots and bursts of violent color. I don't think I can fight something so big. But a few short days ago, I didn't think I could shoot anyone. There's a hardness to Wyatt's eyes that I didn't notice before, a loose confidence in his size and posture. Considering what he's told me, I feel like I should like him less.

And yet I find that I like him more.

Without thinking too much about it, I run my fingertips up his arm to the place where a few harsh, black lines ripple over his skin. Sure enough, I can feel the raised bits, like his skin was burned and stained at the same time.

"Did it hurt?" I ask softly.

"Yeah."

"Why didn't you finish it?"

"Mikey was working on it, and I looked down and saw the twisted needle, the ripped-open pen. And it just hit me, I guess. I wasn't causing anarchy. I was just . . ."

He trails off.

"Acting out? Punishing your parents?" I poke the black marks. "Being a dick?"

He chuckles. "Yeah. Pick one. But I made him stop. We got in a big fight, and he OD'd right in front of me. I dropped him off at the hospital and never saw him again."

"And you feel bad about it?"

"Not bad enough to go back."

I've gone from tracing the tattoo to just touching his arm, enjoying the maplike lines of his veins. His skin jumps when my fingertips skim over the inside of his elbow. "It's kind of funny. You were given everything, and you rebelled. I was given nothing, and I worked my ass off."

"And now here we are, in the back of a mail truck. Being miserable."

I have to force myself to look at him. "I'm not actually miserable," I say.

Wyatt smiles, all soft. "Me neither."

He pushes up from his slump and turns to face me. Matty moves between our knees, her muzzle wiggling back and forth on the bed and her tail going wild. I sit up straighter as Wyatt leans closer, holding my breath as his eyes close and his lips brush mine.

"Is this okay?" he murmurs against my mouth, and I barely nod my head yes, not really knowing what *this* is. His lips catch mine again, and his hand finds the back of my head, holding me to him gently but firmly.

Somewhere, deep behind my ribs, in a place I didn't know existed, my heart opens up like one of those blooming tea bags, the ones that start out tiny and dark and then blossom like a flower. I've never let someone kiss me before. I've never let myself want to let it happen. It's as unreal as everything else, but far more welcome.

He shifts, moving closer, his leg lining up with mine. Matty backs up and barks at us like she can't figure out what's going on, if we're trying to eat each other or what. Wyatt's hand strokes her head, and against my mouth, he whispers, "Shhhh, girl. Shhh." It's the sexiest thing I've ever heard.

My mind floats away, and my body yearns toward his. Misery feels like a long thing, something that eats you, digests you, traps you. I am surely miserable, and misery is a rainstorm. But this moment is an umbrella, a singular thing, a contained thing, a stolen thing, a world infinite in itself. It reminds me of the first time I rode an elevator up a skyscraper downtown and saw how very different things look from above the clouds. As hard as we labor every day, from up above, it's just bright splotches of movement and color.

Wyatt's tongue finds mine, and I wrap my arms around his neck and fall back, pulling him on top of me. He holds himself up on his arms as he kisses me, and I miss that wild freedom from earlier, when he was hugging and tickling me. He's holding something back now, just when I realize I need it most.

"What's wrong?" I say, pulling out of the kiss to gaze into his eyes, breathless.

There's a raw tenderness about him as he strokes my face and says, "Nothing. I just don't want you to regret anything. You already regret too much of what you've done lately."

"It's just kissing." But I feel the heat of a blush creeping up my cheeks.

"Is it?"

He runs a hand up my jeans-clad leg, which has somehow twined itself around his hip without my permission or knowledge. His hand is hot and wide, fingers spread, and I tremble when I realize how firmly we've wound around each other in just a few moments of heated kissing. I think of him, in his flimsy pajamas, straddling me, and I wish the darkness would devour us completely so I could lose myself and not feel the judgment in his eyes.

"I'm less miserable," I whisper.

"Me too," he whispers back.

"Then come here."

My hands are still behind his neck, so I firmly pull him down to me until his chest presses into mine, his weight pinning me to the bed, to the truck, to the ground of what used to be America and is now some bank-owned corporate monarchy.

"I don't know what's going to happen in the next week," I say into his ear. "But right now I just want to not be alone. I don't want to feel cold."

He pulls away violently and lands on his feet beside the bed. His nostrils flare wide, his face screwing up in pain. Before I can ask him what's the matter, what I did wrong, he wrenches up the back door of the truck and jumps out.

"Then hug your fucking dog," he says over his shoulder.

I don't know where Wyatt went, but I burrow into my quilt with Matty's head near mine, feeling sorry for myself and weirdly ashamed. She whines a few times like she knows something is wrong and is sad that she can't fix it. I wipe my tears off on her fur.

"I don't understand boys, Matilda," I whisper to her silky ear.

And it's true. Aside from hanging out with the fun but utterly undateable Jeremy and Roy at work, I've had very little to do with guys. I always have to work a lot, and I won't drink or go to parties, and I won't kiss on a first date, which means there's never been a second date. I've basically come to the conclusion that all the guys at my school are either boring or jerks, and as such, I'm better off without them. I've pretty much decided that I'll meet some awesome, artsy guy in college, and that's when I'll really figure out what love is. It's not like I had any sort of relationship role model.

But I know that I said the wrong thing, that I made Wyatt really angry. So angry that he would rather storm away into the cold fall night than stay in bed with me, which I can't even comprehend. I shiver until I fall asleep, half expecting him to be completely gone when I wake up. But there he is in the front seat of the mail truck, drinking a Big Gulp of steaming coffee, his breath coming out in puffs against a lavender sky. A rolled-up fast-food bag and a smaller cup of coffee sit on top of the microwave, and Matty is eyeing it like it's a lesser god. I didn't even feel the truck moving, although I remember dreaming that I was on a pirate ship in the ocean.

I roll out of bed feeling grouchy and sad and embarrassed and ugly. And seriously uncomfortable. I can't remember the last time I slept in jeans, and I think there might be permanent creases all up and down my legs. I want a shower like whoa. And I can smell my hair, which is in no way sexy. Not that I care about sexy, since Wyatt clearly doesn't want anything to do with me.

Whatever. I don't owe him pretty.

"Morning, Wyatt." I take a big, unladylike bite of my sausage biscuit and drink some coffee, which I don't really like but am determined not to complain about.

"Morning," he says, kind of mocking and sad and expectant all at the same time.

"Where'd you sleep?"

"Right here, in the driver's seat."

"That must have sucked."

"It did. Thanks for noticing."

He takes a defiantly deep gulp of his coffee and jerks it away with a muttered, "Shit, that's hot!" Coffee splatters the inside of the truck, and he looks at his lip in the rearview mirror, to see if he's burned it, I guess. I smile a small smile when he's not looking. He's cute when he's pissy. But if he wants to ignore what happened last night, I'm happy to help.

"So where are we?" I ask.

"Outside of Ken Belcher's house." He takes a daintier sip and grins. "And you're not going to believe where he lives."

As I stand and stretch, the bottom of my spine cracks from being curled up on the small bed. Matty almost grabs my biscuit, but I snatch it up as I move to the front of the truck and try not to touch Wyatt as I squeeze between the seats. I plop into the passenger seat, my jaw hanging open.

"This place? He lives here?"

The mail truck is parked in a half-paved turn lane, and just in front of us is a house I've passed a thousand times, asking myself a thousand times why it would even exist. It's a gigantic, immensely sprawling mansion that reminds me of something out of Jane Austen. Like, it actually has wings and a big circular driveway with an outside chandelier, and stables, and a guesthouse, and tennis courts, and its own parking lot. And yet here it is, right next to our Podunk town, with a little sign out front telling everyone that it's important enough to have a name.

"Chateau Tuscano," I murmur.

"Like, do they even care that Chateau is French and Tuscano is both Italian and misspelled?" Wyatt says, and my crush on him grows a little bigger, because that's exactly what bothers me about it too.

"I know, right? And why does it have a parking lot with numbered spaces?" I add. "Like, your billion guests are getting into fights over where to park their limos?"

It's kind of pretty in the early morning for an oversized blight on the countryside. The horses are long gone from the overgrown pastures, and there haven't been grand parties in years. The stupid parking lot used to fill up every weekend, but it's been empty a long time, the snaggletoothed bushes surrounding it taller than me now. I used to imagine Jay Gatsby throwing parties here just to lure Daisy in so she could ruin everything.

And then one day I noticed a For Sale sign in the front yard, the kind that was made just to advertise the exotic allure of Chateau Tuscano. Then that sign was replaced by a standard RE/MAX sign. And then a For Sale by Owner sign—like anyone would just drive on up and knock. And now, for the last few months, a big sign with a Valor Savings Bank logo and FORECLOSURE/BANK OWNED stamped across it in angry red letters.

I gulp the last of my biscuit and swallow it down with coffee. It burns, but I don't mind that. I need all the help I can get keeping the food in my stomach where it belongs. I would have preferred to take my time this morning, to get cleaned up with my wipes and maybe throw a stick for Matty for a while before turning on the GPS machine to find Ken Belcher.

But whether he did it out of malice or kindness, Wyatt brought me here instead. The red clock on the dash gives me a little more than three hours to kill or compel this guy, and my phone is finally dead and can't tell me the actual time.

"Would you mind driving up closer?" I ask.

Without a word, Wyatt cranks the truck on. It rumbles slowly up the long driveway, and he parks just outside of the overhang. Like me, he's probably worried that the rusty chandelier will fall on the truck and flatten it. The concrete is uneven and cracked, with chunks pulling up here and there. The property looks so grand from the street. But up close, it's falling apart like Miss Havisham's cake in *Great Expectations*.

Under the shade of the building, it's even worse. The chandelier is missing crystals, the shards of which glitter on the bricks below. The bushes are overgrown and half-dead. The paint is peeling, and some of the windows are cracked as if they've been shot out by BB guns. It's almost as bad as Uncle Ashley's house, really.

How low the mighty have fallen.

"Are you ready?" Wyatt's dropped the pissy act and just looks worried for me.

I shrug and tuck the gun into my jeans and find the envelope, pulling out Ken Belcher's card. Wyatt says, "Here," and hands me the shirt from under his seat, the signature machine and button still carefully wadded up in the center.

"Thanks."

I shrug it on, stretching my shoulders against the itchy fabric that doesn't get any more comfortable with each wearing. My hand stays clamped around the top button. The damn thing feels like a ticking time bomb with no visible fuse. Half the time, I feel like Valor knows all about Wyatt and is going to swoop in with a SWAT team at any moment to punish me by pumping him full of holes, but most of the time I'm just hoping it's like the security cameras at the store—always recording but rarely watched. Like maybe there's just some crappy mall cop camped out in front of a hundred Valor monitors while he eats his sandwich, occasionally staring when something exciting happens on one of his screens. Maybe they just fast-forward through each tape at the end to make sure I hit the entire list. Maybe they're grading me. Or maybe the button is just a button. Just another lie.

Maybe it's just another bite of their bullshit pie that I keep swallowing down with a fake smile. I shake my head. I've got to get better at covering that button, just in case. And I have to get on with the next name on the list. Three hours doesn't feel like enough time, even though I'm already here.

The hat feels nasty as I slip it over my greasy hair with one hand. After kissing my lucky locket, I jump out through the front of the truck so Matty can't follow me. I don't want her anywhere near me when I'm holding a gun. I don't want her to get hurt accidentally, but I also don't want her to see me kill someone. The way she looks at me, her brown eyes soft with unconditional love and worship—I don't want her to think any less of me, even if she doesn't really know what's going on. I need her, and I need her to look at me like I'm awesome.

The front door is taller than it should be, as if daring me to press the doorbell. *Bluff called, Tuscano.* Inside, an unfamiliar tune plays, something that sounds fancy and French. I roll my eyes. So Ken Belcher's too good for a regular old *ding-dong* bell, huh? Footsteps click crisply within, and there's a moment while I wait for him to inspect me through the peephole. I smile innocently. Cheerfully. And the door unlocks and opens, revealing a thin and angry old man with ruddy skin and graying white hair. I can tell from his pooched-front khakis and slick penny loafers that we would never see eye to eye.

"What is it?" he says sharply, one soft and manicured hand held out expectantly. "Is it from Valor?"

"I think so." I hand him the signature machine. He signs with a long flourish, and I check to make sure it says Ken Belcher. I had completely forgotten to ask him his name. I can't read the scrawl. "Are you Ken Belcher?" I say, just to make sure.

He hands the signature machine back and says, "Dr. Ken Belcher," with a snotty insistence on *doctor*.

"Dr. Ken Belcher," I say, "you owe Valor Savings the sum of . . . Jesus. One-point-two million dollars?" I look around at the house towering above and around me. "Seriously?"

"Is this some sort of joke? Give me the envelope and get off my property immediately. I'm a high-level board member of Valor Savings Bank, and that information is personal."

"Okeydokey." I hand him the envelope and card without really thinking; I'm just so programmed to respond when important-acting guys talk to me like that. "So you really don't know why I'm here?"

"To deliver an empty envelope and a ridiculous forgery?" He holds it up and looks at me like I'm dog crap on his shoe. "Was there a check? Did you steal it?" He glances over my head at the mail truck and stares at my chest like my embroidered name will appear if he just watches my boobs long enough. "I'd like to speak to your supervisor."

But he just stands there. Doesn't go for a cell phone or walk inside or call for anyone.

"So do it," I say. "Go ahead and call."

He gets flustered, licking his thin frog lips. "I don't get a signal out here. I'm sure your manager's number is programmed into your cell." He holds out a hand, fingers wiggling in a "give it here" twitch.

"They turned it off, didn't they?" I say. "Valor cut you off."

"That's a serious accusation, young lady. You don't know who you're dealing with." His face is an ugly shade of orangey-red now. "I'm going to have to ask you to leave my property, or I'll be forced to call the police."

But still he doesn't go for a phone.

"Good luck with that." I pause and peek around him. "Are you here alone?"

He gasps and tries to shut the door in my face, but I wedge my foot in and step closer. I've been scared every other time I've done this. It was always in residential areas, near nosy neighbors and kids. But now we're out in the middle of nowhere. This guy spent millions of dollars that weren't his to buy his own private country estate, and now there's nobody left to hear the gunshots.

"You need to leave now." His voice is quavering, petulant, almost begging. He may have been powerful and untouchable once, but now he's alone and scared of a skinny seventeen-year-old girl.

"Ken Belcher," I say firmly, leaving out the doctor part just to make him angry as I dig fingers into the door to force it open. "You owe Valor Savings a shit-ton of money, and they're calling it in. Can you pay this sum?"

It's not what I'm supposed to say—not by a long shot. But he's still got my envelope and his card, and I can barely remember my own name as we fight for control of the door.

"How dare you."

"Are you willing to work it off as a bounty hunter?"

He shudders and drops the envelope on my foot. He knows now. "I—I don't know what you're talking about, but—"

"I'm pretty sure you just said no."

I pull out the gun as he lets go of the door and turns to run away. The world goes into slow motion. He slips on the polished foyer floor, and I pull the trigger, ready for the recoil and the explosion of echoes in the marble room. The shot slams into him, right under his armpit, and he takes a few lurching steps toward the hall, trying to get away. I remember how to move, how to breathe, and push through the open doorway right behind him, my sneakers squeaking on the marble. The old man is gasping and rattling and holding his side, and I know just enough from watching action movies to guess that I shot one of his lungs.

"This is insane," he splutters, blood bubbling from his lips. "I work for Valor. I'm on the executive board. They wouldn't do this to me. John wouldn't let them. They know I'm . . . solvent. They gave me today off for my birthday, for Chrissakes."

"Of course they did. They wanted you to be home when I got here."

Dr. Ken Belcher's loafers slip in his own blood, and he falls forward, landing on his hands before crumpling on his side like a dead spider. He rolls onto his back, puts his hands up in supplication. I aim my gun at his chest, wanting it to be over, wondering if my hands will ever stop shaking. If anyone deserves it, this prick does; he's part of the debt problem and, if he really was on the Valor board, part of the machine that destroyed my life. But he's also a terrified old man pissing himself on the marble while he drowns in his own blood, and what he deserves now is mercy. I pull the trigger, and his body thrashes backward, his head bouncing against the tiles.

I loom over him, lean past him to take back the envelope he'd crushed in greedy fingers. His shoes probably cost more than my mom used to make in a month, and his collared shirt is utterly without wrinkles. His hair swoops over shiny red skin, and more hair curls out of his ears and nose. I've never really been around someone this wealthy before, but I now know that being rich, or pretending you're really rich, doesn't make you any less gross when you're dead. And it definitely doesn't make you a better person.

I look up at the grand balcony where the curving staircases meet, twenty feet overhead. The house is unnaturally silent.

"Hello?" I yell. "Is anybody here?"

Nothing. No faraway footsteps or slamming doors or the gasp of a fainting maid. I walk in the direction that seems like the logical place for a kitchen, and eventually I find it. It's big and airy and filled with rich textures, from shiny stone to raw brick to unused copper pots that gleam like art. The phone on the wall was made to look old, and when I pick it up, the line is dead.

Still jacked up with that weird mix of adrenaline and nausea and horror and giddiness, I rip off my mail shirt and wad it up inside my hat. Jumping over the puddle of blood, I run outside, chandelier crystals crunching under my sneakers.

"Come on in!"

Matty barks joyously from the back, and Wyatt scratches the back of his head and stares at the huge house like he expects it to slowly collapse. "Seriously?"

"It's empty."

He shrugs and hops out of the front seat while I let Matty out of the back. She yips happily and slurps my hand and lopes into the tall grass, her tail making huge circles like a helicopter's rotor.

"I always wanted to see what this place looked like on the inside," Wyatt says. "You okay?"

Genuine concern is written in his smile, and I wonder if he's forgiven me for whatever he thinks I did or said wrong last night. I want to ask, but I don't know how. Not having a dad in the house means I don't even know how couples fight. My blueprint for a relationship is a quiet woman, alone, struggling to get by and failing. And I'm not going that route. So I just smile back and comically bow Wyatt toward the door like everything in the entire world isn't completely wrong.

"After you, milord."

It's not until I'm standing in the ginormous shower, washing my hair with a forty-dollar bottle of shampoo, that the irony gets to me. That the guy in the million-dollar mansion wasn't actually a millionaire and the poor girl from down the street is now enjoying his big-ass house. I spin under the two showerheads, practically melting under the steaming hot water. I was half surprised to discover that the house still had electricity and plumbing after finding the phone cut off. Then again, it seems like Valor wanted him to be here, thinking nothing had changed. Thinking nothing was wrong but a messed-up phone. They wanted him to die holed up in the beautiful house he had no business buying. And for all his importance, he died here, alone, still thinking he was superior and untouchable right up until the last possible moment.

I rinse the conditioner out of my hair and wonder how to pronounce "babassu oil." What the hell is it, and why does a mostly bald old dude need it? It sounds like it comes from some exotic bird. I've never used any shampoo except Suave, but at least there were lots of different scents to try. When I step out onto the heated floor, the towel waiting for me is so huge and fluffy that it's got to be made of dreams. I wrap myself in it and feel like a child when it falls below my knees. It's a shade they don't carry at Walmart, a strange, rich mauvey plum, perfectly matched to the thick wallpaper. Curling my toes against the cozy-warm tile, I wish I could just hole up here for days, painting my toenails and taking bubble baths and pretending I'm richer than my wildest dreams and that I don't know what worry is.

Matty pads into the room, wagging her tail. There's dark red staining her muzzle, and I sure as hell hope it's not Dr. Ken Belcher's blood. Leaning close, I catch the scent of hamburger and ketchup and breathe a sigh of relief. I scoot her over with a towel-covered knee and realize that I failed to bring a new pair of undies and a new T-shirt in here with me. It's gross, shrugging back into dirty clothes that still smell like sweat and the peculiar tang of the metal mail truck. But at least I find fancy deodorant and scented lotion in the cabinets.

Just as I'm fully dressed and about to put my lucky locket back on, Wyatt knocks on the door.

I drop my necklace on the granite counter and shove the wadded-up Postal Service shirt and hat in a drawer with the Q-tips. I should've put it there in the first place, but I was so overwhelmed at the thought of a hot shower that I just balled it up on the floor like an idiot. At least the camera was covered by cloth so the rent-a-cop didn't get a show to go with his sandwich.

"Come in."

Wyatt leans against the door frame, his hair dark and slick with water from his own spa time in one of the six bathrooms.

"So what now?" he asks.

I grin. "We raid the fridge and watch TV?"

We're downstairs eating ham sandwiches on kaiser rolls and dropping chunks for Matty when the fridge stops humming and the lights flicker off. Wyatt's eyes meet mine across the table.

"I think we need to go," I say.

He just nods. Before, it felt like we had plenty of time and could just play Rich Kids Home from College all day. Now I imagine SWAT teams descending on us with machine guns and grenades as a fleet of robotic guys in black suits storms the mansion with some freaky new bank-owned army. We both stand, and I take off for the stairs to fetch my shoes, hat, and mail shirt as Wyatt starts hunting through the cabinets for supplies.

When I arrive back at the truck with my wadded shirt tucked into the cap, Wyatt's already got the engine running. Matty's head pokes out between the seats, and I close the door to Chateau Tuscano behind me, leaving Dr. Ken Belcher's shrunken form sprawled across the white marble. His eyes are still open, his face frozen in disgust and surprise and the indignity of being forced to crawl across his own floor. I didn't like him, and I didn't mind killing him so much, but I'm glad as hell to be away from his body and the bloody, green-and-white Valor card perched on his chest.

As soon as I'm in the passenger seat, Wyatt starts driving, and I watch his messed-up tattoo flash and flex as he spins the big wheel. I'm amped up from running away, from the feeling of being chased, from the fear of being caught by the only authority left. Yet I'm also strangely relaxed from the most indulgent shower of my life. I feel like I've been washed clean, like the water contained some secret substance with the power to heal and reverse time and generally burn away the bad stuff. And my hair smells amazing, like gardenias made of moonlight. Suave doesn't come in this scent.

"I packed a bag full of food." Wyatt's all business now as he drives. "You might want to put it in the fridge or something before Matty goes crazy."

As I scoot into the back of the truck, my hip grazes his elbow. He grimaces and swallows, and I know then that he still likes me, or at least feels attracted me, no matter which invisible rule I broke last night. I find the bag, one of those reusable grocery bags that looks like it's never been reused, and pull ham and cheese and big, purple grapes out to stuff in the tiny fridge. There's also a few cans of sparkling water, which cracks me up. If you want bubbly water, why not drink soda, which actually tastes good? But I'm running out of money, so I guess I'll drink it when I have to.

We get back onto the main road without a problem, and Wyatt turns in the direction of his old neighborhood. I guess he feels safe there, in that abandoned section where he used to hang out with his brother. With Max. Just thinking about him, this guy I've never met, makes me feel sick to my stomach. I want to get through my list and be free, but I don't want to get to Max. Or, for that matter, to the name before his. But I've got three more deliveries ahead of them, so I'll worry about it later.

I wedge myself back into the passenger seat and stretch, enjoying the breeze. I'm usually in the back, trying not to puke while I deal with the fact that I've just done something horrible. But right now, it feels free and peaceful up here with my feet on the dash and the dying warmth of the fall sun battling with the winter wind whooshing outside the open door. The red clock turns over to 12:00:00, and I wrap my hand firmly around the oh-shit handle and just enjoy feeling young and alive for a moment, in body if not in mind.

"You have a really pretty smile," Wyatt says quietly.

I smile back until I notice the black Humvee barreling toward us, straddling the middle line of the narrow road.

6.

SHARON MULVANEY

Wyatt swerves onto the shoulder as he throws an arm across my chest, pinning me to my seat. "Jesus Christ!" he shouts. "What the hell?"

The mail truck bounces, kicking up a spray of gravel and almost flying down the shoulder and into the woods. Wyatt wrenches the wheel one-handed, and we're suddenly back on the asphalt, squealing.

The Humvee misses us by a bare few inches as it flies over the winding road in the opposite direction. Toward Dr. Ken Belcher and Chateau Tuscano. Just like the SUV outside of Kelsey's neighborhood, the window glass was so dark that I couldn't see anyone or anything inside. I didn't see a logo, but I know it must be someone from Valor, going to the mansion we've just left. Wyatt stomps the gas, and the truck jumps forward and shoots up the hill as fast as an old mail truck can go. As soon as we crest the incline, he realizes that his arm is thrown right across my boobs and lets it drop sheepishly.

"My mom calls that the 'grocery-saving response,'" I say, trying to tone down the awkwardness.

"Groceries saved," he says weakly. "Yay for groceries." He drives for a minute, both hands on the steering wheel, pink splotches high on his cheeks. "So where to next? Food, rest, lucky number six?"

I take a deep breath and blow air through my bangs. Every time I look at the red number on the dash and see the seconds flying away forever, I have a tiny heart attack. I know I need to hurry, that I can get three more done today and be that much closer to freedom. But the exhaustion is setting in, and I want nothing more than to snarf the food from Chateau Tuscano and find some quiet place to nap off the constant squirts of adrenaline and tears. I don't generally have a lot of free time, and the free time I do have I fill with all-ages shows at the Masquerade and exciting nights knitting alone in my room by my old CD player or watching reality TV while graphing out new cross-stitch projects that say rude things. Now free time is a chasm of dread. I want to finish my list. But I don't know how I'm going to live with myself after I scratch through those last two names.

All I really want is to run away and have more time with Wyatt. My brain knows that there's a good chance that I'm going to die and that America is already dead and that the world has ended and that my life, whatever it was, is over. And yet my heart knows that every second of happiness and hope is valuable and special and worth dying for. I feel this demanding pull to make Wyatt like me again. To get him to kiss me again. To cram as much Wyatt as I can into the remaining hours of my life. As soon as it's his brother's turn, our time is up. Forever.

At the very best, his brother takes the deal, and Wyatt goes with him to help, just like he's helping me.

I want to quit for the day, so much. But we're out here already, on the road and pumped full of adrenaline. We're fed and clean and have used real toilets. The only reason not to go to the next house is flat-out cowardice.

One glance at the dashboard clock confirms it for me.

"Lucky number six," I say. And I do feel kind of lethal, kind of badass. I can always get all the easy assignments over with, then balk for the last twenty-four hours.

I lean over and turn on the GPS, scrolling to the next name. Sharon Mulvaney. The address is in a bad neighborhood that's in the news every other week for a meth house being busted or prostitution or, one time, illegals being fenced as slaves. When you drive by the sign, it doesn't look that much different from my own neighborhood, but it's like one of the houses inside went rancid and corrupt with cancer and started just eating up the whole subdivision until it was rotten through and through like a busted pumpkin after Halloween. My bus doesn't even stop there anymore. I guess all of the high school kids dropped out.

"God, I hate Oak Hollow." I lean back against my chair.

"It's pretty skeevy." Wyatt turns right at the bullet-hole-pocked stop sign. "My buddy Mikey used to live in here."

The late morning is pretty and quiet, and the warm fall sun paints the broken-down street in the kindest light possible. If Ashley Cannon's neighborhood had given up, this one has just died an awful death and fallen where it stood and gotten nibbled by rats. Graffiti, boards over windows, mangy pit bulls on chains in the front yards. It's about as bad as things get in our town, and I want out of here as fast as possible. In the back of the truck, Matty growls, low in her throat, and it sets me further on edge. I haven't heard her growl yet, not even when I stood at her door, gun in hand, and shot her owner dead.

The truck rolls to a stop in front of a two-story house that must have been cute, once. It's got little lacy designs on the corners, as if Hansel and Gretel had lived here. Now, the way it's caving in on itself, I imagine the wicked witch lurking inside, waiting by a hot oven. There are no cars out front, and the driveway is a steep hill downward, as if the house had sunk twenty feet into the earth. On the porch of the house next door, three thugs in heavy coats smoke, eyeing us. Each guy slips a hand inside his jacket as they stare us down, and I tuck my own gun into my jeans, flat against my spine.

"You sure you don't want to come back later?" Wyatt says. "Get some more food and wait a while? Those dudes don't look too friendly."

"And who drinks out of paper bags this early in the day? How old are those guys? Like, fifteen?"

That's when I notice a box of empty bottles on the front porch of Sharon Mulvaney's house. And another one by the garage. And a couple of crushed needles in the driveway. Bile rises in my throat when I think about what I'm going to find when I ring that doorbell. Whoever lives here has worse problems than bills from Valor. I'm kind of glad I don't have the fruit basket anymore, because I would probably get jacked just for carrying it around Oak Hollow.

I grab my envelope and slip on my shirt and cap. Sharon's card has a much lower number than the others. But Valor never promised me any answers. They never said it was supposed to make sense.

"Good luck," Wyatt whispers as I hop down. Although I haven't seen it in a while, he has my other gun on the floor at his feet, and I feel a little better, knowing he's got my back. I reach between the seats to pat Matty on the head and let her lick my hand, and that feels like good luck too.

But when I reach for my lucky locket, it's gone. I suck in a breath like I've been punched in the chest.

"Shit. Shit, shit, shit."

My heart's frantic as I claw desperately along the crack of the passenger seat and scramble bitten, Christmas-painted nails along the floorboards.

"What's wrong?"

I look up and meet Wyatt's eyes, my other fist wrapped around the button on my shirt. How can I make him understand? The whole thing seems so stupid, that I could be as upset about a locket as I was about killing someone. But my body doesn't know the difference between real and useless panic, and in this moment, my heart doesn't either.

"My lucky locket. It's one of the only things my dad left behind. I wear it every day." I touch my forehead to the butt-warm plastic seat in resignation. "And I left it on the bathroom counter at Chateau Tuscano."

"Do you want to—"

"We can't. They're already there."

"Can you just—"

"No. Whatever it is, no. It's gone, Wyatt. It's just . . . gone."

Before he can say something annoying or trite, I turn to go. Without my lucky locket, I feel more exposed and doomed than ever. As I jog down to the front door, the eyes of the thugs next door crawl lazily over my body like maggots. I'm glad to get under the overhang, hidden by untended bushes and out of their sight. The doorbell doesn't ring when I press it, so I knock on the door, disgusted by the softness of the wood under my fist. More rot in

Oak Hollow. Big surprise. My stomach's full of acid and my mouth's full of cotton and something nearby stinks to high hell, like an opossum dragged itself under the porch and died.

No one answers my knock. No footsteps, no shadows moving behind the fake stained-glass windows. I knock again, harder. No car, no answer. God, I hope she's home, whoever she is. I don't know how I'll ever get the courage to come here again. When I glance back at the still-running truck, Wyatt is standing in front of the passenger seat, legs spread and arms crossed so that his biceps stretch the arms of his T-shirt. His face is dark and sharp, his jaw jutting out and stubbled. He can be pretty fierce when he wants to, and I wonder how much of a badass he was when he was running with the wrong crowd, how tough he is on the lacrosse field. Has the mild-mannered rich man's son ever killed anyone before yesterday?

"You gonna have to walk in, *chica*," calls a voice from the house next door. "Sherry don't answer the door no more."

I refuse to look around to see what they're doing, but Wyatt's eyes are on the other porch. After tugging my sleeve down over my fingers, I grab the dull door handle and push. It's unlocked. Ever so slowly, the door creaks open, and the scent of raw garbage slaps me in the face. It's dark inside, the only light coming from a sliding glass door to the back porch. That one's ajar too.

Cold ice seeps down my spine. Everything about this place feels wrong. The stench of rot and damp walls, the piles of trash on the floor. The door catches on a teetering tower of papers and mail, and I slip inside, leaving it open. The walls shrink in around me, and it's like being in a haunted house. Nothing can be this ruined and still lived in. Big, rusty stains bloom on the wall, and water drips from a tear in the ceiling. Old, faded prints hang askew, and moldering bits of hardened food drip from strange places, like a food fight happened twenty years ago and was never cleaned up.

I take a deep breath and stop, midgulp. I don't want that much of this air in me.

Something touches my leg, and I jump back into the doorway. It's a skinny old cat covered in sores, and it makes a strangled, pleading sort of meow at me, winking a destroyed eye. It rubs against me again, like it's freezing to death and I'm a space heater. I nudge it aside and press farther into the house, one hand to where my locket should be.

"Sharon Mulvaney?" I call. My voice echoes, and something thumps irritably overhead.

I don't want to, but I head upstairs, testing each drooping step with my shoe before entrusting it with my weight. The stairs are swaybacked and covered in shag carpet the color of smog. I think it used to be blue. Faded photographs march up the wall with me, and I shiver when I see someone I recognize. A little girl from my second-grade class, Ann Filbert. I wanted to be friends with her, but my mom said that she was trash, and I couldn't ever go to her house.

There are several incarnations of bad school pictures of Ann and an older boy who looks progressively more emo. In the last picture, he's dressed like a Juggalo, growling at the camera at a birthday party. There's a creepy man with a pornstache in a few of the early pictures, but not in the most recent ones.

Ann herself just looks like a nice girl, which is how I always thought of her. Pretty, kind of skinny, always dressed in hand-me-down clothes but so sweet that nobody ever said anything about it. After I showed up to spend the night with her in second grade and my mom wouldn't let me get out of the car because her house was so old and dirty, we never talked again. That was a different house in a different neighborhood, and this one is much worse. She still goes to my school and is as popular as a dirt-poor girl can be, although we're invisible to each other now.

Why are Ann's pictures in this house? It's another kill that can't be a coincidence.

I'm almost to the top of the stairs, and there's a new smell up here. Less garbage, more chemical, plus the overhanging funk of cigarettes. A weak cough totters down the hallway, and I follow. As I pass a bathroom that looks like a meth lab, I pull my shirt over my nose to cover the sweet, sickly reek wafting out. The door to the next room is shut, and the one after that has a caved-in hole where the roof should be. The piles of all-black clothes and stompy boots and Insane Clown Posse posters tell me it was the emo guy's room.

Maybe still is, since there's a manky sort of burrow on the bottom bunk of a bunk bed, the sheets crusted around the shape a human body would make.

At the end of the hall, I stop, heart thumping in my ears like a claustrophobic kid locked in a toy chest. Something rustles in the last room, and I imagine a giant snake, doubled back on itself, waiting for me. My hand is on my gun, and I'm about to pull it out when someone coughs raggedly, something a snake just can't do. The door is ajar, so I push it all the way open.

"What are you here for, honey?" Her voice is a rasp, barely more than her cough.

She looks sixty and she sounds eighty, but she's probably only forty. She lounges in a big, flimsy brass bed, her skeletal arms and legs splayed out like a broken puppet. The stained nighty dangling off her sharp collarbone was probably supposed to be sexy, but she's so bony that it just looks like a child's camisole on a coat hanger.

"Are you Sharon Mulvaney?" I ask.

"You here for a tweak?" she rasps. "Joey ain't here."

"Are you Sharon Mulvaney?"

"You a friend of Annie's? She moved out. Didn't leave an address. Little bitch took the car, too. You find her, you tell her I'm gonna beat her ass when she comes crawling back."

"Are. You. Sharon. Mulvaney?" I spit out each word through clenched teeth.

"Is that for me?" She waves one shriveled hand at the envelope. "If it's a subpoena, I ain't taking it. Or did Jesse finally send me my check?"

"I can't give it to you until you tell me that you're Sharon Mulvaney."

"I don't go by Mulvaney." She turns her head to cough into a dirty spot on the pillow. "Went back to my married name. I'm Sharon Filbert. They call me Sherry." I hold the signature machine for her because I'm worried it's so heavy it could break her hand, or maybe she'd try to steal the damn thing and sell it for parts. Her signature is just a ragged X. As I click accept, she looks me up and down, her gaze hungry in a weird, detached sort of way. "Say, you want to make some money? I can't trick anymore, but the boys next door would probably pay. They don't hit too much if you do what they tell you."

"Sharon Mulvaney," I say, stepping back a little. "You owe Valor Savings the sum of $3,455.20. Can you pay this sum in full?"

Sherry giggles madly, and it builds into this rasping, choking laugh that shakes her whole body like it might fall apart. I notice that her toenails are painted bubblegum pink, and that one of her big toenails has flat-out fallen off. The sausage biscuit rises in my throat, and I hope to God I don't puke in here.

"Pay off a debt? Are you shittin' me?" She grasps at her heart, at where her heart should be. "Only people who pay off debts are

· 160 ·

dumb bastards who think the big banks give a crap. They can't do shit! I got more credit cards than I got fingers, and I just let those goddamn bills pile up behind the door. Nothin's fuckin' happened. And every time I apply, damn if they don't send me a new one."

I angle my chest toward her as I read from the card, fast and with as little breathing in as possible. "By Valor Congressional Order number 7B, your account is past due and hereby declared in default. Due to your failure to remit all owed monies and per your signature just witnessed and accepted, you are given two choices. You may either sign your loyalty over to Valor Savings as an indentured collections agent for a period of five days or forfeit your life. Please choose."

"You are just a piece of work, honey," she says, her scrawny chest still shaking with laughter. "You think I don't remember you, but I do. You just about broke my Annie's heart. Y'all rolled up our driveway in your piece-of-shit car, and your mama looked at my house like her crap didn't stink, and you didn't even get out. Annie watched you from the window, and she cried all night. That was some cold shit, girl. She never forgot that. And now you think you can show up and tell me what to do? Well, screw you, kid. The bank can't do shit. And you can't, either."

"It wasn't my choice," I say, and my voice is raw, because it's bothered me. For ten years, it's bothered me. I saw Ann in the window while we drove away that night. I saw her crying, but I didn't stop my mama. And I didn't apologize to Ann at school the next Monday. We never spoke again.

"You always got a choice," she says, mean and sharp as barbed wire.

"Wrong."

She throws her head back on her skinny neck to laugh at me, and I pull out my gun and shoot her, right where the bird bones meet over her chest. Her eyes go round with surprise, but she keeps laughing, blood burbling out of the hole in her chest, out of her mouth. I throw her card at her, scared to get too close, like she might grab me and yank me into her diseased death hole of a bed, the skeleton in a haunted house that really is haunted. The card sticks in the blood, slides down to that dark spot on her pillow. Holding my wrist over my nose to keep the smell out and the puke in, I rush out the door and down the hall. There's nothing I want more than to fly down the stairs and out into the truck and back to Wyatt's secret place, back to where things feel safe, even if they aren't.

But something stops me. I have to see what's behind that closed door.

My hand curls around the cold doorknob, and the door glides open. Inside, it's like a wormhole to another dimension. This room is the only clean, pure, pretty place in the entire house, maybe in the whole neighborhood. Light pink walls, filmy curtains that let the sun in with a delicate glow, pure white carpet, and a bed covered with bows and ruffles. The pillows and stuffed animals, though ratty, are arranged just so, just like the stuffed turtles on my mail truck cot. There's even an air freshener plugged into the wall, coating the whole room in a candy-vanilla cloud. Little photos are stuck under the frame of the vanity mirror, Ann smiling with her friends, the second-tier popular girls. I had forgotten that she was on the JV cheerleading squad, that she was on the homecoming court and the student council.

It's beautiful, this little sanctuary. It's amazing how it can stay pristine surrounded by such decay. And it strikes me to the heart that her mother kept this door shut, this room fresh, like her Annie might come back and make everything better.

I open drawers in the vanity until I find a pad of pink, star-shaped notepaper and an old ballpoint pen. I scribble, *Ann, I'm so sorry about that day. My mom made me leave. I always thought you were a really nice person.* And I sign it with my name. *Patsy.*

I leave the note on her bed and let myself out the door, closing it gently behind me. And that's when I hear a sliding glass door whisper open down below.

"You in here, little *chica?*" a mocking voice calls.

"Her boy still out front. She in here," says another.

I freeze and silently pull the gun back out of my jeans. It shakes in my hand.

"Maybe Sherry got her," one of the guys says. "Sherry, you pop her ass?"

"Maybe she pop Sherry."

"Maybe I pop that cherry."

"Maybe you suck dick."

"Maybe your mom sucked mine this morning."

"Shut up, man. We get her, we get that truck. We get her alone in that truck . . ."

One guy beatboxes, and the other two grunt along like gorillas.

The first heavy foot hits a stair, and I realize that I have only seconds to become a victim or stay a killer. The choice is easy. I unbutton the top button of my shirt, letting the sides hang open so the camera is flopping against my shoulder. I'm pretty sure I'm allowed to kill these guys with no consequences. But if I know Wyatt like I think I do after only two days, he's going to show up as soon as guns start firing. There's no time to warn him. For the first time in my entire life, it's kill or be killed. I step around the wall and aim my gun down the stairs, both arms out straight and my finger on the trigger.

"Oh, here she is. Little bitch thinks she can pull—"

That's all he gets out before I shoot him in the neck. He falls backward, right into the next guy. They all look alike, just general thugs in oversized coats and pants and shoes, like cats puffing up their tails to look bigger. They're younger than they appeared from a distance, and I'm not falling for it.

"Oh, you gonna pay for that, *chica*," says his friend, aiming a sideways gun at me, and a bullet ricochets off the wall over my head. I spin back around the corner, out of sight.

I'm breathing heavily, panting, my hands shaking. Every other assignment, I've had this certain confidence, like I couldn't be touched, like the blanket of silence radiating out from Valor Savings would protect me. Like my lucky locket would protect me. Like I was invincible and as long as I was doing it to protect my mom, I would somehow be safe too. Now I'm trapped, hunted, and scared. Down below, the first guy's body hits the floor, and the other two guys pound up the stairs. There's a crunching, ripping noise, and one of them screams, "Shit, man! My foot!"

The last guy keeps coming, and the front door slams open and bounces off the wall. A dog barks, and my heart sinks. *Please don't let Matty get shot. Don't let Wyatt get hurt.*

These guys that are after me, they're straight-up thugs. They have nothing to lose, and they steal and kill and rape for fun. And now they're mad. What I'm doing is business, necessity. What they're doing is just cruel. My hand stops shaking as I decide that I have to get my only two friends out of this corpse-house in one piece.

I spin back into the stairwell just as the next thug hits the top stair. I smash the gun right up to his chest and shoot him before he really knows what's going on. He mutters, "Fuckin' bitch," as he slumps over, and another bullet thumps into his back. The last guy is stuck on the stairs, his foot caught in a hole in the rotten step. His bloody ankle is comically small between the huge pants and puffy shoes, and I can see thick, jagged splinters ringing it. His face is screwed up, and he's holding his gun sideways as he shoots and screams, calling me every name in the book. But his shots keep going wild or just smashing into his dead friend as he falls away from me in impossibly slow motion.

I aim for the stuck guy, but he ducks at just the right time, and the bullet pings against the door, inches from Matty, who's planted all four fat feet and is barking like crazy. I can't shoot again—I can't risk hitting her, and I'm shaking too hard to aim. My head is nothing but barking and yelling and the high whine of too many gunshots, and each second lasts a million years, and I just want it all to be over.

Wyatt's right behind the dog, gun drawn, and I let him see me before I spin back into the hall and out of range of the thug on the stairs. The last one should be easy pickings for Wyatt now, with me out of the way. I hear gunfire, but I can't tell who is shooting at whom. Matty starts growling, and the thug curses and bumps around, probably trying to pull his foot out of the rotten wood. There's another gunshot, and Matty howls and whimpers. Something heavy thumps and rolls down the steps, and tears burn my eyes. Almost without thinking, I charge down the stairs and shoot the guy in the shoulder. Before he can fire off another shot, I put one in his chest from point-blank range, screaming in his face so hard that my throat hurts.

He flops backward down the stairs, his foot still stuck. I know he's dead. I know it, but I kick him and scream, "Fuck you, you goddamn piece of trash! I hope you rot here!"

Strong hands link around me in a bear hug, and Wyatt hauls me, kicking and screaming, off the crumpled-up thug. As he drags me down the stairs, I can see now that the thug's even younger than me, maybe fifteen. He's so pathetically skinny, under all his puffed-up clothes.

"Are you cool?" Wyatt asks me once we're in the foyer. I dangle in his arms, limp and past fighting him.

"I'm fine," I say, although we both know it's not true. "Where's Matty?"

Wyatt sets me down on my feet, and I almost trip over the first thug. This one's a little older but just as pathetic, and probably a tweaker, judging by how soft and crumbly his teeth look. When I think about what these guys would have done to me if I hadn't had a gun, I shiver. And I'm glad Ann moved away from here, hopefully very far away. I hope that when she still lived here, the doors were shut and locked. I hope she had a knife under her ruffled pillow, anything to protect her from all this goddamn decay.

I kick the thug over and scramble out the door, slipping on blood and trash. Matty's limping toward the truck like it's a real home.

Collapsing next to her, I stroke her head and look for the wound. She whines softly and licks my cheek, but her tongue feels dry. Dammit. When did I last give her water? I can't remember. Two days, and I'm already a shitty pet owner.

"It's okay, girl," I say, petting her and feeling for blood. "It's going to be all right. Who's a good girl?"

Her tail thumps once before she whimpers and rolls over onto her side, and I force myself to stop sweet-talking her if it's only going to cause her pain. I run my hand over her side and find the sticky place, in her neck. When my fingers graze it, she lets out the most mournful sound I've ever heard, and it takes everything in me not to burrow my face into her shoulder and cry.

Wyatt squats beside me and says, "She's not going to die. It didn't hit anything vital. We can fix this."

I meet his eyes and see nothing there but resolve. He's not trying to make me feel better; he actually believes it, the fool.

"I can't afford vet bills," I say. "I can barely afford lunch."

"I can." But a look passes over his face that I can't quite figure out.

He scoops Matty up, and she whines, then growls for a second, then looks surprised at herself for growling at Wyatt and goes back to whining. When he tries to get a better grip on her bulky frame, blood squirts out of the hole, and her eyes roll white all around. I wish it had been me instead of her. At least I would understand what was going on. But her sweet face is just so scared and hurt and shocked, and I can't even tell her not to worry about it because she'll start wagging again.

I lift the truck door, and Wyatt lays the black Lab carefully on the metal floor.

"I'll ride in back with her," I say, scrambling up beside her on stiff legs. "You know the vet by the emissions place on Craley Bridge? Let's go there."

He nods and rolls the door down, leaving Matty and me in the dark. I'm glad I don't have to watch Ann's house as we pull away. It doesn't seem possible that one rotting old building can hold four dead bodies, a meth lab, and a perfectly preserved girl's room. If the ground were to open up in a gigantic sinkhole and swallow it all down forever, I think I would feel better. And the neighborhood's so bad that not a single person came to investigate what had become a flat-out gunfight.

The truck pulls away, and Matty and I slide across the floor as Wyatt turns us around in a cul-de-sac. I've gotten so cocky that I forgot to be safe. We should have parked the truck facing out of the neighborhood for a clean getaway. If the thugs had been alive and chasing us, we would have ended up with busted tires and a truck full of bullet holes, and the rest of my assignments would have been screwed. So many things could go wrong at any moment that I kind of can't believe Valor would expect me to accomplish anything.

Shit, maybe they're counting on me to fail.

As I stroke Matty's head and hold an old sock over the bullet hole, I realize that I'm still wearing my Postal Service shirt. The camera flops uselessly against my shoulder, so hopefully it didn't see Wyatt, but the bottom of the shirt is speckled with Matty's blood. Guess I'll have to tuck it in from here on out. I look at it closely under the tap light before stuffing it into the fridge, but the tag inside doesn't say anything about how to wash it without damaging the special camera. When I turn back, Matty is either asleep or unconscious, her breathing shallow and quick.

"Can't you drive any faster?" I ask, and the truck speeds up with a grumble.

When we bump over the curb and screech to a stop in the vet's driveway, Matty wakes up and starts whining again. Wyatt lifts the door, and I help him carry the shaking dog to the vet's front door. She's damn heavy, and my arms flop like stretched-out rubber bands. The vet is open, and the waiting room is empty, thank goodness. I've never had a pet, and I've never been to a vet before, but I always had this one picked out as the one I would use. There's this stone statue outside of a dog carrying a basket of flowers in its mouth, and for different holidays, they dress the dog up in bunny ears or a Santa hat or a pirate eye patch. I always thought they must be nice people, to keep that stupid statue dressed up all year.

The smell inside is homey and horrible at the same time, a mix of wet fur, doctor smell, and some weird dog perfume wafting from the groomer's door. Wyatt takes Matty's weight from me and carries her to the front counter.

"Please, it's an emergency. Somebody shot my dog."

My temper flares for just a second. She's *my* dog. My inheritance. My responsibility. And one I royally screwed up, I guess. Still, if he's paying, let him lie all he wants to.

Just fix my dog.

The receptionist's face crumples up like she's never seen a dying dog before. She opens a door to the back, and I trail behind Wyatt as she leads us down a long, empty white hall. A single drop of blood plops to the ground, and I've stepped in it before I can make my foot work. My sneaker spreads it around, and my heart tightens in my chest. I don't know anything about vets or sick dogs or bullet wounds, but I hope Wyatt is right. I hope this is fixable.

A youngish lady in scrubs that match her bright green eyes meets us in the exam room, and I'm glad that she looks kind.

"What happened?" she says, putting on blue gloves and feeling gently around the wound.

"Jackass kids shooting in their backyard hit her while we were walking in the woods," Wyatt says, and it comes out so smoothly and matter-of-factly that I almost believe it's real. That it could have happened.

"Kids and guns around here." The vet shakes her head. "Did you catch 'em?"

"We were too worried about Matilda," Wyatt says. "They ran away."

"You should probably call the police anyway. They might hit a person next time." The vet's doing things with her hands, with a little instrument thing, that I can't really see. Matty's coat is so black and glossy that the blood just makes it look shinier. She whines and tries to lick the vet's wrist, and the vet says, "You're a good girl, aren't you?"

Matty's tail whacks the table. *Thump, whine. Thump, whine.*

"We'll call them as soon as we can," I say, voice shaking.

I know very well that even if the police are around and listening, they sure as hell wouldn't waste any breath today on redneck kids shooting guns in the woods. This kind of crap happens all the time, and no one did a damn thing about it even when they could have, even when the police were still the police.

"We need to get her into surgery to make sure there aren't any bullet fragments, but I think she'll be fine," the vet says. "Looks like it just grazed her. I don't think it hit anything major. Do you guys want to wait around, or do you want me to call you?"

Wyatt's eyes meet mine, both our mouths open and empty of words. He looks as confused as I feel. I guess neither of us has a working cell, which is just ridiculous. Telling this lady that we don't have a phone is about the same as announcing that we're space aliens.

Still, whether it's because he can't pay the bill and Valor cut off his service, or he's smart enough to know I'm being tracked, it's a relief that Wyatt is just as disconnected as I am.

That means he can't call his brother.

"We'll wait outside in our truck," I say.

"Yeah, I'm allergic to cats," Wyatt offers.

"I'll let you know what I find, but I think things should go smoothly. You did well, getting her here quickly. We'll take good care of her."

With murmured thanks and one last pet, Wyatt and I walk out the door, through the waiting room, and back out to the truck. I don't realize until he lets go that he's been holding my hand ever since we put Matty on the examining table.

7.

TOM MORRISON

I'm exhausted but filled with nervous energy, still too spooked to talk. Without a word to Wyatt, I pick up my yarn bag and grab a ball of black yarn to add to the flagpole scarf. I stare into space as my needles click furiously, row after row of tight stitches appearing from thin air.

Wyatt watches me for a few minutes and says, "I'm going across the street to Subway. You want anything?"

"I just can't," I say, and he nods once and leaves.

My stitches are so taut that the flagpole scarf pulls in at the middle, like it's wearing a black corset. With a sigh that turns into a groan, I set the needles down before I ruin it. I want to finish this piece and get it up on the flagpole before my assignment is over. For some reason, it's really important to me that it gets done. Like some small part of me thinks everything will change afterward, and I just want to finish one thing for myself, instead of taking care of a big, stupid bank's bloody business.

Speaking of which, there's a blood smudge on the floor where Matty fell over. I scrounge up some fast-food napkins from the trash and try to wipe it clean, but I need something wet, because it's all crusty and I don't have any saliva left to lick the napkins. By the time Wyatt gets back and erupts from between the front seats with a plastic sack and two large drinks, I'm scratching at the bloodstain with my bare fingers, crying.

"Out, damned spot?" he says with a frightened chuckle.

All I can do is growl at him, a ragged, feral sound that starts in what used to be my heart.

Gently, his hands catch mine and hold them still.

"Don't do this," he says, his cheek warm against mine. "It's not your fault."

"Everything is my fault."

"No. If anyone's to blame, it's Valor. It's this big, faceless corporation that's using dirty tricks to make you do horrible things."

"But those guys back there . . ." I trail off with a sob.

"They were going to hurt you, Patsy. I mean, this is kind of my fault."

I glance up in surprise. "What? Why?"

"I saw them whisper and go into their front door, and I thought I didn't have to worry about them. I just figured they were dumbass tweakers. And they snuck right out the back door and trapped you in that hell house." His hands rotate around mine, from holding them away from the bloodstain to holding them gently and warmly. "Jesus, I'm so sorry that I let that happen."

"Not your fault," I whisper.

"Then we both agree it's neither of our faults," he says, and he trips over it like it doesn't make sense grammatically or seriously. "Shake on it?"

"You're already holding my hand," I mumble, and he smiles and shakes both of my hands like a dork before sheepishly letting them go. They drop to my lap, useless. That's when I realize that the gun has been in the back of my jeans this whole time, that I walked right into an animal hospital with a loaded gun casually tucked into my pants and sliding around in butt sweat and Dr. Ken Belcher's fancy lotion. Suddenly it's the most uncomfortable thing ever.

"Excuse me a minute." I pull it out and check the clip like it's as normal as brushing my teeth.

"You got more bullets?" Wyatt asks, and I pull a cardboard box out of my backpack and put it between us on the floor. He opens the box and looks at me quizzically. "So they gave you two guns and two hundred bullets to take care of ten people?"

I smirk.

"Nope, they gave me one gun with a loaded clip. I already had the bullets, so I brought them, just in case."

"Where'd this one come from, then?" He holds up his gun, careful to point it away from me and to keep his fingers far from the trigger.

"It was my dad's. Only thing I have of his besides my locket." I flinch at the way he's waving it around, even if he's doing so safely. "That one isn't stamped." I show him the words VALOR SAVINGS on my gun. The gun he's been using is also a 9mm, but it's a different brand, much older and more dinged up.

"Smart move."

He slips the bullets into his clip one by one and slides it home like a pro, confident and sure. I load mine up too. After shit went sideways at Sharon Mulvaney's, I never want to be caught by surprise again. If I'd run out of bullets in there, I'd probably be just another dead thing in a dead house. The dashboard clock is already ticking down on my next assignment. I'm going in angry, and I'm going in fully loaded. Provided Matty is okay, that is.

There's a distinct smell of gun oil and metal in the truck as Wyatt opens up the Subway bag. His hands are covered in oil and dog hair and dried blood, and I hurry to hand him a shower wipe before he can touch the food. I need one too, considering all the crap I touched in that nasty house.

Wyatt sucks down two foot-long sandwiches with his usual,

freaky grace, and I manage to get down half a meatball sub and some chips. I'm so hungry and messed up that I don't even notice the cheap, plastic taste. I wonder, for just a moment, when food will start having an appeal again. As soon as I'm done with my service, I'm going to gather up whatever money I have left and take my mom out for a big-ass restaurant meal, the kind where they ask you how you want your steak cooked and you order an appetizer and an entrée and a dessert and eat three baskets of bread and don't worry if you finished everything. And I'm getting a big ol' doggy bag for my dog, too.

I drink all of my Coke and go into the animal hospital to see if I can use their bathroom.

The receptionist lights up when I walk through the door. "Oh, good! Dr. Godfrey was just about to go out and look for you. Your dog is out of surgery."

"Is she okay?" I ask, just about peeing myself. "Is she alive?"

With a motherly smile, she pats my arm. "She's just fine, honey. She won't be awake for a while, and she'll need to stay overnight for observation, but she's going to be just fine."

I'm so grateful that I hug her, and she just laughs and pets me like she's used to that sort of thing. I can't think of the last time I hugged someone besides my mom or Wyatt, and it's weird to feel her hair against my face and smell her old-lady perfume. But I really am about to pee my pants, so she points me to the restroom.

"You want me to go out and tell your boyfriend?" she asks, and I just blush and nod.

When I come back out, Wyatt is looking at some X-rays with the lady in scrubs, who I guess must be Dr. Godfrey.

"You're just in time," she says to me with a big smile. "Everything went great. The bullet just grazed her. No organs or major arteries were damaged, just some soft tissue. She only needed a couple of stitches. For getting shot, it was about the best place to take a bullet."

My face starts scrunching up for an uglycry as I think about poor Matty, charging toward those stairs to save me, never knowing how many bullets were flying around. Not even knowing what bullets are, but knowing that I was in danger. That's bravery, right there. That's love. And she's only known me for a couple of days.

Whatever it costs to fix her, it's worth it.

Dr. Godfrey tells us we can pick up Matty tomorrow afternoon, after two. She hands me some forms on a clipboard, and I fill them out with my address and a bunch of made-up answers about Matty's age and health, but I leave all the phone numbers blank. I don't want them calling my mom, making her wonder what the hell is going on. The receptionist looks over the form and asks for a cell number, and Wyatt rattles one off, and I wonder if it's real or made-up.

"I hate to bother y'all, but we're going to need to go ahead and run a credit card to cover the surgery and boarding," the receptionist says, looking pained, like requesting payment gives her indigestion.

"No problem," Wyatt says, handing her a credit card.

Seeing the Valor Savings Bank logo flash for just a second between their hands makes a cold chill shudder through me. The receptionist swipes the card. As Wyatt waits to sign the slip, he rocks back and forth on his heels, tapping his fingers nervously on the counter. He signs, and the receptionist says, "Thank you, Mr. Beard. We'll see you tomorrow. We'll take real good care of Matilda."

"She goes by Matty," I holler back.

Once we're in the parking lot, I curl angry fingers into his shirt. "A Valor card? Do you really think that's a smart idea, Mr. Beard?"

"Do you want your dog alive or not?" He whips his shirt back out of my grasp.

"I don't want you on someone else's list."

"Maybe I deserve to be on someone else's list," he says. "Did you ever think about that? Maybe I'm one of the bad guys. My dad and my brother are on there. Why not me?"

Something's got him pissed off, and I just want everything to be normal. I want to soothe him. I want to hug him. I want a few moments of peace before I have to go kill someone else.

"I don't think you're a bad person," I say softly. "Any more than I am."

He almost says something but stops himself. We climb into opposite sides of the mail truck, him on the driver's side and me on the passenger side. For just a moment, I flash on a lesson from world history when an overexcited Dr. Terry showed us a picture of a chariot in which the warrior shot a bow and arrow while his trusted charioteer drove and carried the warrior's shield. And that's us. Wyatt drives and protects me, and I'm just here to kill. I slump down farther.

"I don't see the point in getting philosophical about it," he says. "It's all going to end the same, either way. Let's just get the next one out of the way. Three in one day is enough, right?"

"I don't know." I flick on the GPS. "It's just one long-ass nightmare. I've got ten hours. But you're right. Let's get the next one over with. If I'm going to feel crappy anyway, I might as well do all the crappy things at once."

The GPS barks out the first line of directions in that weird, British accent, and Wyatt takes off driving. He normally seems relaxed when he's behind the wheel, and I would imagine he's one of those guys who digs cars and goes for long drives when he needs to think. I bet he loves road trips. But he's tense now, and I feel like there's something he both wants very much to say and never, ever wants to say. I don't know much about guys, but I know that pressing him will probably make him explode like a popped balloon, so I just sit back and try to get mentally prepared for the next assignment and not think about my mom or my forever lost locket or poor Matty all doped up on doggy drugs and alone in a cage.

As always, my thoughts stick to the list like duct tape, like it's a catechism. Lucky number seven is Tom Morrison.

The name conjures up a school teacher, maybe a principal. The kind of guy who wears a tweed jacket with those silly brown patches on the elbows. The kind of guy who smokes a pipe. In my head, Tom Morrison becomes a first-class swindler, using his credit cards to wine and dine unwitting students before trading BJs for good grades in his all-wood study. I can kill this version of Tom Morrison. I can kill him without crying about it afterward.

Wyatt turns down a long driveway deep in the woods. The truck rumbles over the pavement, then bumps over the dirt tracks when the driveway disappears. Tree branches scrape the roof, making my teeth itch.

"At least the neighbors aren't going to sneak up on you out here," Wyatt says.

A house appears, framed by the trees, and it's like the place I've always dreamed of living. It's almost a tree house, or a fairy house, with beautiful wood shingles and fancy shutters and a porch swing. It's in a little clearing surrounded by berry bushes, and the sun shines down on a perfect circle of soft green grass where stuffed bears are having a picnic at a tiny set of table and chairs. I imagine Disney animals dancing out of the woods to sing a song about how whoever must live here is the happiest kid on earth.

"I so do not want to shoot this guy," I murmur. Wyatt wisely doesn't comment.

I shrug into my Postal Service shirt and cap before I can guilt myself out of it. Every assignment so far has had some sort of personal connection to me, and I no longer believe there's any way it could be a coincidence. What exactly is hiding behind that door that's going to kill a little piece of me even more than murdering a stranger should?

With the fully loaded gun in my jeans and a fake smile plastered over my face, I walk along the perfectly placed paving stones and up three steps to the front door. When I ring the doorbell, it plays the song "Once Upon a Dream" from *Sleeping Beauty*.

"I'll get it!" a small voice cries from inside.

I almost expect a fairy or an elf, but the truth is even more painfully adorable.

The door opens, and I'm met with two smiling faces. Level with my eyes is a kind-looking man with a beard and glasses. Hovering around his waist is a little girl with dark curls and bright blue eyes wearing a pink princess dress.

"Did you bring me a present?" she asks, and I choke on nothing and go into a coughing fit. All I'm holding is his card, my fingers sweating against the green printing.

"Are you okay?" asks the man. "Do you want to come inside and have a glass of water?"

I look back at the truck, and Wyatt is biting his lip. He holds up his hands as if to say, "I got nothing."

"Sure, thanks," I say. I can't shoot this guy in front of his kid, that's for sure.

I step inside, and he shuts the door behind me. The little girl grabs the end of my shirt, which I've forgotten to tuck in. Her tiny, pink hand is wound up in the blood-spattered cloth, but she doesn't notice as she tugs me down a hallway lined with photographs and framed drawings of stick figures and hearts.

"You can use my Belle glass," she says, chin up like a queen. "But I get Rapunzel."

She escorts me to a cheerful table under a skylight. There are only two chairs, and one of them is covered in dried-jelly fingerprints and globs of granola bar, but that's the one she pulls out for me, so I sit. Her father places a plastic glass on the table and watches me with the innocent, curious eyes of a deer in the forest. Belle's face smiles at me as I sip water I don't need and don't want.

"So is that for me?" he says, pointing at the card.

The little girl perks up. "Did Mommy send our check this time like she promised?"

He picks her up and snuggles her in his lap, and she buries her face in his shoulder, giggling.

"Don't worry, Jilly Bean. We'll be fine," he says.

"Are you Tom Morrison?" I ask.

"That's me." He smiles and nods at the machine weighing down my pocket. "Do you need me to sign?"

I slide the signature machine across the table, and he signs it, one arm snug around Jilly Bean. But I don't give him the card. I don't want him to read it yet. I don't want to see the little girl's face fall.

"Can we talk somewhere private?" I ask.

He glances from the official-looking card under my hand to the top of his daughter's curly hair.

"Run outside and show the nice lady how high you can swing, okay, Jilly?"

He stands and opens the French doors, and she runs outside, yelling, "Watch this!"

Goddammit. She's wearing lady bug galoshes with her pink princess dress. I would have given anything I owned for that kind of getup when I was a kid. But my mom didn't have the money for clothes that weren't practical, and she would have scolded me for looking silly. There's a nice wooden play set out there, and the kid climbs on the swing and starts pumping, but she can't quite get the rhythm right, and it reminds me of myself at that age, somewhere around five, trying to teach myself to pump after my dad left and there was no one left to push me anymore.

"What's all this about?" Tom asks, and I blink out of my sunny reverie. "Is it another subpoena? I swear, my ex-wife doesn't want custody of Jilly so much as she just wants to drive me crazy."

I clear my throat and hold up the card, but I can barely read it through wet eyes.

"Tom Morrison, you owe Valor Savings bank the sum of $43,575.98. Can you pay this sum in full?"

His laugh is gentle, disbelieving. "Right now? No. Of course not. Am I missing something? They usually just call when my payments get this late." His eyes dart to Jilly as if wolves are waiting in the forest to grab her away the second he isn't looking.

"By . . . um . . ." I don't want to say it, and I can't remember the words. I have to hold up his card and read it while he squints at the fine print on the back. "By Valor Congressional Order number 7B, your account is past due and hereby declared in default. Due to your failure to remit all owed monies and per your signature just witnessed and accepted, you are given two choices. You may either sign your loyalty over to Valor Savings as an indentured collections agent for a period of five days or forfeit your life. Please choose."

"I don't understand. Valor Savings is still a bank, right?"

"It's the government now. And they can do anything they want to." My eyes shoot meaningfully to Jilly outside, and I lay my gun on the table between us, but I don't let go of the grip. He covers his face with his hands.

"It was a house loan," he says, confused and pleading. "To build the cabin. I've got twenty-eight more years to pay it, and I know

I missed a couple of payments, but it's my ex-wife. She's draining me. She won't pay alimony. I do freelance, but it's not enough. And I can't pull Jilly out of preschool." He runs a hand over his beard, and I realize that under all the facial hair, he's pretty young. He can't be more than twenty-five. He walks over to the counter and comes back with a checkbook. "Look, I'll make up all those missed payments now, at least. We'll find the money somewhere."

"It doesn't work that way." My voice is soft. Like I'm afraid Jilly might hear me. "You've only got three choices. Two, really. Valor is calling in your debt. You either pay now, in cash, or you agree to be a bounty collector, like me. Or I have to shoot you, and I really, really don't want to do that."

I hand him the card, and he scans it. The color drains out of his face, and he turns to watch his daughter swinging in the afternoon sunshine, the gold threads in her pink gown glinting as bright as her smile.

"I just wanted her to be happy," he whispers.

"So take the deal. Ten people, and then you're free. It's not so bad. It's better than losing your daughter. Better than letting her lose you."

"Is that what happened to you?" he asks, looking me up and down. "You're young. You can't have any debt. Are you doing this for money? Or what?"

"My mom lost a lot of money." My voice catches. I rub a hand

· 187 ·

over the camera button, holding it there, covering it. "She's sick. She needs hospital care. It was my only choice."

His eyes go from the card to his daughter to me. He stares at my face, my shirt, my gun, and I try to imagine what he's seeing. My wild dark hair, like his daughter's. Cloudy blue eyes just like hers, looking older and more exhausted than they should. Painted, chewed fingernails and mismatched socks at odds with the seriousness of my errand.

She'll look just like me one day, and he knows it.

"How many people have you killed?" he asks, voice low.

"You're number seven on my list. Five wouldn't take the deal."

"Five people," he says to himself. "You killed five people."

I don't mention the guy I shot in the stomach or the thugs on the stairs.

In the silence, a bird sings, a mockingbird. It must live right outside the house, because it's imitating the doorbell. Hearing it, the little girl laughs and leaves the swing to climb up on the slide. She stands on her tiptoes in the galoshes and reaches toward a branch that's stark and leafless against the sky.

"Here, birdie," she calls. "Come here!"

"It's going to be worth it," I say. "She's worth it. Whatever you have to do."

"I . . ."

His voice chokes off, and I shiver over with goose bumps as I realize that if he doesn't take the deal, I either leave a helpless child alone in the woods or take her with me on my killing spree. I flash on a vision of a small figure in a princess dress curled up on my cot, crying, covered in blood, a too-big gun under her tiny hand.

"She needs me." He flips the card over and over in his hands. "I can't leave my little girl alone. I'll do it."

I let out the breath I was holding and flip the button back toward him. "Say it again, Tom."

"I'll do it," he says. Then, more quietly, "I'll do anything for her."

Feeling a thousand years older, I stand up and push my chair back.

"Thank you," I say, voice shaking. I slip the gun back into my waistband.

"Go to hell." It comes out soft, his leaking eyes never leaving his daughter as she strains toward a bird she'll never catch.

I let myself out and plod to the truck. I don't look back. I can't. My arms are numb, and it's all I can do to wrap my fingers around the top button of the mail shirt and wish to God that I could suffocate it, that it was a living thing I could choke to death in a fair match instead of a cold piece of tattling technology.

"No gunshots?" Wyatt asks.

"No."

"That's a good thing, right?"

I'm silent.

"Are you okay? What happened in there?"

"Please take me somewhere quiet and safe," I whisper.

I crawl into the back of the truck and climb into my bed, clutching the button with cold fingers. There's an empty space where Matty should be, a horrible silence where her tail should be thumping against the metal. My only kindness is that Wyatt is turning the truck around and driving me away from this place, from the tranquillity that I've ruined forever.

I had some level of sorrow for everyone on my list so far. Not so much for Robert Beard or Dr. Ken Belcher, maybe, but everyone was a victim of one kind or another, even if they were just victims of their own failures or addictions or dreams. But this guy—he was trying to do the right thing. He wanted to be there for his daughter, be a good daddy, the perfect daddy.

He was doing the exact opposite of what my own daddy did.

Tom Morrison didn't run away from his kid, from responsibility, from life. He made sacrifices for her, used his money to create a paradise for her. And, yes, some of that was money he didn't have. But it seems to me like a thirty-year mortgage on a small fifty-thousand-dollar house is a lot different from credit card debt to buy crap you don't need or a million dollars for a stupid mansion. I didn't have a lot of sympathy for some of the names on my list. But this guy is killing me.

Worst of all, though, is thinking about that little girl. Will she go away with an aunt for a week while her father rushes around town, killing people to get home in time for a bedtime story read with dried blood under his fingernails? Will he tell her he has to take a work trip? Will he bring her back a stuffed unicorn and tell her that he'd been on an airplane? Will she sleep on the cot in the back of a mail truck and eat Happy Meals while wearing pink earmuffs to block out the gunshots and screams? And what if someone shoots him? Where will Jilly Bean go if he's gone?

She has everything I ever wanted, and now it might be taken away from her too.

My heart fills with anger at Valor Savings, at the world, at people and their stupid goddamn choices. Why are all these assholes spending money they don't have for crap they don't need? If Tom Morrison had just rented an apartment and walked his kid to a park instead of trying to build her a Disney set on borrowed money, maybe he wouldn't be in there waiting for his Junior Assassin package from Valor to show up behind a black suit and a crocodile smile. What kind of messed-up system is strangling my country, where people expect to buy things when they don't even have a job? And why does it cost more to die from cancer than to become a goddamn doctor in the first place?

The truck crunches over dirt and rocks and rolls to a stop. I can tell from the silence outside that we're in that quiet place in Wyatt's neighborhood. In his private wilderness. I tear my face off the pillow and try to wipe some of the tears and snot away on my blanket. I've cried more this week than in the rest of my life combined, probably, including the year my dad left. Wyatt turns in his seat, looking at me, trying to figure out how to handle me. I guess he's seen me at my worst now—sad, hopeless, vicious, screaming in a kid's face as I shoot him dead. How do you handle a girl who's going through some totally messed-up shit? How do you hold an unwilling assassin in your arms and tell her everything's going to be fine when you both know it's not?

"You can come back here." I sniff. "I think I got it all out."

"You needed a good cry worse than anyone on earth," he says. "But, for the record, I wasn't listening, and you didn't make any weird snerk noises."

I laugh, but it comes out as another weird snerk noise. He lumbers into the back of the truck and sits on the edge of the bed, putting one hand on my shoulder. It feels good, being touched. I had almost forgotten that skin was warm. He rubs my back, just one hand moving up and down lightly, and I close my eyes and relax a little.

"I guess you get a bonus when they take the deal," he says. "The clock reset with enough time to get you through noon tomorrow. You hungry?"

I snort into my pillow. Wyatt is more food driven than anyone I've ever met. Instead of answering, I turn over onto my back, praying that my face doesn't look horrible after everything I've been through today.

"What do *you* want to do?" I ask. "I feel like I'm just dragging you all over the place. Like you're my chauffeur."

"And your cook," he says. "And your master of hounds."

"Is that what you rich guys have for fox hunts in the Preserve?"

His face goes dark, and he starts to stand up. Another sore point. I reach out to grab his shirt and tug him back down with the hand not holding the button.

"Stay," I say. "Please."

He sits, just barely hovering on the edge of the bed. I wish for that playful moment yesterday when he all but smothered me to death. Things were weird then, sure. But they're weirder now. I tug on his shirt again, then grab his belt and tug him toward me. A smile threatens at the corner of his mouth as he slides back and turns to me, his hip against mine.

I look up at him and smile, trying to put what I feel into my eyes. Trying to make them say, "Look, I'm messed up, and this situation is messed up, but I like you."

"Don't do that," he says. "Just don't."

"Is there something wrong with me?" I ask, my hand dropping from his belt to my belly. "Because sometimes you look at me one way, and sometimes you look at me another way, and this isn't who I am. I mean, I'm just . . . just a girl."

"You're not the problem," he says, his voice gruff.

"Oh, so *you're* the problem?"

"Maybe."

"Liar. What's really wrong?"

"It's me. It's just . . ." He stops and looks down, his face bleak. "I don't know. I have my reasons for being here, but I don't want you to use me just because you need comfort and I'm the only one around. You calling me your chauffeur. I mean, I charged into a fucking gunfight for you today. I deserve better than being used like that."

I bolt upright, my face going red.

"You think I just, what? Want you for your body? Like you're some disposable comfort fuck on my exciting adventure? Oh my God. Could that be any more insulting? And isn't it usually the other way around?"

"It's just, yesterday you said . . ."

"Forget yesterday. I'm here right now. And I'm not using you. I've never even . . . I mean . . ." I blush deeper, and the arm attached to the hand around the camera button is suddenly struggling to cover my chest in shyness. His mouth quirks up at the corner like he knows what I'm trying to say and thinks it's cute. "When you kissed me, that was the first time for me. I wouldn't even know how to use your body, okay? So sue me for liking you and wanting to be close to you and not knowing how to show it."

"I'm not really the suing type."

He turns toward me, and the hardness is gone from his eyes. He actually looks relieved. It's kind of sweet. Out of the entire world, I get stuck with Wyatt, with this hot guy, and he's afraid I'm trying to use him for sex. As if there were any reason in the world not to like him. Kind, funny, cute, brave. Strong enough to realize he'd screwed up and smart enough to start turning his life around.

"Knock, knock," I say.

Wyatt looks at me sideways, like I'm crazy. "Who's there?"

"Lilac."

He grins.

"Lilac who?"

"Lilac you."

It's as close as I can come to telling him that I have feelings for him the day after meeting him and killing his father. But it seems to do the trick. He moves closer to me, his hip against mine, his hand on my other side, pressing into the bed. I kind of wish I were still lying down on my back, because sitting up this way, I can barely keep myself from crashing into him. After all my chasing around, it would be nice if something just came to me easy.

My breathing speeds up as he cups my face with one hand. I close my eyes and lean in to his touch, and I realize that I'm shaking. Not like I have so recently with fear and adrenaline. With hope, with anticipation. Can it be possible that he likes me too? Is it just the apocalypse talking, the fear in each of us reaching out like magnets for safety and comfort? Were my teachers right, and we're really just animals driven to rut before a battle in a last, desperate bid to keep the species going?

Wyatt's lips brush over mine, just barely, and I open my eyes as he pulls away.

It's none of that. It's too sweet to be that simple.

"Lilac you, too," he says gently.

And hearing those words gives me the guts to do the scariest thing I've done today: I rip the button off my shirt and throw it under the bed and lean forward and kiss him for real, one hand in his shaggy hair. His lips are warm and dry, and they curl up in a smile as he presses closer. I want more, and I twine my other hand behind his head and pull him down with me until I'm on my back. His forearms line up on either side of my head as the kiss gets deeper, and I moan and slide my fingers down his neck.

What I'm doing, what I'm feeling—I have no blueprint for this. I never saw my parents kiss, never saw my grandparents so much as touch when passing in the hall. My mom never had any boyfriends, and neither did I. The kids I hang out with at school and at work pair up, and some stay together and some break apart, but I think of the way they make out as a show, like they're doing it more to shock or impress other people than to please themselves. Half of what they do is on the phone, anyway, which is the least sexy sex I can think of. I've always wondered what two people who like each other do when they're alone. How they learn the way of things. I guess I'm finding out now, and it's a welcome oblivion.

The kiss is deep and long, and by the time he pulls away, I feel like I've been underwater for an hour, like air is some foreign substance that doesn't taste as sweet as it used to. He hovers over me, and I'm amazed by the details of his existence, by his eyelashes and the gold sparks in his eyes and the stubble on his throat. I reach out to run a finger along the golden bristles, and he closes his eyes and sighs.

"If I asked you to kiss me again, would you?" I ask.

"Gladly," he says. "I didn't want to rush things."

"I did," I say. "Just come here."

With a sultry smile that makes me all tingly, his body lines up with mine, and he murmurs, "Yes, ma'am," as our lips meet, and it's the happiest I've felt in years, another umbrella against a rainstorm of suck.

It's full dark before we pull away from each other. We don't go all the way, not even close. But I've thrown my caution and fear out the window and given myself the freedom to experience things, and I'll be damned if they didn't feel freaking awesome.

Wyatt shifts uncomfortably and sits up. His hair is messed and his face is red, but part of that is probably due to the red numbers on the dashboard clock. These extra hours with Wyatt make for one hell of a decent bonus. I feel overheated myself, like I'm a size bigger all over than I was before I pulled Wyatt down on top of me, my lips puffy and my back permanently arched from pressing against him, into him. I feel loose and relaxed, almost brazen. If I knew how to swagger, I might swagger. I'm not even sure yet if I can stand.

I feel around on the bed and find my wadded-up Postal Service shirt. Without the button, it's deceptively light, and I drag a hand around under the bed, fumbling with stuffed turtles and pillows until I find the damn thing. For the millionth time, I pray that it's unbroken and doesn't have sound.

Wyatt starts to say something, but I make a fist around the button and shush him. He motions that he's going outside, and I nod my head. I have to pee too, but peeing outside is so awful that I've been ignoring the urge.

And then it strikes me that I may have had at least an audio audience for my first hard-core make-out session. I've been trying to keep Wyatt hidden from the damn button, but if that thing records or broadcasts sound, it probably caught some moans and grunts. But what was I supposed to do—stop macking to get up and stuff it in the fridge? There's so much on my mind that it's hard to stay on top of everything. I guess if he was a major problem, they would do something about him. He'd be dead already, right? It's odd, basically having a giant corporation as a boss but never receiving any sort of feedback about what you'd done well or badly. Aside from time bonuses for Kelsey and Tom, there's no report card until the end. If then.

I've broken pretty much every rule they've given me. I've messed up my speeches, I've told the debtors things I wasn't supposed to, I signed for Ashley Cannon, and I spent a few hours luxuriating in Dr. Ken Belcher's mansion and eating his food. I feel like I should be in trouble, but I'm not being punished. No surprise packages in the passenger seat or dropped out of a helicopter. I wonder if maybe they tried to call me, but my phone ran out of juice a long time ago. Forgetting the power cord was a convenient sort of almost-accident. I didn't want any calls from Valor, checking up on me. And I didn't want to be tempted to call my mom.

It's actually the longest I've ever gone without any kind of media. No phone, no Internet, no TV to drown out my constant anxiety. No outside communication of any kind. It's been utter radio silence while I complete my assignment. Except for Wyatt, of course. But I never dreamed I would end up with a partner in crime, much less a partner who could kiss like that.

The bed is still warm from our bodies and hard for me to abandon. I stripped off my socks while we were entangled, and now the metal floor stings my bare feet with cold as I sit up to get my bearings. I turn on the tap light and run a finger all around the button, trying to puzzle out how it might work, what it's hearing or seeing. There's no seam, no obvious way to open it. They want whatever

happens inside it to be a secret, and it's a secret that's far beyond anything I could discover without a hammer. With a sly smile, I put the
button under my pillow and make a mental note to get one of those
flimsy travel sewing kits when we stop at a gas station tomorrow
morning for biscuits.

Finally, I'm forced to face the fact that I'm about to pee myself.
I grab a wad of toilet paper and hop down from the truck, looking
around for a shadowy but safe place to squat. I hear a thump and
almost pee myself for the second time in a day, but it's just Wyatt
dragging a big-ass log across the field.

"We've got a fire pit," he says. "I thought we could start a
bonfire."

"Won't we get in trouble?"

He drops the log and laughs. It's a cross between bitter and crazy.
"You shot, like, five people today. I don't think anyone's around to
send you to jail for roasting some marshmallows in a field."

"You brought marshmallows?" I ask tentatively.

He shrugs. "Imaginary ones."

"I've never actually seen a bonfire before."

He drags the log over to a circle of black ash surrounded by a
ring of stones and concrete blocks. He's already got some smaller
branches set up in the middle of the ring, and I sneak off behind
some trees to pee in skinny jeans, which is pretty much the most
awkward and difficult thing ever. I don't know what to do with

the used toilet paper, so I stuff it under an old log covered in fallen leaves. I've never been camping, either.

When I return to the circle of stones, Wyatt is holding a metal lighter up to some twigs, trying to get them to catch fire.

"Where'd you get the lighter?" I ask.

"It was my friend Mikey's." He clicks the thing again and again, trying to get the flame to hold. He shakes it in frustration. "We left it out here in a Tupperware box, along with a couple of water bottles, a Swiss Army Knife, and some metal sporks. When we were younger, we were always afraid the apocalypse was going to come, zombies and everything. We figured we'd be safer alone, out in the woods. There's a perfect climbing tree over there. If you sit still long enough, sometimes you see deer. Max and I used to come out here to watch them."

"And the lighter still works?" I ask.

"It was in an airtight container. It's not made out of solid silver or anything," he says with a smirk. "They cost, like, nine dollars on eBay." His smile turns down. "Or they did. I guess eBay is gone now, if Valor owns the mail trucks."

The fire finally catches, and the twigs begin to burn. A thin column of smoke rises up against the deep purple sky, and a star winks into existence. Then another, then another. We're less than five miles from my house, but it's like we're all alone on a frontier, far away from the city lights. Even the moon looks bigger and prettier, pristine and bluish white. But there's a chill in the air. I rush to the back of the truck and slip on a sweater. While I'm there, I grab my quilt and the leftover food from Dr. Ken Belcher's mansion. But I leave the sparkling water behind. We're not that desperate yet.

"You still got that bottle of water out here?" I ask. "I think I saw a zombie."

Wyatt grins. "I hope it's one of the slow ones." He jogs off into the woods, and I suddenly feel very alone. Two people in a wilderness is exciting. One person alone in the wilderness is a sitting duck.

I go back to the truck again, this time for my gun. If there's anything I learned from Dave and from Sharon Mulvaney's house, it's that you never know when something badder than you is going to show up and give you a taste of your own medicine. As I settle down on my quilt by the fire, Wyatt appears with a single bottle of water. It looks a little beat-up, but I guess it's not like water's going to go bad. I open it and take a sip, then pass it to him. He sits down beside me on the blanket, and I lean my head against his shoulder. Being this close to him makes me forget all the other batshit crazy stuff. It just feels natural, even if there's a Glock under my knee.

"It's kind of weird," he says, poking a stick into the growing fire to make sparks. "I feel like I know you, but I don't, really. I mean, how old are you? What do you do for fun? What's your middle name?"

The fire's glow warms my cheeks, and his arm snuggles over

my shoulder, pulling me closer against him. I wonder if this is how it felt the first time a caveman stood up beside a fire and told a story. The words are unfamiliar in my mouth, almost holy.

"My name is Patricia Louise Klein," I tell him, speaking to the flames. "My mom wanted to call me Patricia, but my dad called me Patsy, which my mom thought was stupid. Who names a kid Patsy Klein? He left us when I was four, and I refused to answer to anything but Patsy, so now I'm kind of stuck with it. I'm seventeen. I get good grades, work at a pizza restaurant, and take care of my mom. I guess the only things I really do for me are music and crafting. Yarn bombing and cross-stitching."

"Sounds fun," he says. "Tell me more."

When I gaze into the fire, I can almost see through it and into the past, when things were easy. "I always liked yarn. Like, when I was little, I would do that finger-weaving thing and make these long, useless snakes. I would hang them around my room, put them on the Christmas tree, wrap presents with them. So when I got older, I taught myself how to knit from YouTube videos, and I made hundreds of scarves and gave them to everybody I knew and then donated the rest to the food bank for winter. And then I saw an article about yarn bombing and knew I had to do it."

"Why?"

"Because we live in this crappy suburb, right? We have to drive everywhere, and nobody puts any thought into making things pretty. In New York or Paris, people put up beautiful statues, have outdoor festivals and markets, gather inspiring artwork in museums. Here it's just ugly. Even the wild spaces are surrounded by treeless neighborhoods or rednecks. You're never just driving or walking along and then think, 'Oh, that's such a pretty, random surprise.'"

"What about when a deer runs across the road?" he asks.

"Yeah, but that's out of your control. And you might hit it and destroy your car."

"But that's free meat."

I can't tell if he's serious or not until his mouth twitches.

I knock my shoulder back against his. "Ew. They have ticks, weirdo. But yarn bombing is thoughtful. Planned. You can almost guarantee that you're going to make people think, maybe even feel something. At the very least, they'll question it."

He's silent, but he puts his chin over my head and nuzzles back and forth. I watch the fire and enjoy the quiet. After a few moments, he says, all in a rush, "Do you think you would knit a scarf for me, one day?"

I laugh against him.

"Sure," I say. "I can take time out of my busy assassination and yarn bombing schedule for that. But what about you? What do you do? What's your middle name? And did you actually go to all the concerts, or did you just get the shirts online?"

He drags me onto his lap and wraps both arms around me, and

for just a moment, I feel like a little kid. Cared for, hugged, wanted. In between Wyatt and the fire, I've never been so warm from head to toe.

"My name is Wyatt Dane Beard," he says. "I like music, I play bass, I have a pet snake, and I used to skateboard a lot. Now I do lacrosse so I can take out my anger by beating on other guys with a stick. It was my therapist's idea. My parents got divorced when I was eleven, and it royally screwed up my life. I wasn't a decent person again until I turned sixteen and watched my friend Mikey OD. I'm nineteen now but a year behind in school. I get good grades and hope they'll balance out my old grades. I've never worked a day in my life, and I kind of hate myself for it."

"You shouldn't."

"It's just one more thing I've got to fix," he says firmly, and I settle myself against his chest.

"I don't know if I would work if we weren't poor." I sigh, thinking about how weird my hands feel when I get home every night, powdery and greasy at the same time, aching from making dozens of pizzas. "It's not like I have a passion for crappy pizza or anything. And the customers are major jerks."

"Are they paying you for this?" he says suddenly.

"Valor, you mean?" I shrug, my shoulders rubbing against his chest. "Kind of. They said there might be a bonus, but they didn't say how much. I mean, it was basically a case of *do this or we kill your mom and then you*, so I didn't ask about the pay scale. The guy who came to my house said her medical bills would be covered, so maybe they're paying something. I guess I didn't think that far ahead." I swallow. "He had a gun. To her chest. I would have signed anything."

"What about the truck? Do you get to keep it?"

I look past the fire to the hulking shadow of the mail truck. So normal and trustworthy and boringly governmental. Such a brilliant way to sneak up on people. Everyone's excited to get a package. The fruit basket was pretty clever, too, and I consider that I might want to find a fake box or something, to make it look less like "It could be a check or a subpoena" and more like "Happy birthday!" At least one person on my list is going to need major incentive to open the door for me.

And what would I even do with a mail truck after this? Sell it? Park it in my driveway and take it to school every morning? And will there even be a Postal Service anymore, now that Valor Savings owns the government? Will there even be school? I snort to myself, considering that my life now brings new meaning to the term "going postal."

"I don't know," I finally say. "They seriously went out of their way to keep me in the dark. I couldn't see past the first five days and keeping that gun off my mom."

"She's lucky to have you as a daughter," he whispers.

His voice sounds so sad and far away that I twist in his lap and kiss him gently on the lips.

"You do what you have to do to survive," I say.

"But what about what you do before survival is even a problem? What if you make the wrong choices when there are dozens of choices? What if you can't fix it?"

"There's always another choice," I say. "And you're a good person."

"I'm . . . glad you think so."

He kisses me again, deeper this time, and I cup his face. There are tears caught in his eyelashes, and they tickle my fingertips as his arms wrap around me, hotter than the fire. He smells like smoke and detergent and boy, and I can't get close enough.

Later, after we've kissed each other until our lips are nearly numb, Wyatt makes sandwiches with the food from the fridge and slices an apple with the Swiss Army Knife from his secret tree-house hidey-hole. The fire slowly dies as we sit there, talking and holding hands. He feeds me huge grapes too fast, stuffing them in my mouth until I nearly choke with laughter. I trace his broken tattoo by the firelight, and he lets me this time.

"You should get a new one," I say. "Something beautiful."

He chuckles softly. "How do you cover up something that screwy?"

"With something bigger."

He stands and kicks dirt over the embers of the fire, helps me up and follows me to the mail truck. The quilt is wrapped around me, dragging on the ground, and he takes it from me and shakes it clean.

We fall asleep curled together on the narrow cot under my quilt. I wonder for just a second if our tender whispers will carry to the camera under the pillow, but before I can move it, I'm asleep, held snugly in his arms.

Sometime in the night, he sleepily, slurringly says, "I'm so sorry."

But he doesn't say about what.

I'm about to ask when the first bullet rips through the wall.

8.

ALISTAIR MEADE

Wyatt rolls on top of me like some kind of idiot hero.

"Tell me that was your gun," he grunts. "Tell me that was an accidental discharge."

My hand slips under the pillow and past the button, and I've never felt so good about wrapping my fingers around the Glock's grip.

"Not mine. Someone's outside."

Three more shots go off, punching random holes in the truck. Wyatt rolls us both onto the floor, as if that's going to help. He lands on top of me like a sack of dumb rocks and tries to shove me under the cot.

"Come out, or we're coming in!" someone yells from outside,

kinda like they're unsure. Another shot backs up the demand. The voice is familiar, and I go cold all over and slam my other fist into the floor. Goddammit.

"What the hell, Jeremy?" I scream with what little air I can find. "Stop shooting, you moron!"

The shots stop, and I hear whispering. Of course Roy's with him. Of course. But why are my redneck buddies here at all? And why are they shooting? And are they going to start again? My relief at the pause in gunfire spills uneasily over into doubt that I hear echoed in Jeremy's voice.

"Patsy?"

"Yeah?"

"Is that really you?"

I shove Wyatt off me and crawl to the front of the truck, pausing between the seats, just in case Roy's holding a gun too. His eyesight's notoriously bad, and his trigger finger is shaky. Sure enough, there they are, standing out in the middle of the field like dorks. They're both wearing camo and have their faces painted, badly, in streaks. It would be hilarious if they didn't have guns pointed right at me. What kind of game are they playing?

"Yeah, it's me." I wave the gun. "Are you done with trying to kill me now? Cuz my aim's better and you know it. What the hell are y'all doing?"

They whisper together again. "Wanna parley?" Jeremy yells.

I snort. "Your obsession with *Pirates of the Caribbean* needs to stop now. But yes. Please. If you promise not to shoot."

They whisper again, and Wyatt's hand lands on my leg. He shows me his gun and raises his eyebrows. "They're idiots, but they're my idiots," I whisper.

"I don't trust them."

"I do. But stay hidden and keep them in your sights. There's something weird going on. Valor said there would be nobody around to stop me."

Wyatt nods, and his eyes shift sideways. "Is one of them your boyfriend?"

I eject the magazine and shove it back home to make my point. "Don't insult me like that when I'm holding a gun." Then, loud enough for the guys outside to hear, "I'm coming out now. I'm armed. Put your guns on the ground."

Roy tosses his without a second thought, but Jeremy stares at his for a second and yells, "Ain't gonna happen, Cowpatty. This shit's for real."

I take a deep breath and stare at them. My two lovable, moronic, geeky redneck friends. Whatever's going on, I'm betting they wouldn't be here if they had a choice. And I don't want to hurt them. And even if Jeremy's still holding his gun and glaring at me through his badly done face paint, I know that underneath the bravado, he doesn't want to hurt me, either. My first thought is that maybe they work for Valor, that I'm finally in trouble for everything I've done wrong. But I don't see a mail truck or mail shirts. And nobody's offering me a fruit basket and a signature machine. And there are still three names on my list.

It can't be Valor. Can it? And if not them, who?

Shit.

Jeremy's staring at me like he's running restaurant close-out numbers that insult him by not adding up. But the Patsy I am now is not the same Patsy I was last Friday night, playing Six Degrees of Separation as we mopped the kitchen floor and threw chunks of old pizza dough at one another. I'm not going to shoot them in cold blood. And I'm not going to let them shoot me, although I know that would be a surefire way to keep my mom safe. I'm not ready to give up. Not yet.

I'm not going to let them stop me. My heart hardens, goes cold and dark, and falls to some wet place in my stomach.

"Have it your way," I holler. "But remember who's a faster draw."

Wearing only my thin tank top and skinny jeans, I point my gun at Jeremy's heart and squeeze between the seats and into firing range. When I hop down from the mail truck, Roy takes a step back, and Jeremy's gun wavers.

I wish I had a pistol to cock, to let them know I mean business. Considering how quiet the night got after the shots stopped echoing, that click would be awfully satisfying. Still, my matte black Glock looks sharp and evil in the moonlight, and I hope that's good enough. "Now, why are you guys shooting at me in the middle of nowhere?"

I can hear Jeremy swallow from twenty feet away, and I force myself to walk forward, my bare feet numb in the frosty grass. Goose bumps slam up my arms, and every hair on my body is at attention, and for just a second, my vision goes double, like there are four guys here instead of just two. My gun and Jeremy's gun are identical, pointed right at each other, blue light glinting off stamped gold letters.

Goddammit, Valor.

"We didn't know it was you," Roy says, soft and lost.

"Oh, so you just thought, *Hey, let's go randomly shoot up a mail truck in the middle of a field. That would be fun.* Because I don't think so."

"They never said who." Jeremy's voice is stronger than Roy's. It always is. Up close now, but not close enough to touch, his bright blue eyes glare at me from their jacket of camo, resentful and sullen and sorry. I've never seen him like this before, hard and desperate. He's usually just a good-natured clown. But he's never tried to shoot me before either. I glance back at the mail truck, but I can't see a hint of Wyatt. Still, I know he's there, watching, finger on the trigger of my dad's old gun, the one I used when Jeremy taught me to shoot.

"They who?"

Roy sniffles and turns away, roughing up the high-and-tight under his army cap like he's not about to start crying. Jeremy sighs and lets the shaking gun fall to his side. I let mine fall too.

"This guy showed up at our trailer. Gave us some card about how my dad owes a bunch of money from his new truck. Said the debt would be forgiven if we . . ."

He halts. It's hard to condense what Valor has done to us into one sentence that makes any sense.

"If you became a bounty hunter."

His head jerks up, and he looks at me hard. "Yeah."

"Where's your mail truck?"

He stares at me like I'm an idiot. "Mail truck?"

"They gave me this truck. And a stupid Postal Service outfit. And a fake fruit basket so I could ring people's doorbells for a good reason."

"That's totally gay," he says, and I reflexively punch him in the arm with my left fist, surprising us both.

"Don't say that, asshole. It's so offensive."

He stifles a laugh. "Born a redneck, die a redneck." Same thing he always says when I get onto him for using ugly words. But it's different now. Something in me goes tense when he says the word "die."

I clear my throat. All joking is gone. "So I'm on your list?"

He shakes his head, and Roy says, "Unidentified female, seventeen, armed and dangerous in a stolen mail truck. The GPS sent us here."

"So you were going to shoot me first, then read me my rights?"

Jeremy spits a wad of tobacco at my feet. "Read you your rights? Shit, Cowpatty. What do you think? You don't *have* any rights. We're just supposed to kill the ones that bolt before they can kill us."

My brain digests it. I'm the alpha squad, and these guys are, what? Cleanup? They're just a bumbling team of redneck nerds who can barely hit the broad side of a barn.

"Is this because I messed up or something? Because I broke the rules?"

Jeremy makes a jack-off motion with his empty hand. "There ain't no rules. You're the first person who lived long enough to ask us anything. Which is good, cuz we don't have any answers."

"How many have you done?" I ask.

"You're the third."

"You know any of the others?"

He rolls his eyes, shrugs so that his gun goes sideways. "Why would we?"

So it's just me, then.

"What happens if y'all don't kill me?" I ask.

The night goes dead quiet. Even the wind stops shivering in the grass. A mourning dove calls, and we all startle.

Jeremy looks down, rubs a boot toe in the grass. "Then I die, I guess. My family, too. Ain't gonna happen, Cowpatty."

"Even Dotty?"

The thought of his sweet little sister getting shot dead next to her hand-me-down Barbie Dreamhouse makes my blood run cold and backward.

He nods, slow and thoughtful, eyes burning into mine.

"I guess so."

"What about Roy?"

Jeremy shrugs. "He's my stepbrother."

"Will they kill him?"

"What?" Roy's voice quavers, and he steps to Jeremy's side, shaking. "What about me?"

I can't get past the lump in my throat, the burn of a meatball sub on the back of my tongue. "If you don't kill me, are they gonna kill Roy, too?"

With careful intensity, Jeremy says, "I reckon not. His name was never mentioned."

I lock eyes with Jeremy. He's breathing through his nose, his dry, bitten lips pinned together.

"Run, Roy," I whisper.

And thank heavens that for once the stubborn idiot does the right thing. He turns around and runs into the forest, tripping over shit and catching himself and crashing in the underbrush like he's being chased by a bear, his forgotten gun dark on the ground beside my bare white foot.

"What now?" Jeremy says.

My gun is so heavy, my fingers so slick. It's like Ashley Cannon all over again. I stare at him, trying to merge the boy I know into the killer in front of me. We struck up a friendship in math class, sitting in back and making fun of the brownnosing preps in the front row. Turns out a smart redneck and a geeky poor girl who don't want to date make pretty good friends. Roy started hanging around with us as soon as his mom married Jeremy's dad, and since then, they've been a safe source of comfort for me and a reason that work didn't suck.

"What now?" I echo.

He turns his gun over, runs a finger over words stamped in gold. That same finger points to a familiar black button on his camo shirt pocket. "One of us has got to die, Cowpie. Who's got more to lose?"

My fingers clench. "Don't you do that, asshole. Don't you try to play on my soft spot just because I'm a girl. Don't you fucking dare."

"Just talkin' sense."

"Bullshit. You're trying to soften me up. And I'm not soft anymore. So cut it out."

"I am disinclined to acquiesce to your request," he says, eyes gone hard and his Southern accent rounding out the words. He tenses a second before I do, and I throw myself to the ground as his gun whips up.

My arms curl over my head as a shot rings out. Jeremy hits the ground beside me a heartbeat after his dropped gun. I can't move, can't pull my hands away from my face and the dirt and tears that appeared there the moment my instincts took over my kindness. My friend's breath rattles, and he groans and tries to roll over. A heavy form pants out of the darkness, and I wait to feel Roy's boot in my ribs.

But it's Wyatt. Of course it's Wyatt. Roy's a coward, always has been. And Wyatt just shot another person to keep me alive. He kicks Jeremy's gun away and gently pries my arms from my head, pulling me into his lap.

"Patsy, are you okay? Speak to me. Are you okay?"

"Means no," I whisper. "Means no."

There's a deep rattle and then Jeremy whispers, "Means . . . no . . ."

I spring away from Wyatt and look down into Jeremy's face. Tears streak the camo paint, but his eyes don't see me. His acne-spattered cheeks flash green and black as his head rolls from side to side, and he coughs as his hands struggle to plug the hole in his stomach that won't stop oozing blood and worse.

"I'm so sorry, Jer," I say. "I'm so sorry."

"Not your fault," he mutters. "Least you and Dotty . . . both alive."

"But you . . ."

My tears fall on his smeared paint. He flaps a blood-and-shit-covered hand at me like he always does when I'm being ridiculous. "Broke-ass country boys are a dime a dozen. Just promise me one thing, Cowpatty." He chokes, and red oozes between his teeth. "Kill at least one of them green-suit *Matrix* assholes. For me."

"As you wish," I whisper.

He chuckles blood. "*The Princess Bride*. Good one, Cowpatty."

And then he's gone.

I don't know how I end up in bed in the mail truck, but I wake up amazed to see sunlight, wholly surprised that the world still exists. At my house, I never slept well. The next-door neighbors had a lot of cats, and there were attempted break-ins sometimes, and kids would let off fireworks and get the dogs barking. My mom was always so timid that I felt like I was our only line of defense against the world. Every little bump or creak, even the heater coming on with a swoosh, and I was awake, groping for the old baseball bat under my bed and then lying awake, thinking about how much that heat was going to cost.

It doesn't seem fair, that I could sleep so well and so long after watching Jeremy die. But I guess my body gets to the point where it doesn't so much fall asleep as collapse in rebellion, and all I can do is trust that Wyatt will keep me safe while I'm dead to the world. I know that the truck moved sometime in the night, and I'm grateful. Roy's not a courageous dude, and I'm pretty sure he peed himself as he ran away, but I'm glad he didn't have the opportunity to come back and get himself killed, messing with us.

Wyatt is curled around me, and birds are singing outside. For just a moment, I feel safe. Protected. I'm facing the wall, and he's snuggled up behind me, breathing softly. I smile to myself and scoot back a little, into the welcoming curve of his body, and his arm lazily sweeps over me, easy as pie. I sigh, and I feel him wake up. He makes a happy groan and pulls me even closer, and it's so perfect it feels like a dream, even if I'm repressing last night so hard that I'm about to grind open a badly done filling.

"You're safe," he murmurs into my ear.

I lean back to kiss his cheek. "Why wouldn't I be?"

He nuzzles my neck, breath hot in that tender place behind my ear. "I was pretty sure that kid was going to shoot you last night. I still can't believe we got out of there alive. I guess I don't really trust anything good anymore. I don't expect it to last."

"I don't want to talk about last night. But I know what you mean."

"It's almost like I don't deserve it." He pulls me closer, holds me tighter, like he's drowning. I turn in his arms and look into his eyes from inches away. The whites are tinged red, maybe from the bonfire or the crying, and it makes little sparks of gold stand out in the brown.

"Don't be silly," I say. "It's not about deserving. Things just happen."

"Sometimes they happen for a reason."

"I still don't know why my dad left or why my mom got cancer," I say, matching his serious tone and veering toward grumpy. "But I don't think it's because I deserve to suffer." I put my hands on either side of his face, and inside, I'm thrilling at the openness, of touching his sleep-warm stubble. "What's wrong? Did you have a bad dream?"

"Something like that. Are you hungry?"

I smile indulgently as he rolls onto the floor, stands, and stretches, his arms bent to keep from scraping the low ceiling.

"You're a walking appetite," I say, and he grins wolfishly.

"I ran into a gunfight yesterday." He rubs his tummy. "Two, actually. A Croissan'wich isn't asking a lot."

My stomach sinks and burbles. *Repress, repress, repress.*

I will not think about Jeremy.

I will not think about crows pecking out his eyes and frost in his mustache stubble.

I will not think about how he said "green-suit *Matrix* assholes," but all the Valor guys wear black.

I will not think about how I prefer hunting to being hunted.

There has to be something good left in the world, but I can't think of it right now.

Oh, wait. Yes, I can.

"And we get Matty back today." I sit up and stretch, my body stiff and aching. With the truck's back door up a few inches, there's a chill in the air, outside of the blankets. I'm glad this stupid assignment happened just as fall was getting crisp and not in the still suffocation of summer or the cold steel of winter.

"You want to knock out the next person on the list first?"

He stretches again as he looks at the list, and I see his hip bones and the top of his boxers and a line of golden hair. I almost reach out to touch him, but I'm not that brave yet.

"Alistair Meade," I say from memory. "Sounds old. Maybe British."

"Sounds like the killer in a horror flick."

"Maybe he's an elderly ax murderer, then," I say. "I just hope it's . . ."

"Easy?"

I wince and hug myself. "Yeah. That last one hurt."

"You never told me what happened with Tom Morrison. But he took the deal, right?"

"Yeah. Damned if you do, damned if you don't. He had a little girl."

"I saw her. When they opened the door."

"She looked just like me when I was a kid. He's a single dad. It was a mortgage, or whatever, to buy the house. It wasn't even that expensive. I just felt bad."

Wyatt's eyebrows draw down. "That doesn't seem fair."

"I know, right?" I put a firm hand over the pillow to make sure the button is muffled, like I'm talking to myself, maybe. "I mean, no offense, but Dr. Ken Belcher buying more fancy cars and expensive countertops and handmade shoes or whatever, guys like him kind of deserve what they get. But Tom was being responsible. Reasonable. He was trying to be good. He was going to pay it off."

"So you think guys like my dad deserve it, huh?" Wyatt says, voice ragged.

"I just mean . . ."

I look down. We haven't really talked about what happened that first day.

"No. I know what you mean. And I get it. My dad's an asshole. *Was* an asshole. But say somebody ran up a bunch of debt and then felt bad and wanted to pay it all back. Do they still deserve it then?"

"Wait. I'm confused. Was your dad paying off his debt?"

"Forget it," Wyatt says. He ruffles my hair like he's distracted and rolls up the truck door.

The scene outside is unfamiliar, a ripped-up old fence and trees. As he lumbers off in the woods to do whatever guys do when they wake up in the morning, I whip out one of my disposable finger toothbrushes and exhale in relief as the dead-skunk morning breath is replaced with perky mint. I want to ask him more about his dad, and about his brother, too. And I know he wants to ask me more about the list and what happens when we get to the tenth name. To his brother. If Wyatt will inherit their debt and be scared of doorbells and fruit baskets for the rest of his life. If his brother will take the deal.

But we're both holding back from talking about any of that, and I don't want to be the one to bring it up. Hell, I can't even ask him how he's going to pay for the rest of Matty's surgery bill, why he has a Valor Savings Bank card in the first place. We didn't ask how much it was going to cost, but he didn't flinch when he handed over his credit card. Not like my mom always does.

I stare at the list and contemplate what kind of guy Alistair Meade will be. I wonder if he lives alone and if his house has a nice shower. I wonder if Valor has taken over Chateau Tuscano as a headquarters, or given it to some high-ranking official. Or maybe burned it to the ground. If there's one thing I learned from history class, it's that whoever wins the war finishes the story.

While Wyatt is gone, I roll down the door and give myself a frantically fast bird bath with shower wipes and slip on a new tank top and panties, a long-sleeved T-shirt, and my other pair of jeans. The whole plain, white uniform is making me feel bland and utilitarian. The blood-spattered, crinkled postal shirt is beyond pathetic by this point, like some leftover prop from a horror movie. And I have to sew that button back on, quick.

I roll up the back door, and Wyatt's standing there, smiling.

"Oh my God, creeper! Were you watching me under the door?"

I say with mock outrage, although secretly I'm amused and can't stop grinning and blushing.

"Just your feet," he says with an answering grin. "I like your blue toenails."

He takes the driver's seat on the hunt for breakfast, which is fine with me. I have my license and have never been in an accident or anything, but we definitely can't afford two cars at home. I've just never been comfortable with driving the way that my friends are, and I always marvel at our delivery guys at work, that they're perfectly happy doing nothing but driving around for six hours a night, delivering pizza to strangers in cars that permanently reek of cigarettes and greasy pepperoni.

"Where were we?" I ask as the truck bumps up old asphalt.

"Just another place I know, where me and Mikey used to hang. I figure that if that Jeremy kid could find us, either your shirt or the truck is being tracked. I didn't want to abandon it without discussing it first, so I just moved it while you were asleep. Are they going to keep sending twerpy vigilantes after you? Why would they try to kill you, anyway? Don't you work for them?"

I snort. These are the same questions that are driving me crazy, but I can't come up with any good answers, and I can't let worry tear me apart when I have a job to do. And that makes me angry. "How the hell am I supposed to know? I don't have an itinerary with *almost get shot by your friends in an empty field after midnight* penciled in. All

I know is what they told me. And that without the GPS, we don't know how to find the people on the list. And without the shirt button, I don't get credit for the kills. And without the kills, my mom fucking dies."

He takes it in stride, just absorbs my rage and nods. "Can we just pull the info out of the GPS?"

I prod the screwed-down machine with a blue-nailed toe. "Be my guest. That thing's tech is tighter than a turtle's butt."

Wyatt pulls into a different gas station, one in the opposite direction of where my mom and I do most of our business. When they cleared the land to build, they seriously destroyed everything around it, and it looks ugly and unnatural, rising out of the dead yellow grass beside a tree-covered mountain. There's a long, paved road down the hill that dead-ends into the asphalt, crisscrossed with chains and No Trespassing signs.

I sigh, the anger draining away. *Repress, repress, repress.* Who needs yoga or therapy when you can be an ostrich with your head up your own ass? "I always wanted to go sledding down that hill," I say.

"I'm in." Wyatt holds out his pinkie. "First time it snows, we're sledding here."

I hold out my pinkie, and we shake on it. And then I blush hot when I realize that he's making plans with me for something that won't happen for at least two months, if it even snows at all this year.

That he's thinking of me beyond the end of this assignment—and in a way that involves both of us alive and not hating or regretting each other. I hop out and follow him into the gas station's artificial warmth.

He goes straight for the hot biscuits and coffee. I make a beeline for the random collection of housewares and find a sewing kit. When we meet at the counter, I realize that I've forgotten to bring cash. I was too busy navigating my feelings for Wyatt and pondering Alistair Meade and remembering the night Jeremy and Roy and I came here and had a Slushie-drinking contest and purple ice came out of my nose. My head hurts so much I feel like I'm about to have a nosebleed.

"I'll be right back," I whisper, and Wyatt has to notice me blushing, my hands in my empty pockets.

"Don't worry. I've got it." He dumps his stuff on the counter, just a corner of the Valor card flashing as he pays. Does he not want me to see it? He signs his receipt, grabs his plastic bag, and we're out the door. He shoves a hot biscuit into my hands, and I waffle on whether or not to bring up how extremely stupid it is to owe Valor any money right now. But I'm so happy in the moment that I don't want to ruin the morning. Not until it has to be ruined, which will be sooner than I'd prefer. The problem with repressing things, with sticking your head in the sand and ignoring them, is that they're eventually going to bite your butt when you least expect it.

Which is pretty much why America is owned by a bank now.

So instead of saying something scathing, I just smile and take a bite of my biscuit.

We can't drive back to our usual hideout because Jeremy—oh God, Jeremy!—so Wyatt takes the truck down a long dirt road with huge pipes piled up at the end amid the bonfire-singed remains of industrial drums. I give him a look, one eyebrow up.

"I know every dead end in this county, darlin'." He's smirking now, and I roll my eyes.

We eat in the back of the truck in companionable silence. The door is rolled up, and our view of the field and forest is the sort of thing rich people pay mad cash to enjoy on the other side of their breakfast nooks. It occurs to me that I haven't had breakfast with anyone except my mom in years, and that I miss the way she blows on her oatmeal between bites, even when it's cooled off. She never talks much at breakfast—she prefers to read the romance novels she checks out of the library and stacks on her bedside table in impossibly tall towers. I tried one once, but it was embarrassingly hokey. I'm just too practical to believe in all that magic and vampires and fairies and true love. But I'm glad my mom still has dreams, locked somewhere inside her. I need to think about her having hope.

I glance at the clock. Ten thirty. An hour and a half to kill a guy or ruin his life, and then it's time to pick up Matty, and I want to be there the second they'll let us take her home. Home to the mail truck, I guess. We'll have to dump it after this Alistair guy, in case they're sending more Jeremys after me. That doesn't matter. I know where the last two people live, although I'll miss having a bed. I wish I had the time and money to get Matty a really nice dog bed too, something fluffy that she would like. But I already owe Wyatt enough, and I don't want to run up his card any more for something as silly as a dog bed. Maybe I can knit her a blanket when all this is over.

I toss my rest of my biscuit in the trash and wipe the buttery crumbs off my hands and jeans before pulling out my knitting bag. The black stripe I was working on last time is totally wonky, so I frog it and grab some rainbow yarn that feels scratchy but looks cheerful. When I'm done with Valor, I'll get some nice, soft yarn for Matty from the actual yarn store—mohair, maybe, not my usual Goodwill trash yarn. I've never knit a blanket before, but it can't be that hard. A few rows in, and I exhale, enjoying the familiar, reassuring click of the needles. I look over when I hear Wyatt crumple up his third biscuit wrapper, and it turns out he bought a small crossword puzzle book in the gas station and has it open to the first page as he chews on a cheap pen.

"Oh my God. What are you, sixty?" I say with a giggle.

He scowls at me. "Oh, yeah. Because knitting is a hobby of the young and nubile."

"But I'm knitting for anarchy." I hold up the almost-done flag-pole cozy, a few rows of rainbow stitches followed by neon green, sunshine yellow, and bubblegum pink.

"And I'm doing crossword puzzles to up my vocab on the SATs."

"Hey, did your school do that career aptitude test thing?" I ask as I start knitting.

I had almost forgotten about how scared I was as I filled out each oval bubble with my sharp pencil, terrified that my answers would doom me to a life as a janitor or a plumber. I nibbled my pencil just like he's nibbling his pen. The resulting career options that showed up in an envelope a month later were bland and boring and nothing at all that I could see for myself and my future. And it really bothered me.

Accounting. Telemarketing. Project management. Words that meant nothing, jobs that seemed to create nothing and do no good in the world. The person whose future held those options—that wasn't me. I was so angry and embarrassed afterward. Like the test looked into my heart and saw that I didn't have the smarts to be a veterinarian or the passion to be an artist or the guts to be a police-man or a fireman. I don't know what I want to do with my life; I just know I want more than my mother ever had. I know I want to kick ass.

"Yeah, I took it. I think everyone in the state had to do it." He nibbles his lip before penciling in another word.

"What'd you get as your future career options?"

Wyatt looks up, his anger a good match for my own. "Sales. Stocks. Executive. Basic heartless desk-monkey crap, like my dad."

"Yours were better than mine. I guess I'm qualified to be the girl who brings you coffee one day when you're a heartless executive."

Just like my mom and your dad, I think. But I don't say it.

He puts down his crossword and joins me in the back of the truck and lays a hand on my arm, and I realize that during my last couple of rows, I was knitting superfast again, pulling the stitches too tight. I wiggle my shoulders, trying to relax. He rubs my arm a little, and the hairs stand up at his touch.

"It's just a test, Patsy Klein. A stupid test. It doesn't mean anything. You can be whatever you want to be. That's the whole point of America, right? Freedom?"

I snort.

"Maybe that *was* the point of America, but something tells me the Valor Nation is going to be about something different."

For a charming and too-short half hour, we sit there in the open back of the truck, just a few feet apart, surrounded by the warm and comforting smell of cheap biscuits and cooling coffee. The silence is companionable, like we're old people happy just to exist. Like we don't need to say anything because nothing needs to be said. I knit, forcing myself to slow down and stay loose. He works through a crossword puzzle, carefully crossing out each clue as he solves it.

"Did you ever wear glasses?" I ask. Doing the puzzle, he looks like he should have some hipster glasses perched at the end of his nose.

"I got Lasik," he says without looking up. "My eyes are better than perfect now."

I finish out my skein of rainbow yarn just as he's marking through the last clue on his second puzzle. After tying on a ball of lavender, I start the next row, then stow my bag back under the bed with the stuffed turtles. I didn't get that much done, but every little row helps. I get through knitting the same way I'm getting through my list: one step at a time.

"Oh." Wyatt looks pained, and I follow his line of sight to the dashboard. The red numbers have started blinking. "Ready to take care of Alistair Meade and convince him not to die and then take the rest of the day off with Matty?" he asks. He pulls me to my feet, and I nod grudgingly.

"I guess."

"Then let's get it over with and pick up our dog."

A little thrill goes through me whenever he says "we." The thought that not only do I have a dog, but that *we* have a dog, makes me feel like there are all these avenues in the world that I never considered. I never bothered to dream that I would have the freedom of "we."

Wyatt drives, and I take out the sewing kit and sew the button back onto my mail shirt. I should have done it sooner, but it's not like I could sew it back on with Wyatt leaning over his crossword right in front of me, his eyebrows drawn down and the back of his shirt riding up adorably. I swear to God, I jump every time I hear a noise, expecting them to finally punish me for keeping him around. For keeping him alive. A secret that sweet and good is just asking for trouble. Every time the truck slows down at a stop sign, every time a car waits beside us at a light, I expect a kid in camo to pop up, waving a gun and making accusations with bullets. If Jeremy was the B squad, who's batting cleanup?

Getting the button back on my shirt feels like an act of atonement. The needle is pathetic, like it's made out of plastic, and the thread is almost too thick to fit through the hole, especially with the mail truck bouncing around like crazy. I may be poor, but if there's one thing I know about crafting—real crafting—it's that you need quality materials to produce anything worthwhile. I might use crap yarn for bombing, but that sweater I made for my mom last year was superfine angora, and I only use the nicest thread for embroidery. It's almost an insult, this gas station needle. I finally get the damn button back on, and it doesn't look that nice, but how nice did that government-issued mail shirt ever look? I take a second to trace the little eagle patch stitched on the front. Aren't eagles supposed to stand for honor or something? I guess they used to.

The GPS announces that we've almost reached our destination, so I feel around under the pillow for my gun. I'm never going into another situation without a full clip. But when I open up my backpack for the box of bullets, there's another gun there.

"Is this your gun, Wyatt?"

He waits a moment before answering. "No. It's from last night."

The gun goes heavy and cold in my hands, and I turn it over to trace the VALOR SAVINGS logo stamped on the side in gold.

Except it doesn't say VALOR SAVINGS.

The letters are in a slightly different font and read SECOND UNION.

My hearing goes wonky as my hands go numb, and I almost drop the gun because that means Valor didn't send Jeremy after me.

Because this is not a Valor gun.

So what the fuck is Second Union?

"You took this off Jeremy?" I ask, trying to make the words sound normal and not like I'm freaking the hell out.

"Yeah. I figured we might need all the guns we can get. The other kid dropped his shotgun, too, so I shoved it behind all your turtles. Only has one shell in it, though." After another uncomfortable pause and a few big bumps in the road, he mutters, "I hope you don't mind. I know they were your friends."

I shove Jeremy's gun back into my backpack, deep, under the dirty clothes. My head is spinning like clothes in a dryer, hot and thick, but still it doesn't add up. So Jeremy didn't work for Valor, wasn't punishing me for anything I'd done wrong. That means there's another group out there, a rival, another bank or government or faction or whatever. Hell, maybe it's even a rebellion. Whatever Second Union is, it's big and important and powerful enough to stamp a gun and put it in a kid's hands and trick him into murdering his friend.

That doesn't tell me what's happening in the world, but it does tell me that maybe, just maybe, Valor isn't as badass as they seem to think they are. That this conflict is about more than just innocent people against one big, corporate villain. All I know for sure is that I'm collecting weapons and kills like a video game hero. But I feel nothing like a hero. And whoever Second Union is, their methods are just as cruel as Valor and depend on pitting kids with guns against one another by threatening their families.

So which is worse: us versus them, or them versus them with us as collateral damage?

"Almost there," Wyatt says.

Not even close, I think.

I put on the shirt and cap and tuck the gun into my jeans. I'm starting to get used to it, the feeling of cold metal warming against my spine, sticking to my skin a little at first and then slithering around in sweat. I wonder if I'll have this gun forever, or if a robotic man in black will find me someday to collect it. If maybe it will disappear one night from under my pillow while I'm asleep. There's no telling where this deadly tool will end up: Maybe in Kelsey Mackey's hand. Maybe in Tom Morrison's. Maybe in Max Beard's.

The mail truck rolls to a halt, and Wyatt motions with his hand for me to cover the button.

"I don't feel so good about you going in alone," he whispers. "This place is creepsville."

Still covering the button, I edge into the front seat. Disaster settles in my tummy on top of the biscuit. I would feel naked without my lucky locket no matter where I was, but Wyatt's right—total creepsville, like something out of a horror movie.

We're out in the boonies, and I realize that all the bumps I felt earlier must have been the truck tackling an overgrown dirt road. Just ahead of us on the other side of a mimosa tree is a single-wide trailer that's definitely seen better days, if not better decades. It's rusted in places, with shredded towels over the windows and an old-fashioned TV antenna sticking out the top. I don't even think those things work anymore, but I'm guessing Alistair Meade is too lazy or drunk or ancient to take the damn thing down.

The trailer is surrounded by an old orchard, the eerily lined up trees long past bearing fruit and the grass grown to waist height. There's a slight path up to the trailer, and I hope it's too cold for snakes. A blue truck with a camper top sits out front, pointed toward the road, not quite as decrepit as the trailer. I hope to God

Alistair Meade is home, because this place deeply unsettles me in more ways than usual.

I shake my head and swallow down the biscuit and bile. "Just have your gun ready and leave the truck running," I whisper back.

I grab the card and signing machine and check my gun one more time. I haven't fired it since before Tom Morrison, thankfully, took the deal. Who knows? Maybe this guy will too. I don't know what would have happened last night if it had come down to me shooting my friend or dying, but I'm damn glad I didn't have to pull the trigger. I want to thank Wyatt for what he did, but I also hate him for it. And I'm glad I never have to find out if Jeremy would have shot me first.

Walking up to the door slowly, trying to look harmless, I hold the signing machine and card out in front of me like a shield. Nobody shoots the mail carrier, right? The sunny clearing is eerily quiet, like the birds know I'm not supposed to be here and have dark intentions. A blue jay's scolding pierces the silence, making me jump about five feet and trip over an ancient garden hose.

Standing in front of the trailer, I can barely breathe. Neighborhoods are familiar, with the safety of society protecting even the most annoying doorbell ringers, but I wouldn't come out here under any other circumstance I can imagine. No one lives this badly, this far out, for any legal reason. But I don't see the usual trash I know surrounds every meth house. It looks abandoned, which is almost worse. I don't bother stepping onto the concrete blocks that serve as front steps; I want to have as much balance as possible, whatever happens. I knock, and the dented metal door shakes under my knuckles like it's a paper mask about to fall off a skull.

I don't hear the footsteps so much as see the trailer vibrate. One of the towels over the window twitches, but I can't see what's behind it. I knock again, but there's no answer, and the door remains shut.

"Hello? Y'all home?" I call, putting as much friendly Waffle House waitress accent into my words as I can. "I got a delivery for Alistair Meade here. I think it's a check. Mr. Meade, is that you?" I hold up the signature machine and give my dumbest smile.

The towel twitches aside, revealing a ripped piece of yellow legal paper. Heavy black marker reads TAKE OFF THE SHIRT AND WE'LL TALK.

"Excuse me?" I shout, cocking my hip and itching for the gun.

The paper disappears, and a finger appears, stabbing the air in a "wait a minute" gesture.

"You've got to be kidding me," I mutter. I look back over my shoulder at Wyatt in the truck and give him an exaggerated shrug. He's spread out in the front seat, gun in hand, taking up space with his Angry Alpha Male face on. He raises one eyebrow as if to say, "Yeah, I'm sure this is legit."

A new piece of paper appears. GET RID OF THE CAMERA.

My mouth goes dry. This guy . . . knows. And if he knows about the camera, then he knows about the gun, and he knows what's going to happen if he signs the machine, which means he'll never fucking sign it.

And, of course, if I get rid of the camera, that means that whatever happens here isn't recorded and doesn't count toward my goal.

I sigh deeply and unbutton the postal shirt, letting the collar flop to the side and obscure the button. The hand appears again, angry and violent in a "cut it off" motion. Jesus, this guy's annoying. But I'm not taking off this shirt to show the white tank below it. I feel exposed enough as it is.

So I compromise. I shove the signature machine in the shirt pocket, wrap my hand around the button, pull my gun, and press the muzzle right up to the glass.

"That good enough for you, dick?"

Painful seconds pass. A new piece of paper appears, the words scrawled even more hastily. TELL YOUR BOYFRIEND TO DROP THE GUN. YOU TOO. DO AS I SAY, OR YOU BOTH DIE.

A thump tells me Wyatt's hopped down from the truck. I check over my shoulder and shake my head at him. I'm cold and shaking like a Chihuahua, my jaw so tense that I can hear my teeth rubbing together. "Put down the gun," I whisper. "Get back in the truck. Let me handle it."

"Are you sure?"

There's a bang and a ping, and we both turn, and one of the truck tires goes flat.

"Goddammit. Yes. Yes, I'm sure."

Wyatt's hands are up, and he places his gun on the seat with exaggerated care. I nod but don't drop my gun.

When the *shick-shick* of a shotgun echoes within the trailer—that's when I drop it.

A series of locks jangles and clicks inside before the flimsy door opens, just a little.

"Give me the camera. It's recording everything," he whispers, so low I can barely hear.

All I see are glasses and a reaching hand, and I stumble back and trip on that damn hose again and fall, arms wheeling, letting go of the button in the process of not breaking my head open. I land hard on my back, my breath knocked flat out of me. The guy's out the door fast, standing over me, his boot raised like he's going to stomp in my face, and I watch the heavy sole come down toward the button, to crush it against the ground, and that's when a gun cracks and the guy screams and staggers against the trailer.

Wyatt runs closer, shoots again, and I want to yell "No!" and "Stop!" and "He wasn't going to hurt me," but I can't even take a breath, and it doesn't matter because blood spatters my cheeks and the guy's writhing on the ground.

I sit up, mouth wide open like a fish out of water as Wyatt rolls the guy over and pins him with a knee across the chest, but not before I see where the second bullet caught him in the lower back, right where I figure his spine must be. I finally draw a breath, but all I taste is copper and the blood on my lips. The guy's not going anywhere, so I motion Wyatt away, farther back behind me, where the button can't see him. He's breathing hard and looks like he would gladly rip this guy's arms off and beat his dying body with them if he could, but he nods and steps back. I mouth, "Thank you," and give him a big smile so he knows I'm okay and rebutton my shirt so that the camera is facing forward. I feel safer with Wyatt at my back, standing sentinel. This wasn't what I wanted to happen, but everything about number eight has felt wrong since we pulled up here.

Whoever this guy is, whatever he thinks he knows, I still need the same thing from him. And I don't have long to get it.

"Are you Alistair Meade?" I say.

The guy's on his back, panting, a poppy-red stain spreading through his white undershirt like the bullet's still trying to escape his belly. He's skinny, with reddish skin and hair the color of nothing, like those see-through noodles you get with Chinese food sometimes, and there's something uncomfortably familiar about him. Scowling up at me, he shakes his head no.

"Just tell me," I say. "You're dead either way. 911 doesn't work anymore."

He shakes his head again and groans, the sweat standing out on his forehead under the precise line of his haircut. He's in his thirties probably, and his eyes are such a light blue they're almost see-through, but he just looks like a sunburned weasel to me.

I reach around him, fumbling for his back pocket, and he groans and spits blood into the grass. The first pocket of his black dress pants is empty. His wallet's in the other one, and I whip it out. As I flip open the worn black leather, the guy on the ground lets out a wheezy laugh and shudders.

Inside the wallet, there are no credit cards. Not even a debit card. No insurance card. Just a fat wad of cash and three different licenses, each with this same guy's picture on it.

Alex Hancock.

Angus Harrison.

Andrew McHowell.

"Close enough," I say. Tossing the wallet onto his chest, I hold out his Valor card. "Alistair Meade, you owe Valor Savings the sum of $36,936.22. Can you pay this debt in full?"

He barks one harsh laugh, and blood leaks out of the corner of his mouth.

"Don't . . . owe . . . anybody . . . anything . . . ," he wheezes. "No debt."

"By Valor Congressional Order number 7B, your account is past due and hereby declared in default. Due to your failure to remit all owed monies and per your signature just witnessed and accepted, you are given two choices. You may either sign your loyalty over to

Valor Savings as an indentured collections agent for a period of five days or forfeit your life. Please choose."

"No."

I stare up at the sky for a heartbeat, feeling totally lost and tiny. No? No's not a choice.

"Listen. It's not too late. You can either die here or take on bounty hunting to pay off your debt," I say, feeling nervous at how every instinct I have says he's telling the truth about not having debt. "If you want to work it off, we'll take you in to the hospital. Or the veterinarian, if the hospital's closed or full or whatever. Take the deal. It's not so bad."

"Just . . . make . . . more . . . debt," he wheezes, his face going red as he tries to laugh and can't. "Fucking . . . medical . . . bills. Might as well . . . shoot." His eyes flash up to Wyatt. "Again," he adds, too wryly for a guy who's dying.

"I'm sorry," I say. "But I'll make it quick."

He holds up his hands like we're playing, like I'm the sheriff and he's the bad guy. And then, quicker than he has any right to be, he grabs the button off my shirt in a bloody fist and pulls me close, dry lips trembling against my ear.

"Not your fault," he manages to whisper. "Conspiracy. Valor. Inside . . . trailer . . ." He coughs and turns his head away. "Don't take the button in there."

"What's inside the trailer?"

"Adelaide. Just . . . Adelaide. Will tell you . . . everything." His lips move, but no sound comes out. When he goes limp and drops the button, I cover it with my own hand and lean in. Barely even a breath, he whispers, "You have to burn it all. They're coming."

His head falls to the side, the light in his eyes gone. Panic rips through me, and I grab my gun, stand up on my knees, aim the button at him, and shoot him right in the chest. Valor never said anything about what happened if someone died before I could kill them myself, not that they know about Wyatt and the other gun. I hope.

The earth soaks up through my jeans as I kneel before the trailer, my gun cooling off in my limp hand. The birds are silent again, even that one mocking jay. We're in the middle of nowhere, another pocket of beautiful nothing surrounded by ugly roads and uglier buildings. It'll be so much prettier when nature swallows up the trailer and just takes back over. I can imagine a flock of turkeys here in the early morning, maybe deer, too. Maybe coyotes at night. It's not bad, for a final resting place. At least, that's what I tell myself as I drop the gun, unbutton my shirt so the button is turned away, pick up the signature machine, wrap Alistair Meade's cold hand around the stylus, and sign a ragged X. God, I hope that's good enough. When I click the accept button, it logs normally, and I exhale. If they're keeping tabs, they have to know I faked signatures on Alistair Meade and Ashley Cannon, and I can only hope I'll still get a passing grade when they do the final tally.

For just one moment, it occurs to me that I could be jumping through completely bullshit hoops, that maybe there's never been a security guy with a sandwich. Maybe there's not even a bank of monitors. Maybe that camera goes nowhere. Maybe my mom's already dead.

Or maybe, considering how important covering that button up was to this dead man, they're watching even more closely than I thought.

Doesn't matter. I can't stop now. I'll play by the rules as much as I can, as long as they'll let me if it keeps me and my mom alive.

Gun in one hand and signature machine in the other, I look down on the body of the man who had better be Alistair Meade. With his face gone slack and expressionless, I realize why he's familiar.

This guy is the Black Suit who tried to hand me a card in the gas station.

It's the white-blond hair, cut so precisely, so Valor, that sticks it for me. I couldn't see his eyes behind the sunglasses, but I know it's him. Which tells me that I have to get in that trailer—now—and find out what "Adelaide" means.

He said, "They're coming." Those were his last words. And goddammit, I believe him. Which means I have to hurry.

Wyatt is careful to stay out of view as I shuck off my shirt, wad it up, and stuff it in the cap. I don't want the camera to see anything of what I'm about to do.

"What the hell was that all about?" Wyatt says. "Who's Adelaide? How did he know about Valor? And what's inside the trailer?"

"Who knows?" I say, steeling myself with one hand against the trailer door. Something keeps me from telling Wyatt that I've seen this guy before, dressed in the standard Valor goon costume. "Out here by himself? Maybe he's cooking meth. Maybe he's a kidnapper and Adelaide is the girl he has locked up in there. Maybe he makes moonshine or has an ex-wife looking for him. Maybe he's just a crazy dude who thinks there's a conspiracy against him." I look at what's left of the shirt balled up in my hat. "Maybe he saw the blood."

"I guess," Wyatt says. The trailer door squeaks as I push it open, and he grimaces. "Are you really going in there?"

"'Inside trailer.' Those were his dying words. Whatever is in there, it was important to him. Maybe it's Adelaide." But I don't think there's anyone else in the trailer. There's definitely something in there, and I get the idea that it's very, very dangerous. But I don't think it's a person.

"Maybe he's got it rigged. Maybe there's a bomb named Adelaide."

I shrug. "Maybe. But probably not. Stay out here and keep watch, okay?"

"You sure you want to do this?" he says. "Want me to go in instead?"

"Just let me look real quick." Before he can stop me, I push the door open and slip inside, gun drawn and senses on high alert. "Hello? Adelaide?"

It's quiet in the trailer except for some weird electrical buzzing noise. At least there's no drug paraphernalia lying around, no needles or big stacks of cough suppressants or a chemistry set like at Sharon Mulvaney's house.

There's crap everywhere, but not like a hoarder's crap, not trash. It's all paperwork, printouts, envelopes, photos, file boxes. Three laptops range across the counter, a forest of wires tangling behind them and an array of devices clicking and whirring and twinkling like Christmas lights.

"You okay in there?" Wyatt calls, and I yell back, "Yeah. Just a bunch of weird paperwork."

Out of curiosity, I run my finger over the touchpads on the laptops, and they all buzz awake to a password-protected lock screen. But something catches my eye where it rests on top of a stack of papers by the laptops.

An expandable file folder is marked POSSIBLE SLEEPER AGENTS, and one of the file folders is labeled CANDLEWOOD. Inside is a typed list of names, hundreds of them, all in alphabetical order. Mine is on there, and so is Wyatt but not Max. Not Jeremy or Roy, either. I glance through quickly and see some other kids from my school, including a creeper who's big into Nazi history. Dozens of similar folders surround it, wearing the names of nearby towns. The stack of papers underneath are bad photocopies of bubbled-in test answers. They're very familiar, because I took one just a few weeks ago. It told me I was qualified to be an accountant or a secretary. I pick up the standardized-test sheets and flip through, but there are hundreds of them. A red notebook draws my attention, and it falls open to pages and pages of lists and cramped writing. Scribbled in the margins are things like, *They always send innocents to fight wars,* and *Anarchy. Fear and chaos. No answers. No one wants to shoot a child.*

Moving more quickly now, I drop the notebook and hurry to the card table with its lone folding chair, looking for more clues to whatever the hell is going on. Most of it makes no sense—lots of printouts in code, or graphs, or maps with stars and circles at regular intervals. There are photo albums filled with newspaper clippings and the printouts of online articles, all of them dealing with China, the debt ceiling, banking, loan rates, business acquisitions, stocks, the recession, and politicians. One piece of paper pinned to the wall says CONTENDERS: FIRST UNION, VALOR SAVINGS BANK, STAGECOACH.

Well, I know two of those banks are in the running—although Valor is now just Valor Savings and First Union is now apparently Second Union, which explains a lot about why Jeremy was sent to kill me. Assassinating the enemy's assassins is just another part of war. But does that mean that the two ex-banks are battling for supremacy? Or does that mean that Second Union is part of the resistance? And what's Stagecoach going to become—Drone?

I move to the counter. An old jewelry box holds pieces of a shirt button much like my own, careful piles of tiny components and a computer chip and wires that make no sense to me. Draped over a chair is a crisp white shirt, black tie, and black jacket, the one Alistair was wearing when I saw him at the gas station. I dig in a pocket and find the tiny headset thing with its see-through wires and a minuscule *gold V*. In the other pocket is a stack of cards, the same kind he tried to give to me before I freaked out. They're poorly printed, tear-apart business cards that read simply: WANT TO FIGHT THE BANKS? YOU'RE NOT ALONE. And then a phone number. In the breast pocket is a full magazine for a 9mm just like mine. I want to drop it like it's a baby rattlesnake, but instead, I shove it in my back pocket.

Jesus. Alistair Meade—or whatever his name was—was a double agent. I wish I knew what happened first. Was he tapped as a Black Suit and later found reason to rebel, or was he a conspiracy theorist just praying for the chance to work for his worst enemy? Or maybe he killed one of the real Black Suits and got a robot haircut and stole the dude's uniform. But why would he be standing around at gas stations with homemade business cards when it was easy to see that Valor didn't want anyone to know what was going on?

And even if my name is on that list of possibilities, how did he recognize me?

I have more questions than answers, and I just shot the only dude around who knows the truth and will never get a chance to talk to him. I spin around, hungry for more, my heartbeat thumping in my ears in the silent trailer.

Again and again, scrawled or printed on almost every surface, I see one word. "Valor."

This guy knew what was going on. He knew even before he put on those sunglasses. And he was trying to change things.

"Patsy? You okay? What's going on in there?" Wyatt shouts. He sounds pissed and antsy, but I'm not done in here. And now that I've seen his name on something, I don't really want him inside the trailer until I figure out a little more for myself.

"I'm just looking around," I say. "Lots of papers. On my way out."

I turn and trip on a cardboard box. Inside are dozens of photocopies, and I pull out the top sheet.

> *Attention, patriotic Americans:*
> *You do not know it, but you no longer live in the United States of America. Our government has sold us out for the last time, thanks to our greed and lack of foresight. No, friends, we now belong to the deep pockets of Valor Savings Bank.*
>
> *Their new dictatorship is called Valor Savings, and*

the first step of their very hostile takeover will involve using our own children in the war against us. Using complex algorithms and the much-maligned system of certified testing, they've identified troubled teens to help cut the deadweight of useless debtors who require the most state help to produce the least bounty.

But that's not me! *you say.*

Think again, friend.

Did you sign up for that Valor Savings Bank platinum credit card? The one they advertised on TV and in every magazine? The one that had an unbelievably low rate, welcomed balance transfers, and didn't require a strict credit check? If so, you signed a waiver to forfeit your life or work as a bounty hunter. Chances are, if you have an able teen between the ages of sixteen and eighteen, they'll be working off your debt for you in exchange for your life. As always, the despots are glad to turn children into killers, to sow anarchy and fear. And you can't complain to the president because he's never been more than a figurehead. Congress has finally taken their biggest cash-out ever. The police have been assassinated, the armed forces incarcerated. We are truly on our own.

Sound like a scary movie?

It's not.

It's our country.

And we want to fight back.

They're monitoring the Internet. They're listening in on your phone calls. But they can't track your body. Join your local Citizens for Freedom group at the date, time, and place listed below to find out how you can live through the Valor regime and help take back what made our nation great:

FREEDOM.

JOIN US.

It gives a date and time at an abandoned high school, just two days from now, right before my five days are up. I fold the paper and shove it into my back pocket along with the photo of my dad with Ashley Cannon.

Just as I take a shuddering breath, a far-off noise catches my attention. A helicopter.

Shit. Valor might not know about Alistair Meade's conspiracy theories and his double-dealing, but they sure as shit know where I am right now. Whether it's the truck's GPS or my stupid button, they always knew. Second Union might know too.

"Patsy! Helicopter! Hurry your ass!" Wyatt yells from outside.

I run to check the other room before he gets too crazy waiting for me, but it's just a tidy and spare sleeping space. A small bed made with military precision, a lamp, a stack of paperback books. A picture of Alistair Meade, younger, with a pretty girl and a tiny baby. I wonder where they are, if they're still alive. Did Valor kill them? Or was Meade a lone crackpot who left his family to pursue a conspiracy that just so happened to be real?

It's not in a frame—just lying on the table with worn corners exposed. I pick it up. On the back, in the same surprisingly exact handwriting as the folder labels, it says, ALISTAIR, MARIE, AND ADELAIDE, FEBRUARY 2002.

I don't think he was lying to me. I don't think he has debt. I don't think he's a crackpot.

I think he knew exactly what's going on, and I only wish I had all day to search through his trailer.

But I don't want Valor or Second Union to know anything about him that they don't already, and I would bet my life that the helicopter getting louder and louder is stamped with one of their logos.

"I'm coming in," Wyatt yells.

I shout back, "No. I'm coming out now!"

I rush to the front of the trailer and unplug the power strip that controls all three laptops. After closing and stacking them and dumping all their cords on top, I chuck them into a box and shove it out the door and into Wyatt's waiting hands. Before he can ask me what the hell I'm doing, I say, "Did you bring your lighter?"

"Yeah, why?"

"Just go put that box in the truck and get ready to run."

"Why?"

"Do you trust me?"

He looks at me, eyes narrowed. Of course he doesn't trust me. I killed his dad.

"I shouldn't, but I kind of do," he admits. "Just tell me what's in the trailer."

"I will after you put those in the truck," I say.

He hurries away with the box, and I rush back to the fridge I saw under a stack of folders. I take a Sunkist for each of us and a beer, too. Wyatt is waiting outside the door by the time I get back.

"Help me get him inside the trailer." I pick up Alistair's feet, and Wyatt grabs him under his arms, and he's all floppy and wet, but we manage to get him inside and close the door.

The helicopter is getting louder.

"So what's going on?" he says.

"This guy's a conspiracy theorist." I pop open the beer can. "Lighter, please." Wyatt puts the silver rectangle in my hand and looks from it to the beer can like I'm six shades of crazy, but he doesn't stop me.

"Grab that towel out of the window, will you?" I say. I point to the open window where Alistair must've stood to shoot out our tire. Wyatt yanks it out, and I pour beer all over half of it. I light the other half with the lighter, although it takes me three tries to get the damn thing to light. Apparently, beer isn't very flammable. Then I throw the towel through the door, aiming for a pile of paper. It catches fire with a *whoosh.* I light the carpet, too. Bright orange flames are licking up the walls when I finally close the door again.

"So why are you burning down his trailer?" Wyatt asks.

"Because I don't know if Valor knows what he knows, but I don't want them to know that I know anything."

"So what's on the laptops?"

"I have no idea. They just seemed more portable than a thousand pounds of paper and maps and crap. If we can crack the passwords, I bet we can find out a lot more about our new government."

"I don't know if you're crazy or crazy," Wyatt admits. "But I think you're pretty cool."

About that time, we realize we're standing next to a trailer that's going to explode, and we run for the mail truck in nothing like the slow motion you see in movies. Wyatt leaps into the driver's side as I land in the passenger seat, and I look at the reset red clock and realize that wherever this truck goes, they can find it. With one tire shot out, it's practically useless anyway.

"Stop. Grab your stuff and the laptops. We're abandoning ship."

Bless his heart, he doesn't question it. We roll up the back door and start throwing all our shit out into the yard. There's not much. My backpack, my knitting bag, Jeremy's shotgun, Wyatt's backpack. On last thought, my quilt.

He jumps down with the box of laptops, and I say, "Go make sure that old truck has keys in the ignition. I bet it does. Dude knew he might have to run."

As he jogs over, I grab one of the concrete blocks that serve as the front step of the trailer.

"Yup. Got keys. It runs," he hollers.

"Load it up with our stuff and get ready to floor it."

Hands shaking, ears pounding with helicopter rotors, I use the concrete block to pin down the mail truck's gas pedal, crank the key, put it in gear, and jump the hell out of the door. I trip and fall on the rough ground but scramble up and away with my heart busting and the gun slipping against my butt crack.

The mail truck barrels into the flaming trailer and catches fire, still trying to ram through and digging holes in the dirt. I run to the camper truck and jump in, and Wyatt guns it in a cloud of dust. It's clean but worn inside, anonymous and well preserved. The keys jangling in the ignition have a red rabbit's foot on the chain. I roll down my window and lean out to look back, and it's kind of beautiful, the trailer and mail truck ablaze in the old orchard, billowing black smoke. I hope it doesn't set the whole field of trees and grass on fire. But it's too late now. What's done is done. If Valor doesn't like the fire, they can put it out. The shadow of the helicopter sniffs the corner of the orchard, and I duck back inside the truck just as we scoot under some pine trees. Maybe they'll think we died in the truck.

I lean back, grab the handle, and take a deep breath. "That went well."

"At least nobody shot at you this time," Wyatt says.

"I just don't get why he was so stupid." I open the glove box, but it's empty, aside from the registration, made out to Axel McDaniel. I wonder what his real name was. "He could have told me what was up first. You can't just grab jumpy people with guns who already want you dead."

"No telling," Wyatt says.

And that's when I wish I had more fully searched Alistair Meade's body for clues. He might have had more information in his back pockets. Jesus, and I just tossed his wallet away without looking past the fake IDs and the money. I didn't even check to see if he had a phone—maybe the one that would ring if you called the number on the business card he tried to give me.

I shake my head. Maybe they succeeded in making me an assassin, a cold-blooded killer. But they didn't make me a decent detective. I just did something impossibly rash and, yeah, kind of stupid. And now all the clues are on fire, including my mail truck and all my posters and my stuffed turtles. I guess I didn't really think that through. I just knew that I had to keep Valor out of that trailer and that truck away from me.

They wanted to keep me in the dark. Now, as much as possible, I'll take a gleeful turn at keeping *them* in the dark. I still have the possibly bugged button on my wadded-up shirt, but as long as I get the next two people on the list today, I should be able to toss it by nightfall.

But, Jesus—what about the truck? They never said that I had to turn it in at the end. Was there something about it on that paper I signed without looking? Are they going to be pissed? What if they think that without the GPS, I'm going to fail? What if they go after my mom before my time is up?

It's too fucking late to worry about that now.

The truck is gone.

The best I can do is finish the last two names and hurry home to check on my mom once I've done what I promised to do. As long as I have the button on my shirt, they have to know I'm still in the game.

Repress, repress, repress. Keep moving. Next name.

I'm not ready to think about the next person on the list, even though I know I have less than twelve hours to face her.

I can't even begin to imagine what will happen when I'm done.

The old truck bumps back onto asphalt, and my butt's glad for a smoother ride. I yawn and stretch and put my feet up on the dashboard. The gun digs into my back, and I slip it under my thigh instead. The other two are on the floorboard under my feet, and I assume the shotgun is sliding around in the truck bed. It's kind of funny how just a few short days ago, I had a healthy respect for guns.

I wasn't afraid of them, and I kind of liked shooting them with the guys after work, but I understood that they were to be transported unloaded, with the bullets locked in the glove box. That was the legal, safe way to do it. Now I'm slinging my Glock around like it's last year's fancy phone, something I need that kind of gets in my way but isn't particularly exciting.

It's lunchtime, but I'm nowhere close to hungry. I bet Wyatt is, though. Maybe he's going to get a second breakfast, since he's a bottomless pit. Or maybe he's headed back to the vet. I have no idea where we are right now, on back roads in the country. Or maybe he's going to another secret hiding spot in the wilderness, now that we can't go back to the Preserve. I try to think of what I would be doing today if I were at school. But does it even matter? After this week, after what I've done, does schoolwork even signify? Could I just go back to school like nothing happened, like I don't know what I know, my hands washed utterly clean of blood? Will I sit in a desk, pencil in hand, focusing on quizzes and tests and home-work and answering questions about the week I spent at home with measles? Could I get through five minutes of US history without laughing my ass off? Do I even want something as regular as school anymore, now that I know that the future is out of my control? Pre-calculus seems like the dumbest thing on earth when a murderous bank runs your country.

Will Valor and Second Union even let me have a future?

And yet, at the same time, it's not like I'm going to go work for Valor Savings, become a willing cog in their machinery. I'm still the same person I've always been, in my heart. Each of those people I've killed—they had a choice. If they wanted to pretend it wasn't real, that I wasn't serious, that's not my fault. Choice after choice, it was always in their hands. Two out of eight people seems like a pretty high rate of acceptance, and they were the two people who I thought deserved their Valor card the least. That can't be a coincidence.

And that makes me wonder how many people like me opted out on the first round. Was it just kids my age, like on that list in Alistair's trailer and like the Black Suit told my mom? Did they give that career aptitude test to every kid between sixteen and eighteen? Or did they choose all sorts of people to become homemade assassins? How many people didn't live past that first Glock, held in the hands of a black-suited man who didn't quite seem to breathe? And why, of all the people in America, had they targeted me? What did that test tell them? I wasn't dangerous. I wasn't trained. I wasn't particularly brave.

I was, however, expendable.

And I don't look like someone your average American would want to shoot, even though most of them wouldn't want me hanging around their neighborhoods.

Teen daughter of a single mother, no father, no other family.

No money to hire lawyers. A mom too proud and ashamed to ask for help and sick enough to be grateful for any shred of hope. We're poor, and we live in one of the poorest neighborhoods of a poor suburb. Wyatt's Preserve is like a king's castle to most of us, and Chateau Tuscano might as well be Disney World. Ashley Cannon, Sharon Mulvaney, and Alistair Meade—they're at the rougher end of the spectrum, but they're closer to the real heart of Candlewood than Robert Beard and Dr. Ken Belcher. Personally, I've never let myself dream higher than Kelsey Mackey.

And that can't be a coincidence, either. All of my assignments have been in the five-mile radius of my house, and all of the people are somehow connected to my life. Whatever's happening to me is not the same as what happened to Jeremy. According to what I read in Alistair's trailer, my situation is playing out all over the country, where undesirable teens are being sent out to cull the debt-ridden herd, activate new assassins, and generally spread mayhem and fear. It's pretty smart, if you've quietly taken over a country known for freedom but dependent on the government employees on the other end of the phone to get help. If no one answers 911, if the police really were assassinated, people are going to start freaking out pretty quickly. But since most people don't need 911 on a daily basis and Valor appears to be controlling the media, the average person wouldn't know about the problem until they'd already become collateral damage.

The more I think about it, the bigger it gets and the more tiny and helpless I feel. And the more I wish I had had time to ask Alistair Meade a few questions. But Valor was coming, and he told me to burn it all. Maybe destroying the evidence in his trailer helped uphold his memory. Maybe it continued whatever he was fighting.

The truck rolls to a stop, and I look up. I've been so busy thinking that I wasn't really paying attention. I should have been, though. I gasp, and my feet slam down on the floorboard.

"Drive!" It comes out strangled. "Drive fast."

With a confused shake of his head, Wyatt steps on the gas just hard enough to keep it from squealing. He turns so fast in the cul-de-sac that the truck is practically on two wheels, and I have to hold on to my oh-shit handle to keep from falling into his lap. All the stuff in back clatters around, the shotgun banging against the metal. He doesn't say anything until we're out of the neighborhood and onto the road.

"Sorry," he says. "I figured you'd want to knock one more out, so I pulled the directions out of the old GPS before we left the truck. No lucky number nine?"

I just shake my head.

"I want a milk shake," I say darkly.

Maybe a milk shake will settle my stomach. Because the house we were just in front of? Seeing it again was just about enough to make me crap myself. I haven't let myself think about the ninth name on the list. Part of me hoped that something would happen before it came down to this. A Deus ex machina, as my English teacher calls it.

I don't want to go there again.

I don't want to talk to her, much less kill her.

My ex–best friend can wait.

9.

AMBER LANE

To his credit, Wyatt doesn't ask me any questions until we're in the drive-through line.

"What flavor?" he asks, and I mutter, "Surprise me."

After careful consideration, he orders one chocolate, one vanilla, and one peppermint chocolate chip, not to mention a pretty big meal for himself and, on second thought, one for me. I stop stewing and brooding long enough to thank him, and I watch for that Valor credit card, but he's onto me. He hands it to the girl front-side down and slides it back into his jeans pocket.

He hands me all the food, and the smell turns my stomach. I drop the bags on the floorboard and start in on the peppermint choc-olate chip milk shake, stirring in the whipped cream and shoveling it into my mouth with a spoon because I know it's too thick to suck up yet. Wyatt just drives, his face flat and passive. Still, it's like he can read my thoughts, because he parks at the vet even though they're closed for lunch. It softens me up enough to tear the straw wrapper and blow. It hits him right between the eyes, and he can't help grinning.

"Are we cool now?" he says. "Did the milk shake work?"

"The milk shake is starting to work."

I stick the straw in and suck so hard my cheeks hurt. A brain freeze would be really good right now. Any excuse to avoid the discussion that's about to start.

"So what happened back there at number nine, Patsy Klein?"

Grabbing the bags of food and the milk shake carton, I hop to the ground and head around to the back of the old blue truck. Wyatt follows me, and when I jab my chin at the truck bed, he pulls down the tailgate, lifts up the camper hatch, and spreads out my quilt so we can sit. It's a beautiful day, with a perfect blue sky and the unusually warm sunshine that sometimes makes November feel like late summer in Georgia. I take my time with the food, pulling out my sandwich and squeezing mayo onto it, getting the little puddle of ketchup ready for my fries. I'm trying to organize my thoughts, too. Where am I even supposed to start?

"I know her, okay?" I take a big bite and chew so long that he makes a "go on" gesture with his hand. His mouth is full too. He's already on his second sandwich. "Amber Lane. We used to be best friends, a long time ago. Before her family got too rich and we stayed too poor. We look a lot alike, and we used to pretend to be sisters. And then in seventh grade, her grandmother died, and suddenly her family had money, and her mom stopped inviting me over, and Amber said my clothes weren't good enough to be her best friend anymore. She fought it at first. But then she got popular and ruined my life worse."

"She ruined your life . . . worse?"

"I kept following her around like a lovesick puppy, and she trashed me in the cafeteria, in front of everyone. Reminded me that I gave her lice in first grade, told everyone how poor I was, then called me a bastard. Said my dad left because I was such a loser, even though there's no way that could be true or that she could even know. Everybody laughed. I cried. Total movie moment. And I guess that's when I figured that I should just stop trying to fit in."

He puts down what's left of his sandwich and ropes an arm around me.

"And she's on the list? Damn, girl. It's like they're trying to punish you."

"Maybe they are," I say.

"What do you mean?"

I've been pussyfooting around whether or not to tell him about all the connections. I glance at the box of laptops, which is nestled between our backpacks like a really ugly Oreo cookie. Alistair Meade's trailer didn't say anything about me in particular as compared to all the other names, but I know without a shadow of a doubt that I'm different. That something about my current predicament is personal. But I need to make sure we're really, seriously alone before I open my mouth.

"Where's the shirt?" I ask, on the brink of going frantic. I don't remember what happened to it at the orchard, but I know I can't go back for anything we might have left there. And even if I'm terrified that I've already messed up and doomed my mom, my only chance at sanity and survival is to keep pushing forward like I can still win this game. Until all ten names are done, I need that shirt. My mom might be in trouble now, but I'm completely sure that without that shirt, she'll be dead.

"I put it under your seat."

Of course he did.

I lurch to the front of the truck, retrieve the shirt, wad it up tighter, and stuff it in the glove box. Wyatt sits on the edge of the tailgate, swinging long legs, oddly graceful for a big guy. I bet it's something else, watching him play lacrosse. Or bass, which revs my engine even more. His food sits beside him, but he isn't finishing off his last sandwich, and after three days with him, I know that this is a big deal. He must sense that I'm finally about to crack.

I asked him back there if he trusted me.

He has no reason to, and yet he does.

Now I have to trust him.

"That guy back there, he was a conspiracy theorist. That trailer was full of data on Valor, on me, on banking, on debt. He had maps with stars and circles. The results of our career aptitude tests." I pull the poorly folded piece of paper—the call to arms—out of my pocket and put it in his big hands, where it looks like a crushed origami crane as he unfolds it gently. "Alistair Meade, or whatever his name was, he knew what was going on. That's why he was acting so weird. He wanted me to cover the camera so he could talk to me. He was a double agent. Those are his laptops. And if we can get inside them, I bet we can learn a lot about what's going on with Valor Savings." I point to the paper. "And now we know when and where these guys are meeting. It's in two days."

"That is . . . some deep shit." Wyatt reads the paper through several times before picking up his chicken sandwich and taking a bite. He scowls, pulls out the pickles, chews, bites, chews, bites, his face screwed up like he's thinking really hard. After a long slurp on his Coke, he says, "So none of this is a coincidence."

But it's not a question. I shake my head.

"The only thing I don't get is why Valor picked you."

"I don't get it either. But there's more."

Wyatt swallows and turns toward me, waiting. A small dam breaks inside me.

"Every person on the list meant something. My mom worked for your dad. The second person was dying of the same thing my mom has. Ashley Cannon was my uncle. The lady at the crack house was the mom of an old friend. Kelsey Mackey was like looking into a crystal ball of my ideal future. Tom Morrison's little girl was like a carbon copy of me as a kid. Everything is related. There's a pattern. But I don't know why."

He puts the grease-spotted paper in my lap. "So maybe these guys will know. We should go to the meeting."

He finishes his last bite of sandwich and starts in on his fries. I'm pretty sure his brain runs on fast food. But he has a point. This whole time, I felt like I was the only person on earth being forced into a horrific choice and that there was no one to complain to, no one with answers. From what little I can piece together, I'm one of thousands, maybe millions of people—teenagers—in mail trucks with magic GPS machines and stamped Glocks, shaking and puking in the bushes as they walk up strangers' sidewalks and become bad guys. And there are maybe some other crazy guys in army costumes chasing us on behalf of yet another bank. And then there are people holed up in trailers or basements or apartments with weird antennas and stacks of information, trying to figure out what Valor has planned. And, hopefully, what can be done to stop them.

Belatedly, I notice that Wyatt casually used "we" again. That alone is enough to convince me that I'm not the only person in this fight. And feeling like I'm not alone makes me feel, for the first time, that I can win.

"So you think we can fight them?" I say quietly, but before he can answer, the door to the vet's office jangles open, and the receptionist walks out, waving at us.

"Y'all come on in," she shouts. "Matty can't wait to see you!"

Wyatt's smiling as big as I am. That damn dog just has a way of getting under your skin. I jump down off the tailgate and jog inside with Wyatt by my side. I wish I had thought to stop somewhere and buy Matty some biscuits or a toy or something, whatever dogs like. I guess half a chicken sandwich will have to do.

We burst in the door, and there's a frazzled-looking lady in a sweatshirt and yoga pants sitting in the waiting room, holding a crying kid. The woman is shaking and panting, her makeup dripping down her face with tears and snot. She looks like she's being hunted. And considering what's going on, maybe she is.

"Don't worry, honey," she says, rubbing the kid's back. "The doctor's going to fix Coco right up."

"Why dat guy shoot her?" the kid asks between sniffles, a big green snot bubble in his nose. "Why dat mailman shoot the doggie and Miss Carla? She is my neighbor. She is not a bad guy."

"I don't know, honey," the woman says, rocking him back and forth, her voice breaking into a sob. "I don't know."

I look at Wyatt quickly, worry written across my face. Now we know without a doubt that it's true. That other shootings are happening all over the place, even in the same town. That there are more people with Valor-issued guns. And that normal, thus-far-uninvolved people are starting to take notice.

"Here she is!" the receptionist calls, leading Matty through the door on a worn-out lead. She's got one of those horrible neck cone things around her face and a big dressing on her neck, but she's wagging, and her whole body is rippling with happiness. I feel the same way. I drop into a squat and wrap my arms carefully around her.

"How you doing, Matty?" I ask. "You feeling better, girl?"

She wags and wiggles and whines, trying to lick my face, but the cone won't let her. I put my hand in there, and she just slobbers all over it with meaty dog breath. I don't care. I've got my dog back. Wyatt squats on her other side and scratches above her tail, and she makes a funny face and licks her own nose. They even sponged all the blood off her, and she smells like baby powder.

Dr. Godfrey comes out and says, "She's doing great. It should heal up without a problem. And y'all can keep that lead, if you want. Just give her soft dog food for a while, or wet her kibble until it's mushy. Chewing will make her a little sore." She squats beside us, patting the top of the dog's silky head. "Matty's one of the best patients we've ever had. Y'all take good care of her, you hear? Lots of gunshot wounds this week, for some reason."

"We will," I say, and I hope it's true.

Maybe we can lock her in the camper part of the truck to keep her from jumping out and getting in trouble. Then again, I hope neither of my last two assignments will end in a gunfight.

Wyatt grabs four big cans of expensive dog food and hands over his credit card again, just as grimly and secretively as the first time. I think about saying something, but he saved Matty, so I don't. The receptionist gives us some paperwork about how to take care of Matty's wound, and I decide that if everything turns out okay, I'm going to pick up a book on dogs and some nice treats for her. As we walk out the door, Dr. Godfrey kneels in front of the frazzled woman and her kid, saying, "How did you say Coco got shot again? This is our third gunshot this week. Did you call the police?"

I pause in the doorway to help Matty out.

"We called," the lady says, voice shaking and puzzled, "but no one answered. Just a weird recording from the bank. How can no one be at 911? Where are the police? My neighbor—they just shot her and drove away. They left her body. It's in the street. No police. No . . . I just . . ." She wails and doubles over.

I nod to myself as the door shuts behind me. That's all I needed to hear. And I can't listen anymore.

Together, we lift Matty into the truck bed and scoot in with her to finish our food. My appetite is back, but I feed Matty as much of my sandwich and fries as she wants to eat. They said to give her soft food, and I guess this is soft enough. Wyatt finishes up the other two milk shakes while I suck up the crunchy candy cane dregs at the bottom of mine.

We take our time, talking to Matty, petting her, letting her slurp all up and down our hands and arms until we're both slick with chicken-crumb slobber. She's so happy to see us; it's almost like she's forgotten that she got shot yesterday. After a few moments, the air in the truck gets pretty thick with the fact that we're not talking about what to do now. We've got our dog. We've eaten. We either have to go to the next assignment or find someplace to rest. There's no more red clock on the dash, but I can feel the seconds ticking down in my heart.

"Your call," Wyatt says, as if he can read my mind.

I take a deep breath and swallow a ball of air. The milk shake wobbles in my stomach. I've never been big on procrastinating, and it's not like it's going to be any easier to do this tomorrow. And, worst of all, I bet Valor can still find us as long as I have that bugged button. We have to end it. Now.

"Let's go back to Amber's house."

Wyatt nods, his mouth quirking up in a smile. "You're the bravest girl I ever met; you know that?"

"I'm not brave," I say, blushing a little. "I just don't like waiting around for things to suck. Let's get this shit over with, hide the bug in a mailbox, and take a nap. She has to take the deal. I'll make her take it."

· 273 ·

I don't say it, but mentally I add, *Max, too.*

We hop down and climb into the front seats, leaving Matty in the enclosed truck bed, and I open the back window so I can pet her while Wyatt drives. I don't need to see where we're going. I can sense each turn, each stop. I know my way to Amber's house. I know the layout inside, the way the fridge door never shuts all the way unless you bump it, although I guess they probably have a new fridge by now. My name is written on the concrete blocks of her basement wall behind the door, AMBER + PATSY BFF. Unless she erased it. But our friendship didn't end that way. She moved beyond me, destroyed me, forgot about me. I'm the one who still feels petty and spiteful. She probably doesn't even know I exist, just like I had forgotten all about Ann Filbert until I stumbled past her picture. We grow past people and just leave them behind without a second thought. Money is the kind of debt that everyone talks about, but friendship is a debt that's taken for granted until it's lost.

For just a split second, I let myself look at this assignment as the ultimate revenge on Amber Lane. But then I realize that that's the sort of thought that makes God want to smite formerly nice girls with lightning and boils, so I grit my teeth and will myself to believe that she's just another name on the list that burned up in the back of the mail truck. I have to convince her to take the deal.

My eyes are stubbornly closed, but I know when we're in front of her house. I can feel it in my bones. Wyatt stops the truck but leaves it running, as we always do. I gently pull my arm out of the window and away from Matty as Wyatt ducks below my knees to hand me my shirt. I turn away to slip it on, arms as heavy as the concrete block I used to rig the mail truck's gas pedal. Wyatt's hand wraps my fingers around the gun. Matty grumbles in her sleep, and I get out of the truck with a sigh and tuck the bloodstained edges of my shirt into my jeans. If Amber's home, she'll probably take one look at me and decide she was right to cut me off. Dirty, wearing dorky clothes and a stained hat, driving a beat-up truck, working for a place as dumb as the post office.

Will she even be home? She should be in school. But Dr. Ken Belcher should have been at work too, and every door I've come to has had the right person waiting behind it.

I pat the rumpled card and the signature machine in the shirt pocket. The gun's heavy weight against my back has become a comfort. Wyatt comes up behind me and wraps his arms around me, kissing me on the cheek.

"Good luck," he whispers in my ear, and I turn my head to whisper, "Thank you."

He sits in the front seat of the running truck, one arm back to pet Matty. I'm so not ready to do this, but I want it to be over with. I don't even feel for my missing necklace this time, and with a sinking heart, I realize I haven't said my prayers in a few days. I haven't asked for forgiveness.

Heavy with dread, I walk up the familiar sidewalk where we used to draw hopscotch boards with chalk. We found a baby bird out here once, fallen from its nest high up in a maple, and we were home alone because we were in fifth grade and our parents all had to work, so we smashed up worms and tried to feed the bird with Amber's mom's eyebrow tweezers. It died before any grown-ups could come home and tell us what to do, and we cried for hours and had a funeral for it. The bird's tiny headstone is probably still in Amber's backyard, along with the other memorial rocks we painted for random fish, a wild lizard, and her pet bunny, Patches.

Everything looks the exact same, except for the fact that there's no chalk on the concrete. Same trees, just a little higher. Her house is nicer and bigger than mine, and her dad always takes care of the yard. The house itself is the same tan it's always been, with the same dark green shutters and the same fancy white wood blinds that my mom always sighed over like they were made of diamonds. There's a lemon-yellow VW Bug in the driveway that I recognize from school, and my heart pounds as I realize that—big coincidence!—Amber is home too.

I try to pull out her Valor card and fumble everything in my hands. The signature machine, her card, Max's card—they all fall to the ground.

"Shit on a biscuit."

I bend over, feeling like a monumental idiot. I also realize, as

I squat and feel a tug in my britches, that it's going to be hard to pull a gun out from under my tucked-in shirt, so I untuck the back. Who cares if she thinks I'm a dorky slob? Not like she's going to tell anybody this time. Because either she's going to die, or she's going to accept a job she'll never be able to finish and won't want to talk about anyway. If there's one thing I know about Amber, it's that as nasty and snobby as she seems socially, there's not a killer bone in her body. Hurt things just break her heart, and she couldn't shoot an ax murderer any more than she would let herself be seen in public wearing Kmart jeans. I've always felt like there was some reason behind what she did to me. I'm pretty sure she felt bad even as she broke my heart.

I take a deep breath and step onto her porch, right next to the boot scraper that no one ever uses. It's shaped like a hedgehog, and we used to play all sorts of games with it. Now it's looking at me reproachfully, so I spin it around with my foot before I knock on the door. Ringing a doorbell just feels so . . . impersonal.

Inside, slippers slap on parquet floors. I hold up the signature machine and card and smile brightly at the exact moment that I know Amber is looking through the peephole. In the silence, I imagine her scowling, tossing the dark waves of her hair, wondering why the reject has shown up to plague her, terrified that I'll actually say out loud what a selfish bitch she is for leaving me in the dust as soon as she could.

The dead bolt unlocks, and the door opens inward. There she is, prettier and snottier than ever in expensive-looking yoga pants, a school spirit tee, and Minnie Mouse slippers.

"Hey." She says it like a challenge.

"Hi," I say. "Are you Amber Lane?"

"Are you retarded? You know who I am."

I wince. "Look, I'm just trying to do my job."

"Whatever." She rolls her eyes. "Is that for my dad?"

"Yeah. Just sign here."

I hand her the signature machine, and if she notices my hands shaking, she doesn't say anything as she signs her name in perky cursive. I click accept.

"Thanks," I say, but she doesn't say anything back, and she's looking anywhere except at my face. She's gotten really good at being a snob.

She holds out her hand expectantly, and I find that I've completely forgotten my speech. I have to read it from the card.

"Amber Lane, you owe Valor Savings Bank the sum of $21,502.03. Can you pay this sum in full?"

"Are you dicking around with me or what?" she says.

"Definitely not."

"I don't owe anyone anything."

I glare at her, and she has the good taste to look away.

"Look, you either pay up, agree to work for Valor, or . . ."

"Are you threatening me?"

For a moment, I just stare at her. "Yes."

Her mouth drops open. "What?"

"I'm threatening you."

"Are you trying to get me back for dropping you?" she says, voice sharp and loud, like we have an audience in the cafeteria. "Is this some kind of stupid prank? Why are you even out of school? Who told you I was skipping? Did you come here to confront me or get revenge or something?"

"Jesus, Am. Do you ever listen to yourself? Like, at all?"

She rolls her eyes and makes an affronted sound. I guess she's forgotten what it's like to have someone who knows you call you on your bullshit. That's probably why she's tried so hard to avoid me for the past four years.

I clear my throat and read straight from the card, hoping she'll get the picture and not be such a bitch.

"By Valor Congressional Order number 7B, your account is past due and hereby declared in default. Due to your failure to remit all owed monies and per your signature just witnessed and accepted, you are given two choices. You may either sign your loyalty over to Valor Savings as an indentured collections agent for a period of five days or forfeit your life. Please choose."

She gives a snide little laugh and speaks in the overly sweet voice bullies use right before they throw you in a locker. "Okay, that's hilarious. Either I have to give you all this money I don't have and didn't spend, or I have to work with you at a bank? Um, no thanks. How do you come up with this stuff?"

"You weren't listening, Am. There's a third option," I say, licking my lips nervously while hers glitter with lip gloss. "Pay, work . . . or die."

"Holy crap, Patsy!" she cackles. "You seriously think I'm going to believe all that? I've been pretty nice at school, not telling any more of your dirt. And believe me, I know more than you do. But you're gonna get bitch slapped if you keep this shit up."

I hand her the card, and she rips it in half without reading it and throws it on the ground.

"Fuck your reindeer games," she says with a practiced toss of her hair.

"Am, seriously. If you don't listen to me and say the right thing, I am going to pull out a gun and shoot you. I've already killed, like, ten people this week. You're a major bitch, but I don't want you to die."

"You are so demented. I can't believe we were ever friends."

"Why do you have credit card debt, anyway? You're seventeen, for Chrissakes."

I know I'm stalling. I don't care. Let Valor show up in their Humvees if I'm wasting their precious time. I'm still way ahead of schedule.

"I don't have credit card debt. My family does just fine, thank you." She holds up her French-manicured hands as if indicating how awesome her perfect life is.

I squat down and pick the card back up. I hold the two pieces together, up in front of her face. Her eyes were always a prettier, brighter blue than mine, her hair glossier and in perfect waves. She's like the A-plus version of me. Maybe that's why I didn't fight it when she dropped me. I never really deserved to be friends with someone as pretty and talented and special as Amber Lane, did I?

She reads the card, her arms crossed over her bulging chest, in the tight Big Creek Hornets T-shirt.

"This is kind of adorable," she says. "I can't believe you went to the trouble of printing it up on expensive paper. But seriously, even if you thought this little prank was cute? I don't have a credit card."

I know her tells, and she's not lying. I don't know what to do. Everyone else pretty much admitted they owed the money, except for Alistair, who was probably framed. But it's not like Amber's driving a brand-new car or wearing superexpensive clothes. Her family might be doing well by Candlewood standards, but they're not in the Dr. Ken Belcher league or even the Preserve league.

"Um, is there any chance your parents might have taken out a credit card in your name?" I say. "They can do that once you're over sixteen."

"No way," she says. "They would not do that to me."

But her pouty mouth is turned down at the corners. We both

remember when her mom found out her dad was cheating and when her mom lost her job and got caught shoplifting. Her parents have definitely made some mistakes, and by the look on her face, the puzzle is coming together. She glances nervously at her car and back to me, blue eyes gone from hate to fear.

"Look, Am. Maybe you could, I don't know . . . call Valor Savings and ask them. See if you have an account you don't know about. It doesn't have to go down this way."

"Oh, yeah. I'll get right on that," she says. "Just let me call customer service. You're a fucking joke, Patsy."

She tries to close the door on me, but I shove my foot inside.

"This is not a joke," I say. "Take the deal. This is kind of your only chance."

She slams the door on my foot, hard, and I show my teeth instead of whimpering.

"Seriously, Pats. Get your foot out of my door and go bother someone else who doesn't have a life."

Her eyes narrow to slits. She always had a short fuse.

"I really, really don't want to shoot you, but if it comes down to you or my mom . . ."

"You'll what—shoot me? Really? Look at yourself. I can smell you from here. You're filthy. You're dressed like a hobo. You're begging me for attention with this stupid, dumbass prank. You're trash, Patsy, and you're always going to be trash. That's why your dad left. My mom told me. He was rich, and you were an accident, and he disappeared as fast as he fucking could. Nobody wants you. And if you think you can just join the Postal Service mafia or whatever and show up and yell at me in my own house, you can go fuck yourself."

I go cold all over, and not just because of the insults.

"What did you say about my dad?"

She opens the door and puts her hands on her hips. "That's all you heard in that whole thing? Christ. He was rich. He was connected. He was your mom's boss, and he totally screwed her. They were never even married. I told you. You're a bastard, Pats."

I slap her right across the face, just like that. The crack is loud, although not as loud as a gunshot. But she looks just as surprised as if I'd shot her.

"Bitch, you do not want to mess with me," she growls. Her perfectly manicured fingers ball into fists, and her right cheek is a lot more red than her left. God, that felt good. I've been wanting to slap her for years. I should have done that a long time ago, when I still thought she was worth having as a friend.

I laugh, but it's humorless and frosty. I pull the gun out of the back of my jeans and aim it at her. I have never seen her look so surprised in my entire life, and on one level, it's fucking hilarious. On every other level, it is horrible, and I try to make my hand stop shaking. It's impossible.

"Take the deal, Am," I beg. "I already told you that if it came down to you or my mom, you were gone. It's come down to that, okay? Take the goddamn deal and don't make me shoot you."

"You th-think you can scare me?" she stutters. "You think you can show up at my door and wave a toy gun in my face, and I'm just going to do whatever you say?" She whips a smartphone out of her pocket and stares me down while she dials 911 with a smug grin. "You are so dead, Pats."

Far away, I hear ringing and then a recorded message. Her face goes three shades of white.

"Let me guess," I say. "Valor Savings can't come to the phone right now?"

She spins, runs back into her house, and slams the door. I toss the door open and run after her. I've got a straight shot down the hall, and I aim low. Arms outstretched and shaking, I pull the trigger once, and her hall mirror explodes. She gives a little scream, and I shoot again, and she grunts and falls over.

Without looking back at me, she tries to drag herself down the hall on her arms and one leg, but it looks like I got her right through the back of the knee. She's crying, and so am I, and I walk up behind her and catch her ankle with one hand. The other hand points the gun at her head, although I would never hit her there. It would be too much like shooting my own sister in the face, like shooting myself.

"Am, I am serious as a fucking heart attack," I say, the words slow and careful. "Take this deal, or I have to shoot you dead. If I don't, Valor Savings is going to kill my mom and then me, and that's not going to happen."

She tugs her good foot away from my hand, still trying to crawl away to some imaginary hiding place. Like I wouldn't find her, wherever she went. She's crying, her face turned away.

"Your mom ain't worth a sweet goddamn," she says. "I hope she dies. And I hope you rot in hell."

Her leg is shaking, the blood soaking through her yoga pants. The Minnie Mouse slipper lays forgotten on the parquet, and her toenails are painted a weird, warm gray. Her bare foot is turning a milky blue, even paler than usual. I sigh.

"All you have to do is take the deal. Just say it. Just say yes. I'll take you to the hospital. It doesn't have to end like this."

"Fuck. You."

Hearing her say that as she crawls, shot, dragging a trail of blood along her stupid, plushy carpet, breaks me.

"What the hell is it with you people?" I shout at her. I want to put my head in my hands and pull my hair until something snaps, but I can't let go of the gun. "Why can't you just accept what's going on and do whatever it takes to survive? What on earth would make a person ignore reality and be an asshole? It's a freaking gun, okay? This is real blood all over my shirt. I have been killing people all week just because they won't suck it up and take care of business. You're all a bunch of pussies! I fucking hate you, Amber!"

I realize I'm crying too, and it's absurd, the two of us here. Former best friends, alike as peas in a pod, except that her slippers cost more than my entire outfit and I'm the one holding a gun. She curls on her side, clutching her leg and moaning.

"Why aren't the police coming?" she says in a tiny voice. "Why was it Valor on the message?"

"Because Valor Savings owns everything now. Didn't you read the card? Didn't you read the little words above the signature box before you signed it?"

"Nobody reads that shit!" she screams at me, so hard that I can hear the rasp in the back of her throat. A dark spot stains the crotch of her yoga pants. She swallows and coughs. "Why, Patsy? Why are you doing this to me?"

"Because shit happens. Even to perfect, beautiful, popular, special little snowflakes like you, shit happens. I'm doing what they're forcing me to do. I'm sorry if you didn't actually rack up these debts yourself. Or if they're fake. But I will do whatever I have to do to live through this, and if you're smart, you will too. Now: Take. The. Deal."

She curls in tighter, rocking her head back and forth, her hands over her eyes.

"I can't, Patsy," she whispers in a baby voice. "I can't shoot people."

"Don't make me do this," I say. "Please don't."

I look at the gun in my hand, at how easily my chewed-up red and green fingernails curl around it. Like the gun has always been there, like it's a part of me. I'm about to kill my ex–best friend, whether she deserves it or not, and that's bound to change a person. All this time, I've been following the list, following their directions—mostly. I've been looking to the future, putting one foot in front of the next to get through my time. To pay a debt that isn't even mine.

Up until now, I never considered if I really deserved to live through it more than anyone else.

For just a second, I put the gun up to my temple. The metal is oddly cold against the thin skin there. Cold and hard. I press in a little, like a kiss, and I can smell the steel and oil. Why should I get to live? Even I'll admit that my mom's not special—not more special than anyone else. Probably less special than most. Why do I care so much? Why does she deserve to live? Why do I?

And then I laugh, short and humorless and final.

I deserve to live because I'm willing to do whatever it takes.

And I want out of this goddamn house of cards.

"Last chance, Am. Say yes and take the deal, or I kill you and walk away. You know that I'll do it."

She's curled up like a slug in a pool of salt. Her eyes find mine, brighter blue and hot with tears, and she stares at me as if I'm the fairy godmother that never showed up, a strange and magical creature that can't be understood.

"What did they do to you, Patsy? Who are you now?"

I press the gun gently to her head, right in the middle of her forehead. She breathes through her teeth, sobbing, eyes closed.

"You used to know who I was, Am," I say quietly. "Now neither of us knows. Take the deal. Please."

Her body shakes, balled up in a puddle of piss and blood. She tucks her head to the carpet, hands over her ears. Her words are so low and thready, I can almost imagine I didn't hear them. "Would it change anything if I told you we're cousins? And that your dad used to work for Valor?"

"Tell me more," I say.

She shakes her head. "Only if you promise to let me go."

"Say you'll take the deal."

She shakes her head again. "Fuck you, Pats."

I step around her, put the gun in the middle of her back, and pull the trigger.

When I walk out a few minutes later, my tears have dried, and I'm carrying her body in the quilt that matches mine.

10.

MAXWELL BEARD

Wyatt sits in the open driver's seat, his body and attention focused toward Amber's house and a gun in his hand. As if he could keep me alive through sheer force of will. He's got one arm through the window, stroking Matty, who's trying to cram her cone into the front of the truck. That crazy dog must have heard shots and tried to rescue me again. Thank heavens Wyatt didn't let her out.

"You okay?" he shouts. "I heard two . . . uh, firecrackers. And what the hell is that?"

I rush to the back of the truck, struggling under the weird dead-weight of my ex–best friend. She's thin but long, floppy but stiff, and I can barely hold on to the quilt with my bugged shirt wadded up in one hand so they won't know I took her. Wyatt opens the tailgate and helps me slide Amber's body in. Matty sniffs the bundle through her cone and whines, nudging it with her big paw.

"Let it go, girl," I say. "She's gone."

I shove the blood-spattered Postal Service shirt into the glove box and slam the door shut so hard it bounces back.

"Is she dead?"

"Yeah." I sniffle and rub tears onto my arm. Amber was right. I stink. "I even shot her in the leg first, gave her an extra chance. But she cussed at me right to the end. Like she didn't think I would do it."

Damn it all, I'm crying again, and I slump against the truck. Wyatt gets out and comes around to hold me, but I shove him away and say, "Just drive. Please. Get me away from here."

He doesn't ask me why I brought her body, and I'm not sure I know why myself. It just seemed wrong, leaving a girl I used to love lying in a pool of blood outside her parents' bedroom. Her mom and dad made plenty of mistakes and weren't the best folks ever, but they loved Amber in their way. I couldn't stand to think of her mom, Chrissy, coming home and finding that mess, her daughter just left there sprawled in the hallway in a puddle of piss like nobody cared. Even after this girl said the nastiest things she'd ever thought about me right to my face when I had a gun in my hand, I still feel the closeness we used to share. She was the best friend I ever had, until she wasn't my friend anymore.

And she said we were cousins. What the hell was that? Was she just trying to sink a knife in my back with the kind of lie that would cut me deepest? Was she trying to buy time with the topic that would make me drop the gun and beg for an explanation? Or was she trying to tell me a secret she'd known all along, the real reason she ended our friendship? What instinct deep in my heart jerked my trigger finger moments after she and Ashley Cannon each revealed that we were kin?

Now I can't ask either of them. But there has to be a way to find out. Somehow, I know it all goes back to my missing dad.

In the bed of the truck, Matty is on her belly next to the quilt, her cone lying gently along where I know Amber's head is. I put my cheek to the window and sob. I didn't just kill the Amber Lane that swanned around school in her fancy clothes with her rich friends. I also killed Am, the girl I used to watch scary movies with and play dolls with and trade My Little Ponies with. Maybe I killed my cousin.

"I'm so sorry," I whisper, half to her and half to myself, and maybe to Wyatt, too.

I don't know what to do with Amber. I watched her quit breathing, and then I watched some more, just to make sure. And then I realized that I couldn't leave her alone like that. The best thing I can think of is to bury her out at the Preserve with Jeremy, maybe find a nice climbing tree that she would have liked when she was nine and let go of her memory. She never spoke a single word to Jeremy in her life, but I loved them both, and they deserve proper rest.

Maybe her parents will think she just ran away. Or maybe they'll see the blood soaked into the carpet, get the message Valor left on 911, and always wonder, always hope. Maybe, one day, I'll send them an anonymous card or something. I'm not thinking straight right now, and I know it. But I can't escape the fact that I'm stuck with a quilt full of what used to be my friend, and it hurts so goddamn bad.

Matty belly-crawls over to the window, toenails scraping on the metal floor. I unbuckle my seat belt and unlatch her stupid cone hat so she can get her face into the cab. I know the vet said to keep it on, but she seems fine and happy and isn't messing with the shaved spot on her neck, and her square head feels good under my hand. I stroke the silky black fur, and her deep brown eyes roll over to look at me.

"This is one seriously messed-up world," I say.

Her tail thumps against the camper wall a few times, and I can almost imagine her saying, *Honey, you ain't seen nothing yet.*

I guess it's pretty lucky that Alistair had a top on this old Ford. It's not like there's a cot or anything, but at least it's covered from the elements, in case we need to sleep back there. And, yeah, I guess that's exactly why a conspiracy theorist ready to run would go to the trouble to have a truck waiting for the day Valor caught up with him.

I look up, and we're on a familiar street, but I don't know where

Wyatt is taking us. We pass his old neighborhood, that glorious flock of giant floating castles, which could only have been built with credit, with empty promises, with smoke and mirrors. I wish I knew how many rooms in each house sit empty. How many are guest rooms that are never used. How many hold exercise equipment that goes untouched, or sewing machines still in the box. So much waste, and for what? These people weren't happy. Wyatt's father wasn't happy. Fat, balding, anxious, petty, mean. It all meant nothing. They spent nonexistent money on things they didn't need that didn't even make their lives any better.

And for the first time ever, I long for our tiny, lived-in, no-frills house on Bluebird Drive. I wonder what my mom is doing, if she's even alive, if she's made her appointment with the doctor yet or is endlessly saying her rosaries, waiting for me to come home. I realize that we've kind of traded places, that I've become her parent. And maybe that's why I was able to look Amber in the eyes and kill her. I don't have much, but I have to keep what's mine safe.

And what did Amber mean about my dad? He was rich and worked for Valor? And that's why he left us? My mom never said anything about him, ever. I just have vague, sunny memories, an old gun, and the photo from Ashley Cannon's house. I know Ashley is dead, but who is the third man in the photo? All the questions I've asked over the years have been met with stony, tight-lipped silence. For all that my mama was always loving and went out of her way to find answers to most of my questions, she really stuck to her guns on that one thing, the thing I wanted most to know.

But if he was rich, why wouldn't he help us out? Why wouldn't he send checks, or pay off the house, or even drop anonymous birthday cards in the mail? If he had extra money all this time, what was more important than me? Did I get my amazing math skills and tenacity from him? And if he worked for Valor, why would he allow them to target me like this? I wish for the hundredth time that I'd had more time to poke around at Ashley Cannon's house.

I tug the folded photo out of my back pocket and stare at the three people smiling in front of the dead buck. My dad's face in the photograph is the face I remember from when I was four, the face I always saw in my dreams—but more haggard. Uncle Ashley looks about five years younger than my dad. The third man is clearly their father—my grandfather, I guess. He's a broad guy with gray, military hair and a beard that makes him look like a wolf. But it's not like they were posed in front of a Valor-branded Humvee. They could have been hunting in the woods behind the soccer field at school, or they could have been on a private estate somewhere, for all I know. And Uncle Ashley did have a mighty large television for a poor guy, not that that means much anymore.

Could they all be related to Valor somehow?

The truck crunches to a stop, and Wyatt gets out and walks

around to open my door like we're on some freaky date. Or maybe he can sense that my hands don't work anymore.

"Are you—"

I interrupt him by jumping out and throwing my arms around his neck. I don't think I've stopped crying since Amber's house, but now I really let it all out. He freezes at first, like he's not sure what to do, like maybe I'm a bomb that's about to explode. Then his arms wrap around me, warm and sure and strong, and he edges back into the passenger seat and pulls me into his lap. I bawl my eyes out into his two-day-old band shirt. He smells ripe as hell, but there's something comforting about it, something raw and real. He rubs my back and murmurs things to me, nonsense words, just "Come on, now," and "It's going to be okay," that sort of thing. Matty's nose and tongue flop around, hunting for us through the window, but she can't reach us. I'm glued to the boy at every possible juncture like a frightened octopus.

I finally get myself together enough to snuffle, "This fucking sucks."

"I know it does," he whispers in my ear. "I know. But the hard part is over."

Now it's my turn to freeze. I swallow hard and pull back to look at him, wiping my nose on the corner of my blood-spattered tank like it doesn't matter. I guess I always figured I would throw all these shirts out afterward, anyway. Wyatt tries to pull me back close, but I can feel the tension in his body. I heard what he said, and he knows I heard it, and he knows he's going to have to explain.

"What do you mean the hard part is over?" I ask. "Isn't your brother the next name on that list?"

"I didn't mean it that way. I meant the hard part for you. Not me. I mean, you don't know you're going to have to kill Max. He can be pretty smart. And tough. Maybe he'll take the deal."

"Yeah." I cock my head. "But you don't look worried."

"I'm worried about you right now," he says. "We'll worry about Max when it comes to that."

I push back from his chest, scoot away, and stand just outside the reach of his arms. We're back at the end of the dirt road where we started this morning. It feels like that was a million years ago.

"It's now, Wyatt. It comes to it now. He's the last one. I deal with him, and this nightmare is over. There's something you're not telling me."

"Jesus, girl. You just killed your childhood best friend. You're shaken up. Do we have to talk about this now? Do you want some food? Sleep?"

My eyes narrow at him. "I want the truth."

"What truth?"

"The truth about Max. This whole time, you've kind of ignored it, danced around it. But you've never said much about him, aside from y'all hanging out in the woods. You never told me what your brother was like, or how old he is, or if he lives with you, or what he did to run up all that debt."

"I guess I'm guilty of focusing on you," Wyatt says, but he's nervous. His knee is jiggling, and Matty is staring at him solemnly with those big brown eyes of hers. She's like a living lie detector, and she knows something is fishy.

"Do we trust each other, or not?" I say. More tears sting my eyes, but I wipe them away. "I mean, I trust you. I gave you my gun. And now you're not telling me something, and I'm starting to feel like a total dumbass. Do you even like me?"

"You know goddamn well I do!" he growls. "I don't mean to keep bringing it up, but I ran into a gunfight for you. Twice. I've driven you from place to place and watched you kill people. I've helped you chase them. I've fed you. I shot a man because I thought he was going to lay a hand on you. It's the worst damn timing on earth, but you have to know I like you! You feel it too. I know you do."

"What do I know?" I say, bitterness seeping out of me like pickle juice. "I'm just a murderer with bad luck. Why would a guy like you want to get involved with me, outside of keeping his brother alive and maybe getting to second base a few times?"

"Is that really what you think of me?" he asks, just as cold as frozen ground.

My heart screams *no*, but my mouth whispers, "I don't know what to think anymore."

He looks at me, his eyes hard and dark. Everything about him is bigger than me, and in a different world he would be my champion, my knight, my protector. But here he's just been my chauffeur, my chef, my shield. Maybe I pretended he was my boyfriend, but I was naive, and whatever the world is going to become, right now it's all-out war.

Or maybe that's just in my heart.

Real gentle, he moves me aside so he can get out of the truck. He pulls his gun, my other gun, out of the back of his jeans and places it softly on the passenger seat.

"You think about what you just said. And when you realize you're lying to yourself, you come find me. You know where I'll be."

Turning his back on me, Wyatt walks away for the second time while Matty howls like her heart's breaking too.

"Shit, shit, shit!" I shout at the afternoon sky.

He left me in the truck with my dog and a dead girl. And he took the keys when he left. I've got no idea where I am, it's going to be dark in a few hours, and all our food burned up with the mail truck. Maybe I should just go to Wyatt's house and kill his brother and go the fuck home. I pull the postal shirt out from the glove box and look at the last card. Maxwell Beard owes Valor $18,325.63. It doesn't seem possible, unless Robert Beard took out a loan in his older son's name. What does a rich man's kid need that much money for, anyway? Then again, Amber's debt didn't seem possible either. I almost tear up the card in anger, but I'm so close. So close to saving my mom's life.

If she's still alive. If the house hasn't been burned down. If I've followed all the rules closely enough. If they're not mad about the truck. If I can find Max Beard.

If, if, if.

Repress, repress, repress.

The sun is almost down, the air clean and clear and cold. Normally, I love nights like this. It's just the right temperature so that we don't need the air conditioner, heater, or fans, which means I don't fret about paying for them. I love snuggling under thick blankets and sleeping so deeply that I don't dream, that I can't bolt up in the early morning, driven awake by nightmares and worry. Last night I woke up to bullets and tragedy. This morning I woke up in Wyatt's arms. Tonight I'll sleep alone under a quilt, the doppelgänger of the one wrapped around Amber's corpse.

I pull down the tailgate, and Matty jumps to the ground before I can stop her. She whimpers when she lands but charges off into the forest and squats, tail wagging gratefully, poor girl. I think about making a bed in back, but there's no way I could sleep next to Amber. Instead, I pull out my knitting bag and get back in the passenger seat to hunt around for a color that seems right. None of them do, not really, but I grab a new set of needles and cast on twelve stitches in dark green. I knit furiously by the light of the truck cab, the door open to what should be a beautiful night. I knit like my needles are on fire, like something will explode if I don't knit fast enough. At home it was so plodding and normal. Now it's like knitting on crack while Matty watches me patiently from the ground outside, her tail occasionally thumping the dirt. But it's soothing, and I find my thoughts unwinding with the yarn. I wish it were mohair or angora, something soft and lovely, but acrylic will have to do.

I knit it straight through, hundreds and hundreds of rows. I switch back and forth between the green and a ball of heather gray, stripe after stripe after stripe until I'm out of yarn. By the time I finish the scarf, I know exactly what I have to do.

November got cold, fast, especially considering I'm walking up a pitch-dark dirt track in the middle of nowhere. Matty plods by my side, and only the fact that she's perfectly chill keeps me from wigging out. I just hope that when I reach the main road, I'll know where I am, and it won't be too far to where I'm going.

The only comfort is that whatever happens, it will be over soon. I've technically got ten hours left, but I don't want them. And after being confronted by Jeremy, I suspect that Second Union and Valor don't play by the same rules. One name is left on the list. One more task before I can ditch the bugged shirt. Either I take care of Max Beard, or my mom's not going to need any expensive treatments.

I haven't allowed myself to consider it before, but now I have to. For her, knowing what she has to go through and having met Eloise Framingham, a quick death by a Valor bullet might be preferable. For about three seconds, I think about crushing the button, burning the shirt, going home, getting in the car with my mom, and running away, going into hiding. But people hiding from the new government can't get chemo.

Max Beard it is.

I see the turnoff to the real road up ahead, a strange silhouette waiting under the lone streetlight at the top of the hill. It's one of those flashing construction cones, and on it sits an extra-large energy drink, a banana, and the truck keys. So Wyatt came back. Not all the way, not close enough to touch, but close enough to leave transportation and food, both of which I need much more than some stupid love note from a guy who couldn't possibly love me. I'm a practical girl, and I learned at an early age that actions speak louder than words.

Banana in one hand and crappy flavored drink in the other, I walk back down the dirt road with keys in my pocket and a slightly lighter heart. It's full dark now, which means I have to take care of my final task by the truck's dome light. I feed Matty some water-soaked kibble, finish the banana, do my business in the grass, and give myself a chilly but thorough wipe-down with my shower wipes. I don't exactly feel clean, but I feel better. Another pair of white panties out of the package, a fresh white tank, my last pair of jeans. I pull the Postal Service shirt from under the passenger seat and hold it out at arm's length. It's wrinkled, and the black thread on the resewn button gives it an air of Frankenstein. The blood of two people and a dog are impossible to miss against the cheap, light blue fabric. I think about putting it on, but I ball it back up around the signature machine instead.

I'm going in as me, the real me. Not the assassin. Just Patsy. And anyway, he has to know I'm coming. He told me to.

I stare at the blanket-wrapped form nestled in the truck bed. One last adventure for Am and Pats. It doesn't even feel real anymore. Whatever there was of Amber is long gone. But I can barely lift her by myself, and I don't have any way to dig a grave, and I can't leave her out here for the animals to ravage. Bringing her with me made sense at the time, but now I feel like it's one of the stupidest things I've ever done in my life. It's impossible to forget for a single second that there's a body just inches away. There's no way I could sleep out here. So now she's going with me.

I haven't driven a big truck like this before. I feel like a little kid sitting in the driver's seat, figuring out which levers to pull. I have to scoot the seat forward just to reach the pedals. It's weird not to have the GPS for the last name on my list. But I know where he lives.

"Turn around at your earliest convenience if you wish to kill

Maxwell Beard," I say in a fake British accent. "Take the motorway to break Wyatt's heart." I giggle madly and choke on a sob.

The truck bumps over rocks and grass as I turn it around in a wide circle and follow the tire tracks through the mud and back up to the street. I edge the truck around Wyatt's traffic cone and reach into the passenger seat to pat Matty before turning onto the road that leads to the Preserve.

A few short minutes later, I'm parked in front of the house where it all began. I was so scared then. I remember fumbling everything, waiting until the last possible moment. Juggling the basket and the machine and the card and the gun. I was an amateur. Now I'm a professional. An assassin. A stone-cold killer. So why are my hands shaking just like they did then? Why am I on the verge of puking?

Because it's personal now, I guess.

Because Valor Savings made sure it would be personal.

The door is closed, and I wonder what happened to Bob's body. Did Wyatt and Max drag him inside the house and wrap him up, like I did with Amber? If the police weren't answering the phone, was the coroner? Is there a shortage of coffins and preachers? Has anyone outside of the conspiracy wackos even made the connection between Valor Savings and the hundreds, maybe thousands, maybe millions of people killed at their front doors, puzzlement and outraged shame etched in their foreheads forever?

It occurs to me now—I never asked.

I never asked Wyatt what he had done with his dad. If he had cried. If he needed help digging a grave. If he wanted me to come to the funeral, or if there would even be one. I was so wrapped up in what I had to do to keep my mom safe and stay alive that I completely ignored the fact that he had just lost a parent. Because of me. Even if he claimed not to like his dad, it still had to hurt, somewhere inside that he kept hidden. If there's one thing I can relate to, it's the pain of losing a father.

I pretended to be Wyatt's girlfriend for a few days, just for myself. For my own comfort and curiosity and selfishness. And I was a really shitty girlfriend.

I fluff my hair and smooth my bangs. I wish I had some ChapStick, as I can't seem to stop chewing my lip. But at least I'm not covered in blood anymore. Not visibly.

The walk to the front door is the same as before, except that it's midnight, and there's a black Lab at my side, trailing a borrowed leash. The yellow grass, the fallen tree, the strange combination of wealth and absence, the excruciating pain and fear at what awaits—they all combine with the cold stars to make the world seem bleak and past its prime. Matty sniffs everything energetically, and I'm glad that she, at least, can be happy in this moment. I knock on the door, heart in throat, hoping Wyatt will answer.

Not Max. Please don't be Max.

The door swings open, and there he is. Wyatt. Half of my imaginary "we." Freshly showered, in another pair of plaid pajama pants, bigger than life and taller than I remember with a gold and brown snake wrapped around his arm. But why is he wearing the shirt of a band I hate?

"You're early," he says as if nothing happened, and I wonder if this is a trait unique to him or something all boys do, this stubborn ignorance that refuses to face the facts. He kneels to ruffle Matty's neck fur.

"I tried to call you on my banana, but you didn't answer," I say, and he laughs, which is gratifying, because I spent the entire drive over trying to think of a way to thank him that wouldn't make me break down crying. I look down, and he absentmindedly rubs the snake's head.

"Yeah," he says with a grin. "I ate mine."

He stands back, and I walk in with Matty at my side, stepping over a shiny place in the wood where I last saw Robert Beard's body. A lacrosse stick and a rifle lean together in the corner by the door, as if he was expecting trouble. I didn't set a foot inside this house last time, but I remember the unseasonal warmth. It smells like a house without women, without potpourri or fabric softener or perfume. Kind of stale, too warm, with trash left in the kitchen too long.

Wyatt shuts the door behind me and says, "Did you know Matty is the first dog ever to be allowed in this house? Max is hella allergic."

"Is that Max?" I point to the snake.

Wyatt laughs. "That's Monty. Max is taller. Nice attempt at levity, though."

"Is he here?" I ask nervously. "Not because I want to . . . I mean . . ." I look down, hold out my arms. "No ugly shirt, no bugged button, no gun. I just want to talk. Promise." I spin around and hold up my shirt to show that the waistband of my jeans is empty. When I turn back to face him, there's a warm hunger in Wyatt's eyes that makes me blush. I guess these jeans are lowriders, after all.

He swallows hard and says, "He's not here now. We can talk. You still hungry?"

"Yeah," I admit. "Starving."

He leads me to the kitchen and tries to hand me the curled snake. I shake my head, so he places it gently in one of those hanging baskets that is supposed to hold fruit. I'm not big into snakes, so I'm glad I already ate my banana. Wyatt's culinary skills are pretty lacking, but it's hard to mess up buttered toast. I sit on a bar stool, rubbing my feet on Matty's back and keeping an eye on the snake as I watch Wyatt inhale half a bag of bread and an entire stick of butter. I guess he's the reason six-slice toasters exist. My own toast turns to concrete in my stomach as I huddle behind my coffee mug, breathing in the warmth, hoping it will give me the energy I need to start this conversation.

And the guts I need to end it.

"So," I say.

"So," he echoes.

"Where's your dad? Do you need help with anything? I'm . . ." I swallow down the toast like it's a giant, bitter pill. "I'm sorry I didn't ask before."

He winces in pain, inclines his head to the back porch, his jaw tight. "We have a freezer for deer meat, from when we used to hunt. It's been empty a while. Has a lock. It was the best I could do." He stares at his hands a moment, tears in his eyes, and I imagine what it must be like to hold your parent's dead body in your arms. I hope I never have to find out.

"I'm sorry, Wyatt. I'm so sorry."

"Don't say that anymore. Not your fault."

He wipes away tears and slides my coffee closer, and I drink it, forcing the toast back down.

"So I don't want to kill your brother."

"I know."

"Yeah, but . . . I'm not talking philosophically. Like, I obviously don't *want* to kill anyone. But I don't even want to ask him the question and show him the card."

Wyatt looks happy, then puzzled, then cagey. "What changed?" he asks.

"Well . . ." I take a sip of coffee. "I want you to kill me instead."

Wyatt splutters out his coffee, staining his white shirt with brown splotches. I'm kind of pleased with myself—if he's surprised, then maybe everyone else will be surprised too. Plus, I really do hate that band.

"I can't do that," he says, and he's more scared than I've ever seen him. "You can't do that. There has to be another way."

"I have a plan. But I need you to trust me. And I need to know I can trust you."

We stare at each other, knee to knee. Matty sits between us.

"Can I trust you?" I ask. "For real?"

"I . . . It's just . . ."

"Spit it out. Yes or no."

"You can trust me. But I need to tell you something."

I shrug. How bad can it be? "Okay. Tell me."

"Just promise me you'll hear me out."

"No."

"My God, you are a harsh woman," he says, half annoyed and half impressed. "I'm going to try anyway. Okay, so Max is on your list, right?"

"Right."

"He's my brother. He's . . ." He looks down, bites a cuticle. "He's severely autistic. Like, only aware of other people for a few minutes a day, maybe. Most of the time, he's either watching *The Dark Knight* or lost in his own world or a major rage Hulk, really violent. He has to stay under constant watch or he'll hurt himself. Or us. Or me, I guess."

I look up as if I had X-ray vision and could see through the kitchen ceiling. "So he's not actually here?"

Wyatt shakes his head. "As soon as my dad . . . got hurt . . . I called Max's doctor and took him to Calloway House, the hospital facility where he stays when no one is home to watch him. I didn't know he was on your list. I just knew I couldn't take care of things here if he was around. I mean, the only reason I was home when you showed up was because my dad couldn't handle Max alone, and his credit card got rejected at Calloway again. My dad has . . . had . . . a bad back. I'm the only person in the family who can handle Max when he gets dangerous."

"Then why would Valor send me here?" I ask. "Every single person on the list has been exactly where the GPS said they would be, exactly when I showed up. Why would he be completely out of the picture? And how can a severely autistic kid apply for a credit card?"

Wyatt takes a deep breath and sets down his toast.

"He was supposed to be home, but I took him to Calloway. Because he didn't take out the credit card. He didn't run up the debt." Wyatt swallows hard, and looks directly into my eyes. "I did."

Suddenly, it all adds up. Wyatt was a bad boy. He was in trouble. He did horrible things that he's ashamed of. He illegally took out credit cards in his disabled brother's name, and now that brother is on my hit list. That pretty much makes Wyatt a murderer.

"Shit," I whisper. "Does that mean I was supposed to kill you all along?"

"Hell no," he says fiercely. "I would do the exact same thing you did. I would take the deal. In a heartbeat."

"Really?"

"Really."

I throw myself into his arms, which he isn't expecting at all. He catches me and pulls me roughly against his chest, and the spilled coffee bleeds cold into my own shirt. His jaw moves against my head as he says, "Not the reaction I was expecting."

"No," I say, nearly breathless. "I mean, you were a total dick to do that to your own brother. But that was a long time ago. That's not who you are now."

"I've been making payments. For the last year, I've been trying to pay it off. I swear."

"Too bad they decided to eff you over and call it in anyway."

"My dad kept giving me my allowance like nothing was wrong, like he wasn't already in debt. So I just sent it all in to Valor. Sold my bass and my amp, too. I hadn't used that credit card in years, up until you needed it this week."

"I couldn't believe you'd be taking out any more debt, even for Matty. But now I get it," I mumble into his chest.

"They couldn't do anything worse to me than they were doing to you."

I hug him again, hard. He hugs me back and murmurs, "What's that for?" into my hair.

"That's for making me feel human again. Because if you would take the deal too, then I'm not a horrible person. Or, at least, I'm not the only one. This whole time, I've known that I didn't have a choice, but I still felt guilty. Every single second, so much guilt. But if you think it's worth it, if you agree that it's better than the alternative, that it's worth it to fight . . ."

"Then I think you're worth it too," he finishes for me, pulling me close again.

Matty whines, and I reach down to rub her ears as Wyatt strokes my hair.

"So do you forgive me?" he asks.

"If you forgive me," I say. Then, more quietly, "And I trust you."

He pulls my chin up and brushes his lips against mine, and I lean in to him and pull him closer for more. We teeter together, filling the space between the tall stools, our mouths tentative but smiling as they meet.

Matty barks, and we break apart, laughing. But it's a joyous bark, and we each reach out to pet her, making a complete circle.

"Will he ever get better?" I ask. The fridge has a few photos, one of which shows Wyatt with his arm tight around an almost identical version of himself. Max has thick glasses and side-parted hair, and they're standing on top of a mountain. The other kid is looking away, eyes unfocused, as if he might jump off the cliff without Wyatt's arm holding him down. "Max?"

"He doesn't need to get better. He's himself. He's just different," Wyatt says, sounding affronted, and I realize he's probably said this many times. "He's as good to me as he can be, even though I was a pretty annoying brother, wanted to follow him everywhere when he always needed lots of space. He really loves Batman and the Transformers and likes to build robots and draw their insides, really complicated stuff. When my parents divorced, they made me choose who to go with, and I chose my dad because I wanted to give my mom freedom, give her the chance at a real life where she wasn't weighed down by her asshole husband and her difficult kid. I thought I'd have more freedom with my dad, too, that he wouldn't care how much trouble I got into while he was taking care of Max. And I was right. But living with him—I hated him and I wanted out. I tried to change my mind, so I could move in with my mom instead, but my dad said Max and I had to stay together. He said I'd made my decision and had to deal with the consequences. Kind of ironic, really."

"Jesus," I say. "That all . . . just plain sucks."

"Well, at least it means you don't have to shoot him." He reaches out a hand to catch the snake stretching across the counter.

"But I think it means I'm supposed to shoot you, Wyatt Beard."

"But you want me to shoot you instead."

"Exactly," I say. "But put down the snake and kiss me first, before I lose my nerve."

11.

PATSY KLEIN

I'm back in the truck, buttoning on my Postal Service shirt for the last time. Matty knows something is up, and she runs back and forth from the truck to Wyatt's front door. If I could put this nasty shirt on without touching it, I would. I hated it from the first second I felt the cheap, sharp collar against my neck and the scratchy eagle patch against my chest. Now the stiffness is gone, but the essential horror of the thing is exponentially worse. I shove on the mail cap and twirl the camera button between my fingers, wishing I had looked more closely at the one I found spread out in pieces in Alistair Meade's trailer. What exactly can Valor see and hear on the other end of this connection? How well can it see at night? For now I leave it unbuttoned and flopped over against my chest. These final minutes are private.

I grab my signature machine and the last card, the one for Maxwell Beard. Every movement is familiar, rote, just like putting on shoes and socks and tying the laces in a bow. The last thing I do is tuck the gun in my waistband, the weight now as familiar as a hand in mine. I know exactly how hard to squeeze the trigger.

"I'm sorry, girl," I say, tying Matty's leash to the truck's trailer hitch. She strains against it and whines, and I double tie it just to make sure.

Since my first step onto this cracked sidewalk, I've made all sorts of mistakes, all sorts of fumbles. It was unavoidable. There's a learning curve to killing. Every time you pick up the gun, your hands shake less, you don't second-guess yourself as much. Each time it hurts less, until it's just a job, just one more thing scratched off the list, just another justification for something you know is wrong.

But you do it like you do anything: step after step. Because you have to. And with each kill, you lose a little piece of yourself, forever.

I remember when I was little, asking why I had to go to school, and my mom explained that you didn't have a choice.

"I don't want to go to work," she said. "I'd rather stay home and watch TV, clean the house, watch the bird feeder. I'd rather make cookies for you every day and be home when the bus gets here. But adults have to go to work, and it will be that way for the rest of your life, so you might as well get used to it. You might not like it, but for now, school is your work. So do a good job, and one day, you'll be rewarded for your hard work."

It feels weird, knowing that I will never go to school again.

That I will never get to wake up and go to a harmless job I don't like.

That there was never a reward waiting anyway.

My mom said do what you have to, and the world said do what you love, and I ended up a murderer.

I take one last look around the blue truck. I almost miss the mail van, with my old posters and pillows and turtles. But I still have my yarn bag and the scarf that I'll never stitch around the school flagpole. There's my old backpack, full of dirty white underwear and T-shirts stained with dirt and blood and nervous sweat. I squat down and hug Matty hard.

"I love you, girl," I say. She licks my face happily. It's sweet, how dogs don't understand good-byes.

I adjust my cap and stand. My fingers are numb as I button the shirt, all the way to my throat, a hug that strangles. The sidewalk stretches out before me like a tightrope walker's wire, a long straight line that can lead to satisfaction or utter doom with one false step. I do what I've done all along, what I've done my entire life: I put one foot in front of the other, step by step, until I stand again at the front door, under the porch light. There are two small bloodstains on the stairs, and I wonder for just a moment if Bob Beard will haunt this house forever, restless and dissatisfied and angry at everyone but himself.

I reach out and knock, counting the breaths until the door opens.

"Are you Maxwell Beard?" I ask.

"Yes."

He's wearing baggy sweatpants and a black shirt with the Bat symbol on it, his hair side-parted over thick glasses. He shuffles his feet and scratches his back like his shirt tag itches him and looks over my left shoulder like I'm not there.

"Sign this, please."

He takes the signature machine, signs it, and avoids my eyes as I click the accept button.

"Maxwell Beard," I say, just a little too fast. "You owe Valor Savings Bank the sum of $18,325.63. Can you pay this debt in full?"

He shakes his head, his hands in fists and his movements jerky. "Debt. Money. 'You're garbage who kills for money.' *The Dark Knight*, 2008."

I shake my head and hold up a blood-stained green card. "By Valor Congressional Order number 7B, your account is past due and hereby declared in default. Due to your failure to remit all owed monies and per your signature just witnessed and accepted, you are given two choices. You may either sign your loyalty over to Valor Savings as an indentured collections agent for a period of five days or forfeit your life. Please choose."

His hands uncurl as his face goes red. He takes a step out toward me, and I take a step back because he's freaking scary. "Choose what? That doesn't make sense!"

"Just calm down," I say. "I didn't have a choice. But you do. You can either pay it right now or work for Valor Savings as a bounty hunter. Or else I have to kill you." I look meaningfully down at the bloodstains.

"No! You're a villain!" he shouts, spit flying from his mouth. Everything about him is off balance, the way he's moving and the rough childishness of his deep voice. "You hurt my dad. Wyatt told me. Wyatt said you would come back, and I told him I was going to do what Batman would do. You either die a hero or you live long enough to see yourself become the villain. Harvey Dent said that." He shakes his head like he's beating it against a wall. "No, No! You can't just shoot people because a paper says so."

"Max, c'mon," I say, holding out my hands in front of me. "Calm down. We can talk about this. Take the deal. It's not that bad. You can be a hero."

He steps inside the house and comes back pointing a gun at me with both hands, his arms shaking, his face a rictus of fear and rage. I whip mine out too and aim for his chest, but I'm not fast enough. He looks me in the eyes for the first time.

"I'm not a hero!" he yells.

His gun goes off, and my gun goes off, and I'm deaf as I tumble backward into the dry bushes. Overhead, the sky is flat black poked through with white bullet holes, peaceful and cold. I'm numb all over as I lay there and wait for whatever is next.

12.

VALOR SAVINGS

Matty barks like crazy. As I lay there, half on the sidewalk, a bare foot kicks me bonelessly over to my stomach. Once I'm there, my face scratched by dead leaves and my hands buried in bark, I carefully reach in a hand and pop the top button off my shirt, burying it deeper into the mulch. Once it's completely covered with dirt, I sit up and scrape more bark and mulch and dry leaves over it until there's no sign that anything ever happened there.

"You okay?" Wyatt whispers, and he gives me a hand up and pulls me tight into a hug. Max's Batman shirt smells weird, like a kid's banana-scented shampoo, but I hug him back gratefully.

"Yeah," I say. "But that bullet almost nicked me. I heard it whistle past."

"It had to seem real," he says. "Same thing you told me once. That's the hardest thing I've ever done."

"I've done worse," I say, thinking back to Amber's fingernails curling into the carpet. "But it's close. Let's hurry."

When I was coming up with this plan, I thought back to each kill. The only ones that seemed to have reactions from Valor were the ones who took the deal, the one at Chateau Tuscano, and Alistair. All the others, including Wyatt's dad and the neighbor of the lady at the vet—they left the bodies behind. They only seem to care if there's something they need from the name on the list.

We carry Amber's body from inside the house, and I shudder at the cold, clammy touch of her wrists. She's going stiff, and my skin crawls, to see her so Amber but not Amber. Dressing her in my old tee and jeans was almost impossible, but we did it. I'm starting to believe we can do anything.

I unbutton my Postal Service shirt and thread it over her arms. Wyatt helps me lift and turn her body facedown in the spot I've just vacated, and I tie my flagpole cozy around her neck like a scarf and step away from her for the last time. Splayed out in the mulch, right where I was lying a few moments ago, her dark hair cut with my yarn scissors, she looks just like me. I shudder, thinking how close to the truth that is. I throw the mail hat down beside her. I guess my last act as a yarn bomber is to remind Valor that they couldn't change me, much less kill me.

We could have been sisters. Maybe we were cousins.

One had everything. One had nothing.

Now the situation is reversed.

I stand over her, tears streaming down my face for so many reasons. Wyatt seems to understand that I need a few moments, and he
just stands behind me, his hands on my shoulders. A few cold drops
fall from his wet hair onto my neck, shocking me out of my stillness.
A few warm tears fall too.

"We have to go," I whisper.

"Then let's go."

His car is already parked in front of the old blue truck. I untie
Matty and help her hop into the back seat of the gold Lexus, where
she sniffs Monty's traveling aquarium, as Wyatt downright refused
to leave his snake behind. I'd be pissed about that boy's big heart if
it hadn't saved my ass a dozen times. Apparently, snakes don't smell
like food, as Matty immediately presses her nose to the window and
leaves behind a smear of dog slobber. Wyatt's backpack full of band
shirts and jeans is in the trunk, but all of my things are in the back
of the camper truck, right where Valor would expect to find them. I
don't know what I'll wear tomorrow or when I'll get to shower for
real again. But we're keeping all four of the guns and all the bullets.
And we've got Alistair Meade's laptops, too. I have a feeling those are
the key to everything that's happened to me, and I intend to crack
their codes as soon as we're safely away from here.

I take one last look at the front door where it all began. The signature machine is cracked open on the ground, and the last green-printed card has already flapped away in the November wind. Amber's dark, hacked-up hair almost matches the dirty, scattered mulch. I wonder how long she'll lie here before anyone notices.

"Come on," Wyatt says, and he takes my hand. When he helps me into the passenger side of the Lexus, I wrap the green and gray scarf around his neck, hoping it's luckier than my locket was. I pull the photo of my dad, the letter from Alistair's trailer, and the two halves of Amber's card from my back pocket and slip them in the slot of my pull-down mirror. Every clue is important now, and I suspect my dad is at the center of everything.

Wyatt kisses me gently, gets in the car, and drives us away. The farther we get from my house, the heavier my heart grows, but I have to believe that my mom is alive, that they'll help her like they promised. We can't go back to check, and it's the only way to move on. As far as I can see it, I've fulfilled my half of the deal. I just hope it won't break her when they tell her I'm dead.

Matty settles down across the backseat and sighs happily. Wyatt turns on the stereo. It's a song from the band on his shirt, a shirt I used to have too. The dashboard glows blue. No GPS. No list of names. No ticking red clock. I pull one of Alistair Meade's laptops onto my lap and fire it up as Wyatt guns it onto the highway. My fingers itch like they do when I pick up knitting needles, when I cast on my first stitches for a colorful exercise in harmless anarchy.

I type in *Adelaide* and press enter.

It's time for the anarchy to get real.

ACKNOWLEDGMENTS

Big thanks and lilacs to:

My Agent of Awesome, Kate McKean, for ongoing support and waffles, and because when I said, "So I have this teen assassin bank novel sitting around, but . . ." she was all over it.

My amazing editors, Liesa Abrams and Michael Strother, and the entire Simon Pulse team, with special hugs and gluten-free cupcakes for cover magician Regina Flath and Kelsey Dickson and Katy Hershberger in publicity, who performed a miracle in getting me to Chicago.

Ken Lowery, who provided the music for the playlist that powered the edits.

Jessica Banks for a quick beta read and a lesson in writing disability.

Stephanie Constantin for helping in the Great Title Search and for being an amazing friend.

All the wonderful folks who invited me onto panels and to festivals, including Becky at Anderson's Bookshop and the YA Literature Conference, the fabulous Foxes of FoxTale Book Shoppe, Bev Kodak and the YA Track at Dragon Con, Doctor Q and the Alt History Track at Dragon Con, Lee Whiteside and the Phoenix Comicon team, Carol Malcolm of the Urban Fantasy Track at Dragon Con and the Dahlonega Literary Festival, and the JordanCon crew. And thanks to the RT Booklovers Convention for letting me attend and accept two awards, even though I clearly had a zombie disease.

All the bloggers and podcasters who have been kind enough to mention the book or host me, including Reddit Fantasy and Reddit YA Writers, Sword & Laser, SF Signal, Functional Nerds, and the Vaginal Fantasy Book Club. Thanks to RT Book Reviews and Fashion by the Book for revealing the cover!

The students of Tinley Park High School and Glenbard East High School in Illinois, who were attentive and kind during my first school visits as a YA author. And thank you all for following the directions and only using "boobs" once in our Mad Libs.

As always, enormous thanks to my best friend and husband, Craig, who always encourages me and feeds me when I forget. Thanks to my children for putting up with me, and my parents and grandparents for cheering me on. Thanks to Team Capybara and the Holy Taco Church and my LitReactor students and Twitter and everyone who keeps me smiling when the writing gets tough.

The hard part about the acknowledgments is that I want to thank everyone and can't. But just know that if you're reading this, I appreciate you and would gladly SQUEE and hug you one day.

Read your terms of service, folks!